CON

WORLDS COLLIDE

Derek Power, Tim Mendees, Ella Elvery, Patrick Winters, Rachael Boucker, L T Emery, Michael Nadeau. T J Berg, Charlotte Langtree, Joseph Dowling, Teel James Glenn, Deborah Dubas Groom and Jasiah Witkofsky

Ilustrated By Derek Power and Callum Pearce

First Edition
Published by
Nordic Press
Kindlyckevägen 13
Rimforsa, Sweden.
2022

Worlds Collide

978-91-987509-2-8

Cover Design by
Derek Power
Formatted by
Callum Pearce
Illustrations by
Derek Power & Callum Pearce
Compiled and Edited by
Nordic Press

THE LAST ARCADE IN SAN JOSE
By Joseph J Dowling

With a wheeze and a roar, Rufus powered up the old generator. I flicked on the master switch by the open door. There's nothing like the sound of thirty arcade cabs and pinball machines all powering on simultaneously. First you hear the hum from the vast initial power draw, then the monitors buzzing into life. Next, the pins *click and clack* through their mechanical set up. Finally, the piece reaches its climactic crescendo as the games boot up.

Then there's the light. The beautiful neon of the marquees merges with a warm glow from the monitors. Once it's all up and running, our warehouse is so perfectly lit I can't do it justice. I could stay there forever. But we have to ration the fuel to ninety minutes per day, except Sundays or special occasions. It happened to be one of those very days. It was my nineteenth birthday.

I was born on May 23rd, 1967. Ironically, the same day that U.S. strategic command nearly launched a knee-jerk nuclear strike against Russia, after a solar flare jammed all their radars. But in '84 we got the real deal. Maybe the Russians *hated* that Matthew Broderick movie released a few months previously. Or we poked the hornet's nest one too many times. San Francisco got nuked at 3:47pm PST on 11th November 1983. In San Jose we saw a yellow flash light up the cloudy afternoon sky as we streamed out of school. But a few minutes later, standing dumbfounded as the sound wave hit, we knew everything had changed. I remember the warm blood rolling down the sides of my face. I still can't hear well from the left ear.

"Alright Ellie, what are you gonna play first then, birthday girl?" Aaron popped the tops off eight bottles of beer and passed them around. Birthdays were the mother of special occasions, because nobody knew how many more they'd get. We'd saved up enough fuel for a good five or six-hour session. I took my beer, unable to resist a quick peek at the expiry date.

"Wow, only eighteen months gone, you holding out on us with this fresh supply?" I said as I lifted the bottle to my lips and drank. The cold liquid spread inside me, like popping a fire hydrant on a sultry August after-noon, and I pressed the bottle against my forehead, where tiny beads of sweat had pooled.

"Shit man, you even chilled these bad boys," said Rufus in admiration.

"Nothing but the best for our girl," Aaron said as he pulled out two more bottles from his cool box and held them up triumphantly. "It gets better. Check *this* out!" One was a bottle of white tequila, the other gold rum.

Clyde pitched in, licking his lips as he spoke. "Holy fuck, where did you get them?" If anyone loved the hard liquor, he did. "Whoa there, Clyde, ease down. All in good time. I jacked these from the kiosk over on Fruitdale."

Bradley laughed as he said, "Hey, aren't they paying us to protect their shit?"

"Nice work, dude. We're gonna have some fun to-night!" said Rufus. He was right, but not in the way any of us expected. I gulped down the rest of my beer—the first one always slips down too fast.

Putting on a posh British accent, I called over to Aaron. "Sling me another of these fine beverages, old chap."

"Not if you talk like that, you dumb bitch." I laughed and gave him the finger, while he ripped off another top with his teeth and slid the bottle across the makeshift bar.

"Hey, you know these are screw-tops, right?" I said.

"How about screw you?"

I grabbed my crotch. "Anytime, pal."

I sipped the second beer, savouring it this time, and walked around the room. My fingers slid lightly across the control panels and I jabbed buttons while considering what to play. The arcade cabs were up against two of the room's four walls in a long L-shape. The other short wall had the pinballs. The remaining wall housed our homemade bar and a little boxed out compost toilet.

"Where did you guys get these machines, anyway?" asked Sadie, our crew's other girl besides me, and the newest member by almost a year. We'd only initiated her the previous week. A little shiver ran through me as I thought of Scottie, the memory still raw. But I took comfort believing he'd gone to a better place.

"From all over San Jose. You realise how many arcades there were before they dropped the bomb on Frisco? It was absolute peak," explained Cody, our top boy. "Plus, they had a few cabs in every pizza joint. We've been collecting them for two years, only the best of the best." Cody's head dropped as he spoke, and his voice fell to a whisper. "Won't see many more like these now though, most got trashed or scrapped for parts."

"What kind of asshole would break up a working *Space Invaders* machine for capacitors, man? That shit should be punishable by death," I said.

Marty nodded in agreement and loaded one of his dumb mix-tapes into the boombox over by the bar. The mutated samba beat of *Maniac* from the *Flashdance* sound-track started—pop music frozen in time, forever stuck in '83. The Police might never get knocked off number one, British bastards. How come the Brits got out with barely a scratch, anyway? Well, maybe a hundred thousand odd dead in ground operations wasn't exactly a scratch. But nothing compared to the U.S. civilian total of over fifteen million.

"Hey guys, did you see this? I found it when we broke into the old Tower records warehouse last week." Marty held up a thin plastic case. It opened like a gatefold record and he popped out a disc shaped thing, glinting as light from the arcade monitors caught it.

"Shit man, that's one of them new compact discs. I think they came out a few months before we went *kaboom!* An entire album fits on there, don't even need to flip it over," said Bradley.

"Whadya play it on? Lemme have a look-see?" I asked, intrigued.

"No idea, El. I just thought they looked cool, so I grabbed some," Marty said as he frisbeed it over and I caught it. Michael Jackson's *Thriller* album. Shit, even I knew this one.

"Man, I bet this was just a fad. If you can't play it in your car, what's the point?" I said, slinging it back on the bar.

I walked over to admire Tron. It wasn't the best game here, nowhere near, but one of the coolest looking with its blue neon lit control stick and sleek cabinet design. My left pocket was filled with tokens from *Galactican*, the area's biggest arcade. We'd taken at least ten machines from there, including some absolute classics like *Dig-Dug, Pole Position, Mr Do* and *Joust.* I dropped three tokens into the machine, imagining I was standing in a real arcade again, before all this crap happened. I don't know if you've ever played *Tron*, but it's a weird game. It comprises four mini-games that keep repeating as you go up the levels, getting harder each time. The damn tank game always got me. There were six of the fuckers on level three, and I couldn't quite master it. Clyde had, but he wasn't letting his secrets go yet.

"Shit-eating son of a bitch!" I whined. As usual, the bastards got me again, "Hey Clyde, it's my birthday man, can't you tell me how to beat this goddam tank level?"

"Sure, c'mon over here and I'll whisper it to you." I trotted over to him in anticipation and he cupped his hand as I leant towards him. His hot breath whistled in my ear and sent a little shiver through me. It was one of my most vulnerable erogenous zones, although I found nothing sexy about Clyde. A violent ripping sound exploded in my ear as the bastard burped viciously. The smell of stale gas filled my nose.

"Douchebag," I said as he doubled over. Everyone else in the room started laughing, too. It was kinda funny, I had to admit.

***

Shortly after the tequila came out, Cody had his fateful idea.

"Fuck it. You know what? Maybe tonight's the night. Let's go to Sunnyvale and do the raid we've always talked about." The room fell silent. Nobody knew if he was yanking our chains or not, but I could tell. He had that far-away look in him as he lit a cigarette and inhaled a lungful. He meant it alright.

Clyde was first to speak. "If you're not joking, which I assume you are, then have you gone fucking insane?" He looked directly at Cody, challenging him. Cody held his gaze and Clyde backed down. "Look, Cody man. Nothing's changed. Sunnyvale is still Mallrat territory. I know they don't give two shits about video games, but Atari HQ is on their turf, man. You think they'll just let us walk off with a van full of shit? No way, they'll jack the van and beat the crap out of us, or worse." The van was for emergency use only. Normally, for a raid, we'd boost a trolley and wheel the arcade machines over one at a time, but to raid Atari, we'd need much more than a van.

Cody said nothing for a while. He sat there with that look in his eye and stroked his chin with one hand. The other dangled over his knee, holding the cigarette, which burned on ignored. Then his deep voice echoed through the room unexpectedly, making me jump.

"The Mallrats aren't what they used to be. They've been at war with the Baja boys for too long. I heard they got a dozen guys left at most."

We co-existed fine with the Baja as our interests didn't overlap much. Besides, their top guy Axel was kinda in love with me, which made things easier.

Aaron jumped in and everyone listened intently. "Maybe he's right and it's time. They won't expect us to come near their turf. We've got a truce, remember? Besides, they'll be looking out for the Mexicans, not us." We had an uneasy ceasefire with the Rats since about six months ago. They couldn't fight a war on two fronts, and they knew our small crew didn't have the manpower to attack.

Then it clicked in my mind how it might play out and I said, "It's possible. If I can get hold of Axel, get him on board. His crew can raid from the east, we'll come around from the south. Classic pincer movement. Take them all out, split the territory. Atari is ours, obviously. Shit, can you imagine…?" my voice trailed off as visions of pristine Atari cabinets flashed in front of my eyes.

"Easy there, General Patton. This is idiotic. I mean, who knows if Atari isn't burned down or trashed by now?" said Sadie, lighting a cigarette.

"I know it hasn't. A reliable source told me the head of Atari has been paying them off. Protection money. One day this dump will be a functioning city again. He knows that. He's sitting on millions of dollars of inventory." Rufus's explanation made sense.

Bradley said, "So what you're saying, stop me if I'm leaping to the wrong conclusion here." His thumb rested on his chin and a forefinger on his lips as he considered his words. "Not only do we get our pick of shit from Atari, but we can jack them for the protection gig too?"

Now Cody had most of the room. Only Sadie and Clyde remained unconvinced. As the newest, Sadie didn't have any sway, but Clyde did. He seemed deep in thought. "I dunno guys, this is pretty whacko." He shook his head as he wrestled with himself. "What ammo we got left?" he said, looking at Aaron.

"We got enough to take on twelve guys who aren't expecting it." Silence again. Seven sets of eyes turned to Clyde in expectation. We couldn't do it if he wasn't on board. Admittedly the guy was no leader, but at twenty-three he'd become the eldest when Scottie died, and in all honesty the wisest too. I'd known him since summer of 82; he showed me how to get past the third screen on *Donkey Kong* and we'd rolled together ever since. I was a novice player back then, obviously.

"Fuck it. I'm in." There was a mass exhale of breath as the tension released.

"Alright!" Cody pumped his fist.

"C'mon!" Aaron slammed his hand against the bar top. An ashtray made from half a tin can jumped up in the air, spraying cigarette butts across the bar.

"OK then, that's settled. I guess playtime is over. I'll go see Axel," I said. Midnight had passed and it was no longer my birthday. Not that it mattered.

***

I stepped out into the warm early summer night, almost silent except for the sound of our generator rumbling behind me as I walked out of the deserted industrial compound. Soon the streets loomed. It was a couple of miles to Axel's hideout and I hoped he'd be there, but who knew? In my jacket I carried a small revolver, with a hunting knife sheathed on my waist and a much smaller blade strapped to the bottom of my calf. If I saw another living soul between now and reaching Baja territory, I'd disable first, ask questions later. There was a strict curfew from eight, not that the cops had enough bodies to enforce it. No one in their right mind would be out past midnight on innocent business.

I walked fast, without breaking into a jog and drawing attention. My head scanned the lonely streets, low lit in amber monochrome. There were dark shadows everywhere and only every third street light was on, so I walked mostly up the middle of Saratoga Avenue. Hulking in the darkness, relics of junked cars perched silently on metal rims. An occasional vehicle passed, but when I saw lights or heard an engine I ducked off the road, out of sight. San Jose lay well out of the blast radius, so the buildings still stood. But everywhere tall weeds grew between the cracks in the pavements, and two-thirds of houses looked abandoned, smashed up or burned-out. Millions of people fled Cali and moved east after the war to places like Phoenix and Denver, north

to Seattle, Portland or even Canada if they had money.
Those places have jobs, electricity for eighteen hours
a day and even a functional police force. But it could
be worse. Los Angeles—*Hell-A* as they call it now—
suffered far worse than San Jose. Downtown became a
sea of rubble while in the suburbs anything goes. True,
even Frisco was far worse. The place got wrecked and
only the rats stayed behind to fight over scraps. Even
the gangs fled north or east. Little old San Jose wasn't
worth the trouble except for small crews like us.

Soon, I crossed the Junipero Sarra freeway into Baja
turf. It seemed unlikely all Axel's guys would know my
face, so I ducked into the side streets and stayed in the
shadows. After I'd found the right street, my fist banged
on the heavy metal door. A spyhole slid open, revealing
an eye. The challenge came back.

"Password, homes?"

I half whispered, "Mexicali." There came a pause,
followed by the sound of dead bolts sliding open,
before the lock turned. The door opened a crack and a
Latino face eyed me with caution.

"Shit mang, is you. Mexicali was last week's password. You lucky I didn't leave you out there." It was
Cortez, Axel's number two.

Baja was mostly a Mexican crew who came up from
Tijuana when they heard what remained of San Jose's
drug trade was ripe for picking. After a short, brutal
conflict with the main downtown gang, the Baja took
most of the business. Scag for old-fashioned junkies,
but coke and that new methamphetamine shit were the
drugs of choice now. We didn't bother with it, except
slinging a bit of weed or some uppers and downers, a

good reason we never clashed with them. They also ran a couple of bordellos. Our main hustle was weapons, and Baja needed plenty. But so did everyone. The door opened enough to let me slip inside and banged shut with an almighty clang.

"Dude, that is one serious door. Did you guys beef up security?

"You know Axel, baby. He always a little paranoid."

"Talking of the man, is he around?"

"Sure, sit down, take a line, chill." He pointed towards some beaten old couches around a coffee table with a mound of white powder in the middle.

"Nice one," I said and sat down. The thing almost swallowed me whole, and I had to perch on the edge to get in position to hit a line. Usually I wouldn't partake, but some Colombian would throw me back in the zone after the booze. I used my smaller blade to serve up a line on the back of my hand and sucked it up. My head felt as if it was swelling up like a balloon and my cheeks reddened. Electricity surged through me and my heart kicked jerkily into third gear. Lucky I didn't try starting off with a big hit.

I heard heavy steps coming down the metal stairs. "Ellie, what's happenin' dog?" Axel loomed over me, smiling his easy crocodile smile, his gold teeth glinting. Long dreads hung like heavy black cables. Underneath a plain white vest, tattooed arms popped with vein and muscle. Axel was half-Mexican, half-Jamaican and all bad. We slapped hands before he sat down next to me and took a huge hit from his long pinkie fingernail. He snorted and roared like a lion as the drug careered into his dopamine receptors.

"So, what you doin' round here, girl? Don' you know it ain't safe out on the streets after dark?"

"I can take care of myself, Axel."

"I know you can, for real. When you gonna come work for me?"

It was a loaded question. I paused to think. "Shit, Axel dude, you know I ain't into slinging hard stuff. Only wanna play video games and chill. Most of the time anyway." He said nothing, so I continued. "That brings me on to why I'm here." I took a deep breath. "So we have, how do I put this…a conflict of interest with the Mallrats? We're interested in a hostile take-over. Mergers and acquisitions, you know?"

"Huh?" One of his narrow eyebrows poked up like a rabbit from a hole. I'd lost him.

"We wanna join forces, kill the fucking Mallrats and steal their territory!"

Axel's eyes widened and his mouth broke into a grin. He slapped his thigh with his heavily ringed hand. "Shit sister, why didn't you just say?!"

"We can split the territory. All we want is a wedge of Sunnyvale, north of the 101, east of the Lawrence Expressway. The rest is yours."

His smile dropped. "That's all commercial and ware-housing. What, you going into *business* or something?" His shades came off and dark brown eyes stared out, burning with intensity from deep sockets.

"Easy Axel, brother. Ain't nothin' you need to worry 'bout. You ever hear of Atari headquarters on Borregas? They got a few buildings around Moffett Park too. "

His mouth hung open as he leaned into the deep couch to consider the question. Then he sat upright suddenly. "Video games, right?"

I ginned and nodded slowly as I spoke. "Yeah, you got it. They made video games. Lots of 'em."

"It's real nice over there, all clean. Shit, you and your boys are such nerds." He giggled like a naughty school-boy before taking another colossal hit of cocaine. White powder clung to his nostrils like sand from the beach. "What you boys want with Atari anyhow?"

"Mostly we wanna get our hands on the hardware. There's a shit ton of it still on their inventory." He looked me in the eye again. I held his gaze. "Straight up, man. But they're payin' the Mallrats good money for protection, so we wanna jack that too."

He chewed it over for a while, nodding his head to music nobody else could hear. I sat, waiting patiently. Axel wasn't the sort of guy you could sway once he thought he had the picture.

"OK El, so let's say we do it like you say. My boys take 'em from Lawrence, you take 'em from the 280 and boom!" He smashed his fists together horizontally. "Like rats in fuckin' trap, mang. How many bodies you got?"

"Eight, including me," I said, nodding in agreement.

"Ok when you wanna do this?"

"No time like the present." I raised my eyebrows.

"Huh?" I'd lost him again. How small was this guy's vocabulary exactly?

My voice rose a pitch. "Let's hit them bitches to-night!" He smiled again and raised his hand to slap mine. We both grinned. Then his smile dropped again and the serious look returned.

"But you gotta do something for me, girl." He eyed

me up and down and his hand came to rest heavily on my thigh. I'd thought it might come to this.

"Like that, huh?" I said, staring into his unblinking eyes.

"Yeah. Like that."

"Alright soldier." I stood up and he followed, towering over me. "Your room up there, right?" I pointed up the metal stairs he'd come from earlier. He said nothing and I started walking, but his sinewy forearm shot out and grabbed mine. Effortlessly he spun me around back towards him, into his arms.

"How about right here?" he said as he pushed me around to the back of the sofa, pressing his weight behind me. I could feel he was hard. Rough hands were all over me. One snaked around my waist and dropped in between my legs. I'd gotten a little wet. It had been awhile.

"So that's how you like it?" I said. His breath was on my neck and he bit me gently. In a split second, I ducked down and flipped him over the back of the sofa. He landed face up, eyes wide open with surprise. I leapt over the sofa and landed on top, straddling him like a wild horse. It was work, but that didn't mean it couldn't be fun.

"Nice move, homie," he said, nodding with appreciation.

"Thanks, sweetie." I leant down and whispered into his ear before biting it hard, "I'm not the submissive type, sorry."

***

After it was over, we made the arrangements and I left. Breaking into a jog, I got back to the warehouse in twenty minutes and Rufus let me in.

"You took your time."

"Well, Axel needed some… *persuasion*." I left it there and walked across the room. All eyes turned to me. The floor was mine.

"They're in. We hit tonight at three-fifteen. They're gonna strike from the east, we'll come up behind."

Cody got up and stood alongside me. "No prisoners. We got one shot at this, if we do it, we do it properly," he said.

"Alright, let's fuckin' *do this!*" Aaron roared as he jumped behind the bar to get the weapons stash. We kept most of the guns and shit somewhere more secure, but still had enough weaponry to stop a small army.

He threw me a padded vest and I ripped off my jacket. I got my old sawn-off pump-action shotgun and loaded it with six cartridges, alternating between slugs and 00 buckshot rounds. I put a few more in my pockets and loaded up the vest's ammo belt. Cody and Bradley took M-16s, Sadie and Clyde took MP5 subs. Aaron had an old AK-47 that was his lucky talisman. Rufus had some European assault rifle I can't remember the name of. Marty carried a couple of pistols like some stupid gunslinger from the wild-west.

"Go get the van," barked Cody. Rufus and Sadie ran to pick it up from its hiding place. Five minutes later we heard the horn and went outside. I took one last, lingering look around. Would I see this place again? I flipped the master switch and everything powered off with sad *clunk*. The genny died with a splutter as Marty cut the engine, while Aaron triple bolted the re-enforced door. Cody jumped into the second passenger seat and five of us bundled into the rear.

"Take St Wolfe's and pull up after we cross the freeway," he ordered to Rufus, who always drove.

Seven minutes later, the van pulled over. Nothing but the sound of the engine idling. "Sadie, get out and have a look," said Cody. She clambered over him and out the passenger door.

"All clear," came the verdict, thirty seconds later.

"Kill the lights and drive north, but stay on Wolfe. *Slowly.*"

We coasted another two-thirds of a mile before Cody gave the order, Rufus killed the engine and we disembarked into the still night. Any remaining wind had died and the only sound was our footsteps as we jogged northwards. The intersection with Fremont appeared up ahead. We were very close to their main HQ now. Backs against a wall, we lined up while Sadie scouted ahead. Nothing stirred, not a soul nor another car. Deader than downtown Frisco on a Friday night. Then I saw a couple of wild dogs move from out of the shadows and start nosing some trash—the only living things on the street aside from us.

"Shouldn't Axel's boys have lit them up by now?" said Clyde.

"Might take a while to locate 'em," replied Bradley.

"Would it? I mean, they'd be strung up along the other side of the Lawrence looking out for Bajas, right?"

Aaron chipped in. "No chance they can eyeball that much road with twelve warm bodies, man. They probably got a few lookouts and a car. If Axel goes in with all his lot, they'll split."

"Let's head east towards the Lawrence expressway.

Carefully," said Cody. Sadie stayed out in front, dancing from shadow to shadow like a ballerina. Her scouting skills were the reason we took her in, but she hadn't proved herself, not yet. Scottie, I'd always want on my side in *any* fight. I fought off the unwelcome intrusion and concentrated as we inched our way along East Fremont, listening out for the tell-tale pop of small-arms fire slashing the dead air. It was almost 3.15—nothing. We'd be right on top of them soon at this rate.

From nowhere, the silence broke and gunfire cracked like close thunder. I dived for cover as small calibre bullets zinged off the pavement. Return fire waited while we got a bead.

"Anyone hit?!" cried Cody. It seemed not. "On me," he ordered, then lifted his M-16 and loosed off a few rounds at the corner of Eleanor Way, over to our right. A giveaway muzzle flash—we all opened up in the same direction. Then more fire came from straight up ahead, a hundred yards away.

A car burned down from the east, the other side of some thick redwoods separating East Fremont from the freeway. It skidded to a halt diagonally across the road. *They were trying to bracket us.*

"They're on our left and right. Fuck, where's Axel," cried Cody. We assumed a semi-circle perimeter as bullets flew. The car on my side was loaded with at least three 'Rats. I had to get to them before they opened up and we got eaten by the crossfire.

"Cover me!" I shouted to Aaron, who was nearest. Even at that moment of high intensity it sounded like a fucking cliché, but what else could I say? He raised his AK and loosed off controlled bursts at the car as I rolled out into the open street and dashed towards a thick redwood. It would obscure me from the target at least, but I'd remain exposed to whoever was on the opposite side. I hoped they would either be busy or a bad shot, preferably both. Or even better—face down.

Before I dived for the tree, I saw three 'Rats disembarking from the car under Aaron's fire. One of them took a bullet and span around. He lay groaning, out of the fight for now, leaving two to deal with. I risked a little peek around the tree. They were at either ends of the car, distracted by the barking fire of Aaron's AK. I could see the nearest dude's head, but only the muzzle of the second guy's weapon.

I came back around the left side and rolled out, landing in a quarterback spike position with the shotgun in my midriff. The nearest guy turned in time to take a slug full in the chest. He flew back a few feet and hit the deck face up, arms spread. I couldn't see if he was wearing a vest, but I'd taken him out of it, for now. Chambering a round as I dived, I leapt forward under the hood of the car into a prone position. The guy at the back end of the car knew I was there and, before he could come around, I fired at his exposed lower legs. The buckshot shell cut him down with a puff of red as his lower left calf was obliterated. No such thing as bullet proof ankles. I jumped into a kneeling position and rolled to my left, chambering another slug. The guy was trying to crawl back behind the car's flank, same side as me now. He looked up and I shot him in the face—it wasn't pretty.

The guy who I'd hit in the chest lay close by with a gaping, ragged pink hole in his solar plexus, no vest.

He was twitching as the life drained from him. No need to waste another cartridge. I saw movement ahead, the dude who'd taken one of Aaron's heavy 7.62mm rounds crawling away from me trying to get to his weapon. I've never been one to take pleasure in anyone's misery so I walked over, pumped another slug into the chamber and did him quick, in the back of the head.

"Clear!" I shouted while I reloaded behind the car, although sporadic gunfire still cut through the quiet, so I couldn't be sure anyone heard me. It sounded like the only remaining exchange was between the guys who'd come directly from the east.

Suddenly I heard intense gunfire, like the peak of a July fourth fireworks display. It came from even further east and finished in less than ten seconds. I assumed the Baja crew had finally arrived and cleared the remaining 'Rats from the rear. I stood up to see a line of figures strung across the entire width of the freeway, walking towards us. As the smoke from the fire-fight cleared, I recognised the imposing silhouette of Axel and his dreads. It was them alright. I relaxed and my shotgun dropped towards the floor in one hand.

If I'd still had the hearing in my left ear, it wouldn't have happened. I felt a metallic crunch on the back of my skull and lightning zigzags of white flashed across my eyes, before the whole world turned black.

∗

Words buzzed like slow winter flies as I came to. Someone was hitting me across the face with an open hand. It hardly registered because my head hurt so bad a slap was a birthday present. For a second, I couldn't remember *who* I was, let alone *where*. Only that dull throbbing in my skull. I tried to reach up to rub my eyes and check out the damage, but couldn't move my wrists. My vision faded in, revealing a dimly lit empty room with a naked light bulb hanging from the ceiling. The floors were rough concrete, the walls corrugated iron. A damp, musty smell hung in the air. Someone stared into my eyes, but I still couldn't catch their words. Then it hit me. It was Niko Vega. Head honcho of the Mallrats. *Fuck!*

"Can you hear me, bitch? Don't tell me that pistol whip gave you brain damage. Goddamn it."

"Don't think so, retard," I spat back.

"Hey, I thought we had a fucking truce, man. What the hell?" he said, sounding hurt.

"Business is business, you know how it is."

He shrugged and said, "Fair point, but thanks to that little stunt, most of my guys are dead and you're my way out." So I'd been relegated to a mere hostage, a bargaining chip, nothing but a pathetic pawn in the endgame. "I don't expect you'll accommodate, so I'm gonna give you some assistance." He pulled out a needle and jabbed it into my tightly restrained arm. I felt a tiny wasp sting and he pushed down the plunger.

"What the fuck did you just put in me?" I cried.

He laughed. "Something to keep you compliant. Some crazy new hallucinogen we've been working on in our little laboratory. You're privileged, this shit costs mad dollar and hardly anyone can afford it."

Great, so he'd jabbed me with a random dose of some experimental new drug. I was about to take a journey I might never return from. The Mallrats mostly hustled dope, hence the obvious conflict of interests with Axel's crew. Unlike the Mexicans, who brought everything up via Mexico, Niko was some kind of mad scientist. They synthesised most of the shit they sold and now I'd become their guinea pig.

As he left the room, he cackled, "Have fun, darling. See you soon. I'll get some more kicks with you later." As a parting gift, he pulled the cord and the bulb popped off. Once he'd shut the door, I was in total darkness. This kept getting better by the second.

It took about ten minutes for the gear to work, although my perception of time was already pretty skewed by the lack of sensory input. Except for a low, rumbling electrical hum, there wasn't much to go on. It came on slow, like good mescaline—ephemeral hallucinations, flashing colours, nothing I could grasp, so I just sat back and enjoyed the light show. But my panicked conscious mind still had an opinion, and it tried to have its nagging say. My heart rate kicked on from a disco beat into an up-tempo punk song and I could feel sweat dripping down my face in the dark.

I shouted into the void, "Hey, Niko dude, how about turning that light on? Or even cutting me loose?" No reply. "I'm tripping my balls off here, man!" No use. Strapped in for the ride.

It wasn't long before my fear gave way to vivid dreams like nothing I'd ever encountered. The darkness played as a perfect canvas for my psyche to have its moment in the sun. I don't know if you've ever been one of the ghosts from Pac-man after the yellow son of a bitch eats a pill, but it's no fun at all. On the screen, he's just a little yellow dot. In my mind's eye he became a three-dimensional beast, eight-feet tall with a yawning, snapping chasm for a mouth. I ran out of maze and he swallowed me whole.

Back into total darkness momentarily, then another game—*Robotron:2084*. Out of the black came human shapes, all coming for me. Every time I zapped one, two more would appear. I saw their faces, all people I knew. My brother, my parents, Rufus, Aaron, Axel and then finally Scottie, poor Scottie. After that, any semblance of sentient thought ended, and my trip became a hippy montage and an experimental free jazz freak-out. Archie Shepp's *The Magic of Ju-Ju*, the immersive 3D version. Most of it didn't have enough grounding in reality to even explain properly. Time ceased to exist and I *became* time. I was *before* time, witnessing the nascent universe coming into existence.

As the high-tide of my trip slowly subsided, the hallucinations became more dreamlike again. The final vision, one of pure terror, I'll never forget. Back to 1983, November 11th, but this time the bomb didn't hit Frisco, it hit downtown San Jose. I stood on a hill overlooking the city, spread out below like the wings of a butterfly. For a second, it seemed so peaceful, my breathing slowed and I felt Zen. Then, a slow, whining sound, followed by pure fluorescent yellow as downtown San Jose was obliterated. I couldn't move as the blast whistled toward me in slow motion. I tried to scream, but no sound came.

I felt the nuclear wind, then the shock wave hit. I became subsumed in bright white light. Every cell screamed as it burned. How can you feel pain when you're dead? I begged for actual death and an end to this, but it wouldn't come. My flesh had burned away.

JOSEPH J DOWLING

I held my skeletal hands in front of my eyes until they too disintegrated. I was just thinking, feeling atoms in a cloud of radiation, floating back down to earth like confetti from a top-floor window on a still day.

***

Consciousness. First I felt my own mind again, back in my skull. That delirious moment of existence, awaking from a brutal drinking binge, but before reality descends, bringing pain and memories. Then came sounds, voices, not one but several. My eyes tried to open as light stabbed them. It took a few attempts back and forth, like tipping over a soda machine. No use rubbing them, surely? But I found I could move my wrists again and was no longer tied to a damn chair. I managed to hold my eyes open as the light reduced from agony to mere annoyance. From the rear of our parked van, faces peered at mine. Faces I knew and loved.

"Shit, she's awake. You OK babe?" said Bradley.

"Where… where am I? What the fuck happened?"

"We tracked that creep Niko down. He wouldn't tell us where you were until we cut two of his fingers off and promised his balls were next," Cody explained. "When we found you, we thought your mind had snapped. You were speaking in tongues or some mad shit. Man, I wish I'd had a tape recorder."

"Thanks for your concern, dickwad," I said.

"You Ok to move, Ellie?"

"I think so," I said, trying to stand. With the faltering steps of a newly born foal, I stuttered and stumbled as the back doors opened. Rufus and Sadie grabbed from each side and helped lift me out. Then I saw it—the giant Atari logo. We'd made it. A cold jolt shot through me. Urgently I asked, "Anyone buy it back there?"

"Marty's bashed up pretty bad, but I think he'll pull through. We took him to Doc Wily's." Wily, an underground quack, helped all the gangbangers get fixed up, for a significant fee of course. The only legit medical facility left in the city had armed security and a blacklist longer than a mob enforcer's rap sheet.

"A few of us took dings, but nothing to keep us from this raid," said Aaron, examining the bandage wrapped around his arm. "Pussy pop-guns them Mallrats use, good for vermin, maybe."

"Just as well, huh?" said Sadie, limping heavily.

"So, kiddo, here we are. Atari HQ. You wanna see?" My old friend Clyde's arm sat draped over my shoulder.

"Does the pope shit in the woods?" I replied. Bradley pulled out a pair of heavy-duty bolt cutters from the van. He snapped the chain wrapped around the door handles, while Rufus took out the locks with a battery powered drill.

Soon, we were inside, running freely through the corridors of Atari, like unattended kids who'd snuck into high school on a Saturday afternoon. The early morning sun streamed through the windows. We passed office after office with little to differentiate them from any other company headquarters, except the odd videogame cartridge. We exited into a courtyard complex with several smaller buildings, which we broke open one by one, finding stashes of Atari 2600 consoles, games, joysticks, but no arcades. Then we found it. *The mother-load.*

The door swung open, shining a low beam of sunlight into the room as the smell of carpet and old wood hit us. We stood there, staring in awe at what must have been every Atari arcade cab ever released, in a warehouse from paradise. Every nerd's wet dream had been realised. The ache in my skull had subsided to a low, throbbing pulse, but I no longer felt it. Blank screens stared at me in rows. *Star Wars, Asteroids, Missile Command.* Brand new games that I'd never even seen yet, like *Crystal Castles*, and even the original granddaddy—*Pong*. There was no power, of course, but it wouldn't take long to set up a genny.

"I guess we have two headquarters now," I said, jaw still hanging in wonder. No point dragging all this over to our place. It would never fit anyway. I counted nearly a hundred machines.

***

I think now, is it our duty to help rebuild the world our fathers tried so hard to destroy? What do we owe them, truly? We remain deep in nuclear winter, but there are subtle signs of spring. Life is almost normal in many places, and where it isn't, people create a new normality. Even here, in the unrecognisable remnants of California, things will one day recover. A reversal of nature, the way she reclaims our best attempts to make order from chaos, we'll counter again with steel and poured concrete. Survival, the will of instinct, as hard and real as cockroaches hiding in the dark.

THE MADNESS IN THE WILLOWS
By Tim Mendees

"Come up here, Mole!" a wizened and disgruntled voice demanded, echoing down into the whitewashed subterranean abode. "You owe me sixpence!"

"Bother!" Mole spat as he tossed the book of rude jokes he'd borrowed from Toad onto the kitchen table. " I thought I'd given that miserable blighter the slip this time." Old Rabbit demanded a shiny sixpence every time an animal wanted to cross the private road down towards the river; and, as all his friends lived down by the river, he'd given the old miser a small fortune over the year he'd lived there. It had gone past the point of ridiculousness now. Because of the money-grabbing Rabbit... Mole was almost flat broke. The inheritance from his father was dwindling away to nothing. Soon, he would be forced to find gainful employment.

"Come out, Mole... I know you're down there."

"How?" Mole whispered to himself. "He was asleep... I bet it was those darn weasels grassing me up again!" Of all the creatures that called the area their home, it was those pesky weasels that really got Mole's goat... them and that belligerent Rabbit.

"Come on, Mole... I'm not going anywhere without my sixpence!"

"Fine," Mole sighed with resignation. "Up in a minute!"

Rabbit huffed and puffed. Mole could hear it echoing around his house. Every exhalation was like claws down a chalkboard.

Shuffling across the room, Mole took his piggy bank down off the shelf and gave it a good shake... "Blow!" It was completely and utterly empty. He was certain that he had at least a couple of quid's worth of change in there. Then remembrance dawned... he'd lost it all in a game of dominos with some of the crayfish from the river. He was sure they'd been cheating, but he really didn't fancy tangling with those pincers and hard shells.

"Dammit... I'll have to go to the bank. So much for my relaxing afternoon... Oh well..." he shrugged, throwing on his coat. He normally wouldn't bother, but now winter was here, there was a distinct chill in the air.

Leaving his sanctuary from the sun and the elements,

Mole scrabbled with his little paws. "Up we go! Up we go!" Eventually... pop! His grubby snout came out of the ground inches from the Old Rabbit's feet. Carefully avoiding the yellowed claws, he pulled himself out into the daylight.

"Sixpence!" Old Rabbit demanded.

"Uh... I'm sorry, Old Rabbit. I don't have sixpence. I'll have to go to the bank." Mole said sheepishly.

Old Rabbit tapped his back foot impatiently and folded his paws across his wheezing chest. "No trying to wheedle out of it, Mole... a sixpence, if you please."

Mole bristled. "Look, I don't have a blasted sixpence... I don't have a single penny. Giving you a sixpence just to cross a blasted road every day has bled me dry. Every time I go out, it costs me two sixpences!"

Old Rabbit sniffed. "Not my problem. It's more than my job's worth just to let animals cross willy-nilly."

Mole buried his face in his paw and sighed. "Fine... I'll pay you the blasted sixpence. I'll go to the bank this instant."

Old Rabbit grinned, showing his gnarled and blackened front teeth. "That'll be three sixpences you owe me."

"Three?" Mole spluttered.

"Indeed... The one you already owe me, one there, and one back."

That was it, Mole snapped. "Look, you carrot-chomping dingleberry, why don't you just go and boil your head?"

Clutching his chest in shock, Old Rabbit Gasped.

Mole clamped his strong paws over his mouth in case any more vitriol spewed forth.

Old Rabbit fought to catch his breath.

"I... I'll go and get your three sixpences..." Mole stammered and quickly scurried away. Bustling through the seemingly never-ending stream of young rabbits that hopped down the gravel road, he ignored their jeers and reached the peace and serenity of the meadow. Pausing by one of the trees that lined its perimeter, he flopped onto a mattress of deadfall leaves and tried to catch his breath.

His outburst had unsettled him. What was worse than his harsh words was the seething hatred that had pumped through his little fluttering heart. At that moment, he'd wanted that stupid Old Rabbit to drop dead. It was so out of character, Mole was normally such an amiable little fellow, genial and thoughtful. An explosion of rage of that magnitude was so far out of character that it had shaken him to the core.

A stiff wind scythed through the meadow, shaking the tree's skeletal branches, sending the leaves that had futilely clung to life spiralling to the ground. Now he could breathe, Mole's nose was tickled by the smells of ripe decay beneath him. Patches of sickly-looking mushrooms poked through the natural compost; no doubt, colonising various branches and twigs felled in a recent storm.

Getting to his paws, he brushed himself down, shaking any spores that may have infected his coat to their rightful place. Hugging himself, Mole shivered and gazed around him. The once lush hedgerows, so bushy and inviting, were now jagged and vicious-looking... The only greenery aside from the mud-clotted grass was the tangled weeds that clung stubbornly to the borders; no doubt, concealing hordes of many-legged things with sharp mandibles and vicious stings.

Until that point, the meadow had been a haven for Mole, so calming and peaceful, now it seemed threatening somehow. Every furtive rustle and fleeting shadow seemed to herald danger. A din of fluttering and cawing dragged his eyes upwards. A murder of crows looked down at him from the branches, scrutinizing him with their beady black eyes.

"Um... Hullo." Mole said timidly.

The largest of the crows cocked its head... but said nothing.

Mole huddled inside his coat and hurried towards the gate. He'd never seen so many crows in one place before. It was as if they were waiting for something to happen. Cursing his timid soul as he tried to control his panicked breathing once again, Mole told himself over and over that it was all in his imagination... he wasn't at all convincing.

Upon reaching the outskirts of the town, Mole shook himself vigorously to try and banish his morbid thoughts of harbingers and impending doom. Finally pulling himself together, Mole affected an air of cheerfulness and scampered past the gates and fences, calling out a chipper, "hullo," whenever one of the town's denizens appeared. Coming to a fork in the road, Mole stopped sharply to observe some commotion over the way.

Two squirrels, one grey, one red, rolled on the ground spitting and clawing. An overturned bucket nearby had spilt its collection of nuts and berries over the dirt track. Mole winced, some of the blows were vicious... and, the language! His ears had never heard such profanity. Gearing himself up, Mole prepared to wade in and separate the combatants. Before he could act, however, a large buck rabbit appeared, sauntered over to the pile of errant nuts and commenced to stamp them into a thick paste. The squirrels, incensed, quit their squabble and prepared to confront the rabbit.

Showing no fear, the rabbit turned his back on them and wiggled his pom-pom tail at them indignantly before hopping off cackling like an old hen. The squirrels armed themselves with sticks and gave chase. Mole was stunned. He'd never witnessed violence on this scale in the village itself before. He had come to expect it from the weasels and stoats in The Wild Wood, but not here.

"What in several types of onion sauce is going on around here?" Shaking his head in confusion, Mole turned and raced towards the centre of town. The sooner he was done with his tiresome errand, the sooner he could go back home and hide away from the world. At that moment, he really missed his previously secluded life. It was almost like a dark shadow hung over the area... turning everyone a little crazy.

"Botheration!" Mole exploded as he eyed the gone for lunch sign on the bank's oak door with frustration. It said "back in one hour" but had no indication of the time it had been placed there. If they had only just that second gone, he could be stood out there like a prize plum for what would feel like an eternity. Grumbling to himself, Mole pulled out his watch and marked the time. Now he had to amuse himself for at least fifty-five minutes.

"Toad!" He exclaimed cheerfully. "I'll go and see Toad! He's always in a good mood." Since his brush with the law and reclaiming Toad Hall from those dratted weasels, Toad had been something of a recluse. Badger had thought long and hard about how to occupy the amphibious adrenaline junkie harmlessly and had introduced him to the books in the expansive library of the Roman ruins that comprised part of his den. Toad, to the surprise of both himself and his friends, had taken to reading like a duck to water. Toad being Toad, he particularly liked the adventure stories... and the spicy ones. Mr Toad was just the tonic Mole needed. His boundless enthusiasm was infectious, and even in his current funk, he was sure he could perk him up. Turning towards the river with a renewed sense of vigour, he prepared for a leisurely stroll to Toad Hall.

***

"Hullo, Ducks," Mole called out upon sight of his feathered acquaintances. He was almost at Toad Hall and was surprised to see them this far down the water.

The ducks didn't respond. There wasn't a single quack or wing raised in greeting... odd.

"Hullo, Ducks!" Mole tried again, a little louder this time. "How goes the day?"

Again, not even a flutter of recognition.

Mole paused and looked on with a puzzled expression on his face. The ducks were in a line formation and were swimming around in a strange series of curves and bends... it looked like they were drawing some kind of symbol on the water. Mole found himself unable to take his eyes off the rippling waters. It was as though he were momentarily hypnotised.

"Psst! Over 'ere."

Mole looked around, startled. The shock had broken his reverie. "Um... hullo?" He couldn't see where the voice had come from. Then, a reed waved back and forth like a flag.

"Down 'ere."

Mole moved cautiously towards the beckoning voice. "Who... who's there?"

A broad and sleek muzzle with greying whiskers suddenly popped out of the weeds. "It's me, Otter."

"Hullo, Otter," Mole replied. "What's the matter with that lot." He jerked a chubby thumb in the direction of the ducks.

"Beats me," Otter shrugged. "They've been doing it all morning... Just swimming around and around. It's cheesed me off no end," he exclaimed. "This is my favourite fishing spot, and that bunch of demented feather-bottoms have scared off all the blasted fish! I figured they were practising their synchronised swimming for next year's games... but why they have to do it here, I'll never know!" The disgruntled river-dweller shook his body in frustration, splashing Mole's blue coat with muddy water.

"Hey, careful!" Mole squeaked.

"Oh... blow me, I'm sorry, Moley... They just get my goat sometimes, you know. Anyone would think they owned the dratted river." Otter paused and took a deep breath. "Anyway, what are you up to?"

"That's alright, Otter," Mole said as he wiped the droplets off his jacket. "I was just off to see Toad... I could do with some cheering up."

Otter snorted. "I'm not sure he wants company today... the dirty little duck."

"Oh?" Mole cocked his brow.

"Yeah, I saw old Toady earlier lurking down amongst the willows. He was reading again."

"Well, that doesn't sound so bad."

"It was what he was reading that was the problem..."

"Oh, he wasn't reading one of the racier books from Badger's library again, was he?" Mole smirked.

"Nah," Otter wiped his whiskers with his paws. "He wasn't reading a book. He was reading an..." Otter searched for the right word, "artistic magazine."

Mole looked at him, confused.

"You know, one of those glossy ones with lots of artistic photographs."

Mole gasped.

"Exactly... I had to cover young Portly's eyes. All those pictures of lady frogs stretching their long legs out... Well, it's enough to put you off your dinner."

"Well..." Mole shook his head. "The mucky little devil... I think I'd better go and drag him out for some fresh air. It'll do him the world of good... That, or a cold shower."

Otter chuckled. "Good luck with that... I'm going to stay here and keep an eye on this daft lot." He indicated the ducks, who were still swimming around and around, seemingly in some kind of trance.

Mole turned to walk away, then paused. "Before I go, you haven't seen Ratty, have you?"

Otter thought for a second. "Not since this morning. He was heading towards town, muttering about chicken sandwiches and soggy bread."

"Yeah, that sounds like Ratty. Okay, Otter... toodle pip!"

"Toodle pip, Moley!" Otter replied before resuming his vigil.

After one last glance at the silently swimming ducks, Moley rejoined the towpath and continued on his way. It wasn't long before Toad Hall started to become visible through the trees. The frigid wind that had earlier cut him to the bone had all but stopped. It was almost eerily quiet. The only noise was the sluggishly flowing river as it lapped at the jetty of Toad's boathouse. Pulling his coat tighter around him, Mole pressed on towards Toad Hall.

Rustle!

Mole leapt two feet into the air as a shambolic creature came crashing out of the bushes to his left. Fearing for his life, Mole balled his strong paws and prepared for a fight. Imagine his surprise, then, when he was greeted by the startled face of his friend, Mr Toad!

"Fhtagn!" Bellowed Toad, his eyes wide and swivelling beneath his ridged brow.

Mole looked at his friend like he'd just dropped from the moon. "I beg your pardon?"

"What? … Um... Err..." Toad stammered. "Oh, hullo, Moley! You startled me!"

"I startled you? What the devil were you doing sneaking around in the bushes like that?" Mole panted as he tried to slow his racing heartbeat.

Toad had regained his composure somewhat, though he still looked kind of manic... like he'd had one too many cups of coffee. "Oh, you know? I was just taking a shortcut... I... I had some business to take care of." His eyes betrayed his furtive nature. He must have guessed as he gave them a good blinking before continuing. "Anyway, what brings you to Toad Hall?"

Mole was still all of a dither. The morning's weird atmosphere coupled with Toad's odd behaviour had knocked him for a loop. "I... I was coming to see you, actually."

"Me, but why? Aside from me being fabulous, that is!" There it was, the Toad that Mole knew and begrudgingly loved.

Mole sighed. "I've had a bad day, and I needed cheering up." He leaned in close and whispered. "Have you noticed anyone acting odd?"

"Aside from you, you mean?" Toad chortled.

"No, you dolt! Like the ducks down the river, like the squirrels... like the crows..." He put his hands on Toad's chest and found that, to his surprise, it was hard. Mole creased his brow and patted the area with one of his paws. "What have you got up your coat, Toad?"

"Um... Err..." The sneaky look returned to his face in a flash. "It's just a book."

"Up your coat?"

"It's a really old book... I didn't want it to get wet."

Mole remembered what Otter had just told him about Toad's reading habits. "An old book, eh? ... You mucky little devil."

Toad's green cheeks flushed post box red. "It... It's not like that!"

"Really?"

"Really!" Folding his arms over the book-shaped lump in his coat, Toad spluttered. "Anyway... I must be going. Busy, busy... Poop! Poop!" Before Mole could utter a single word in reply, Toad had taken to his heels and charged off towards his abode.

"You'll go blind!" Mole called out after him in exasperation, then sighed once again. "Well, so much for Toady cheering me up." He pulled his watch out of his coat and checked the time. "Oh well, the bank should be open by now... I'll just go home."

Feeling dejected, Mole turned around and started his lonely walk back to town...

***

"Stupid Rabbit... I ought to stick his rotten sixpence right up his..."

"Ha Ha! The yawning void!"

The maniacal yelling stopped Mole mid-rant as he prepared to enter the meadow. Thus far, his wander back from Toad Hall had been uneventful to the point of boredom. Even the ducks had finally dispersed, and Otter was busy fishing. Now, the well of unease that had been subsiding started to bubble up again.

"The red land... The lightless chaos! Yes, yes... I have seen it!"

"What the custard creams?" Slowly and cautiously, he opened the gate and peeked around the leafless bushes. Thankfully, the tree was free from crows. But, a small furry animal was rolling in the leaves, kicking plumes of them into the air as he giggled and babbled inanely.

Creeping towards the tree, recognition suddenly dawned. "Ratty?" Picking up the pace, he ran towards his closest friend. "Ratty... what in God's name are you doing?" Mole had always been befuddled as to why he was called Ratty in the first place, considering he was a water vole... but this behaviour befuddled him even more.

"Hup mud h'ephainog! ... Hup gn'thorr h'ephainog!"

"Eh?" The stream of guttural syllables from Ratty's thorax stunned him rigid. "Ratty... it's me, Moley."

"You'll get no sense out of him, Mr Mole." A small voice squeaked from under the bushes.

Mole let out a squeak of his own, this one in surprise. Peering into the shadow, he saw two twitching snouts. It was The Hedgehogs. "Oh, hello, Mrs Hedgehog, Mr Hedgehog... I didn't see you there."

"We were trying to catch a little nap on our way home," grumbled Mrs Hedgehog. "Then he appeared and started making such a ruckus that I nearly had an attack of the vapours!"

"There, there, dear," Mr Hedgehog cooed as he tickled his wife's bristles to soothe her nerves."

"I'm sorry to hear that... do you know what's wrong with him?" Mole inquired.

Mrs Hedgehog sighed. "If I had to guess, I'd say he's been nibbling on the freaky fungus that pops up at this time of year... You know, the ones that look like little bells?"

"I can't say as I do... you mean, like the ones under this tree?"

"Aye, that's the little beggers... cause no end of trouble they do!"

"There, there, dear." Mr Hedgehog gave her another tickle. "Think about your nerves."

"Fhtagn!"

Mole shivered at the strange word that burst from Ratty's snout like a sneeze. "What did he say?"

"Dunno," Mr Mole shrugged. "It sounded like fart wagon or something."

"Mr Hedgehog!" Mrs Hedgehog cried in outrage. "Don't be so course."

"Sorry, dear... that's what it sounded like."

"It's just gibberish, Mr Mole... he's away with the fairies and no mistake." Mrs Hedgehog sniffed.

"What can we do?" Mole asked, with great concern.

"Well, if it is mushrooms... he'll probably be right as rain in a few hours." Mrs Hedgehog's expression darkened. "Unless..."

"Unless?"

"Unless he's had too many."

"Then what?" Mole's voice had risen in pitch, betraying his hysteria.

"Then..." Mrs Hedgehog paused for an unsettling amount of time. "Then, he'll die."

"No!" Mole yelped. "I'll go and get Badger... he'll know what to do. Can you keep an eye on him until I get back?"

"Sure!" Mrs Hedgehog said sourly. "It's not like we have anything better to do... like hibernating."

"I won't be long, I promise!" Turning to his friend, who was now doing something akin to backstroke in the leaves, he lowered his voice to a calming level. "Ratty... I'm going to get help. The Hedgehogs will keep an eye on you. I'll be as quick as I can, okay?"

Ratty cackled and made odd whistling sounds, oblivious to Mole's words.

Turning back towards the riverbank, Mole scurried as fast as he could towards the Wild Wood...

***

"I'll swing for the little perishers... just you see if I don't!"

It wasn't uncommon to hear grumbling from behind Mr Badger's door, but he sounded especially browned off as Mole reached out to give the knocker a good slam.

"Blasted weasels, they get their mucky paws into everything!"

Mole paused for a second. Under normal circumstances, he would leave Badger to his grumbling, but these were far from normal circumstances. Still, he felt a hint of trepidation as he raised the heavy old knocker. Badger was a kindly old soul... but he could be beastly when in a foul mood. Taking a deep breath, Mole commenced knocking.

Bang! Bang! Bang!

"Who the devil is that now? If that's you thieving blighters again... I'll wring your blasted necks!"

"Um... Badger, it's me, Moley!" He called through the letter flap.

After a period of heavy shuffling noises, the door creaked open. "Upon my soul, Moley!"

"Is everything okay, Badger?"

"No, it darn well isn't!" Badger fumed. "Someone has broken into my library and pinched a couple of very rare and expensive books! Weasels, I'd wager. I tell you when I get my paws on whoever is responsible..." He

made a snapping motion with his paws. "Anyway..."
Badger smiled genially. "What brings you to the Wild
Wood on a cold day like today?"

"I need your help, I'm afraid... it's Ratty. If ear he's
eaten poisonous mushrooms. He's most terribly ill!"

"Slap me sideways!" Badger bellowed. "We don't
have a moment to lose. I'll fetch my first aid bag and
medical books... if those mischievous mustelids haven't
run off with it. Now, where is the poor little fellow?"

"In the meadow. Mr and Mrs Hedgehog are keeping
an eye on him."

"Capital!" Badger grunted as he slung an old brown
satchel with a red cross on the side over his shoulder,
and tucked a book under his arm. "lead the way, my
good fellow, and tell me everything you can about
Ratty's condition, it may help."

As they made their ways through the rapidly
darkening woods and along the riverbank, Mole told
his robust companion all about the day's events. Badger
said nothing the whole time but occasionally made
low grumbling noises. As Mole spoke of the ducks, the
squirrels... and the crows, he found himself becoming
more and more hysterical. Badger made no attempt
to calm him, and his silence only added to Mole's
disquiet.

By the time Mole had finished his disturbing
narrative, they had reached the boundary of the
meadow. This is where Badger finally broke his silence.
"Ratty's over by the tree, you say?"

"Um... yes. Well, he was."

"Come along then, Moley. Let's, not dally. If I'm
right... we have much more to worry about than mere

magic mushrooms." Badger's mighty brows knitted together like a gigantic furry caterpillar. Mole had never seen such a look on Badger's face before. It was a look of fear.

"What is it, Badger?" Mole asked as he opened the gate for his companion. Though he asked, he didn't really want to know the answer.

"Just a nasty suspicion, my good man... I shall know soon enough."

Hastening towards the tree, Mole and Badger scanned the bed of rumpled leaves for their friend. "Oh, fudge!" Mole spat. "Where the devil is he?"

"Ratty!" Badger boomed, his voice carrying for miles. Reaching the tree, he used his omnipresent walking stick to search under clumps of decaying foliage. "Blast! He's not here."

"Excuse me, sirs!" A tiny voice announced. Badger knew it instantly. It was one of the young Hedgehog children."

"Ahh, Young Hedgehog... do you happen to know where Ratty has got to?" Badger asked gently, not wishing to cause the youngster alarm.

"Why, yes, sir!" The Hedgehog replied. "Ratty fell into a deep sleep, so my parents took him to your house, Mr Mole."

"To my house?"

"Yes, sir. They were worried he'd catch his death of cold out here... I hope you're not upset."

Before Mole could answer, Badger cut in. "Of course, he's not upset. They have acted very wisely. Thank you for your message, Young Hedgehog. Now, you run along home, you hear?"

"Yes, Mr Badger, sir," the Hedgehog squeaked before hurrying away.

"Come along, Moley. Lead the way."

"Follow me." Mole sighed as he rummaged in his pockets and pulled out a handful of change.

"What the devil are you up to?" Badger asked as he saw his companion sorting through his coinage.

"Oh, just getting some sixpences ready for that blackguard Old Rabbit... with you here, I'll owe him at least four... he'll probably charge me for Ratty and the two Hedgehogs too. I'll be penniless by the time today is over at this rate."

"What!" Badger exploded. "Is that bonder still up to that old trick? I've warned him before about demanding toll money. What does he think he is, a blasted troll? ... Well, don't you worry about that cheeky old beggar. I'll soon put a stop to his nonsense!"

For the first time that day, Mole felt his spirits rise. He was going to take great delight in watching Badger give Old Rabbit a good dressing down. Unfortunately, as quickly as they rose, they were quickly dampened down then drowned.

Badger and Mole emerged from the meadow to a very strange scene. The gravel road was packed with young rabbits. They sobbed, held hands, and hugged. Something was clearly amiss. Rabbits were usually such boisterous critters, so it was vastly unusual to see them display such emotion.

"Excuse me, my boy." Badger tapped one of the older rabbits on his heaving shoulder. "What the rhubarb has happened?"

The rabbit pointed to an old abandoned barn just over

the way. "In... in there... 'orrible it is, simply 'orrible."
The rabbit answered between sobs. "Poor Old Rabbit...
who would do such a thing?"

Badger and Mole looked at each other. This didn't
sound good. Pushing through the distressed throng,
they hastened towards the barn. Several constables
stood around the door muttering in low tones about
an atrocity and a heinous crime. One of them, a rather
rotund boar, was off to one side violently regurgitating
his breakfast.

"Excuse me, Constable Trotter," Badger called out to
an acquaintance he recognised under his blue helmet.
"What's happened?"

"Oh, Badger. Thank God it's you." Trotter grunted.
"You know about all kinds of unusual things... tell me,
what do you make of this?"

As he swung open the barn door, Badger gasped,
and Mole nearly fainted. They had just gazed into a
ghastly nightmare. Old Rabbit lay in the centre of the
barn with his limbs splayed out in a star formation.
His abdomen had been ripped open, and his intestines
draped over his left shoulder. A glistening pile of organs
sat just over the right, and his lucky foot, his right, had
been removed and taken away. Old Rabbit's blood had
been used to decorate the barn in a vast occult symbol
resembling a swirling Arabesque with a distorted eye in
the centre. Candles had been placed around the design
and Old Rabbit's corpse in a perimeter circle.

"Well," Badger muttered. "I don't think you'll have
to worry about giving him another sixpence."

Mole gagged as a vision assaulted his eyes. He'd
seen that symbol before... it was a close approximation

of the formation the ducks had been swimming in. He whispered this to Badger, who grunted as though it all made perfect sense. "Come on, Moley. I fear we are all in great danger."

"Badger," Mole demanded. "You know something, don't you? … You must tell me! What is going on here?"

"First, tell me," Badger raised his voice to match his friend's. "That word Ratty said. The one that sounded rude. It wasn't, fhtagn perchance?"

"Yes... that's it!" Mole confirmed as they left the barn and headed towards Mole's home.

"Just as I suspected... I didn't tell you this earlier, because I didn't want to alarm you until I was certain. You see, the books that were taken from my library were not ordinary. They were discovered by my ancestors in a bricked-up part of the old Roman library... Gods, I wished they had left them to rot. These books tell of ancient secrets that no creature should ever learn. They speak of old gods and hideous abominations that would plunge the world into chaos and darkness if ever released. The most dangerous of all... is the Necronomicon by the mad poet Abdul Alhazred. Only a fool would dare speak the incantations held within..."

"Toad!" Mole suddenly spluttered. "I knew I'd heard that word before... Toad said it when I bumped into him on the riverbank... and he had a book up his coat! … You don't think..."

"That batrachian bonehead!" Badger exploded, his body shaking with rage. "We need to get to Toad Hall, and fast!"

As they reached the gravel road, the heavens opened, and a peal of thunder boomed above them. Lightning flashed, forking down towards the river in the distance. It was directed at Toad Hall.

"Come on! We haven't much time." Badger grabbed Mole by the sleeve and dragged him through the horde of terrified bunnies. Crows lined the hedgerows, watching their every move. There were hundreds of them... so many, in fact, that the hedge looked like a carpet of fluttering blackness stretching off into the distance.

Badger tossed his medical book and first aid satchel to a couple of rabbits, telling them that they would be well paid if no harm came to them. The rabbits nodded meekly, their usual bravado utterly absent. Grasping his stick in both paws, Badger lashed out at the bushes around the entrance to the meadow, scaring away two large crows that had been eyeing Mole hungrily.

"You don't think Toad had anything to do with what we just saw in the barn, do you?" Mole panted as they raced past the skeletal tree in the direction of the town. "I mean, Toady may be a buffoon, but he's not evil."

"I don't know what to think," Badger confessed. "Though I have to admit, I fear the worst."

As thick rods of icy rain lashed the meadow, quickly turning it into a treacherous quag, Mole and Badger carried on towards the gate in contemplative silence. Neither one wanted to think that their friend could be in any way connected to the atrocity they had just witnessed, never mind being the culprit.

Reaching the gate, their ears were assaulted by a series of blood-curdling screams. "Now what?" Badger wheezed, gripping his stick like a club.

Mole looked around for some kind of weapon and settled on a jagged rock. In his large mitts, strengthened by all the years of frantic digging, a rock could be a deadly bludgeon. "Right, let's go!"

Creeping down the serpentine lanes, the duo kept a constant vigil. Their eyes darted from left to right, scrutinising every dark corner and looming shadow. The screams and shouts grew louder and louder as they turned the corner at the end of the lane and looked down upon the town square... it was like a surrealist painter's vision of hell. The town's populace was being hunted and torn to shreds by hulking toads. Only, these toads were nothing like their Toad. These were hunched and bestial, with a wide yawning maw filled with jagged dagger-like teeth and were seemingly composed of some kind of glutinous protoplasm. Also, where Mr Toad's eyes danced with mischievous light, the eyes of these abominations were merely twin black pools of seething malevolence.

Mole nearly fainted. "Holy sh..."

"Shhh!" Badger put one forepaw over Mole's snout and held him upright with the other. "Don't draw their attention. If they see us, we are lunch."

The town was a mess of torn fur, spilt blood, overturned carts, and broken glass. The monstrously toothy toads leapt on the backs of squirrels and mice, pigs and foxes. Nobody was safe from their savage assault. Many of the townsfolk were dead and devoured. Survivors barricaded themselves inside shops and cafes. Though they had a temporary reprieve, the toads would soon make short work of their fortifications

"Quickly, down here." Badger yanked Mole down a secluded alleyway that ran behind the shops towards the church. "If we go around the graveyard and through the bushes, we will come out by Toad Hall."

"That must be where Toad came from earlier." Mole mused. "Shouldn't we try and help the other animals in the town."

"By going to Toad Hall, we will be helping the other animals. If we are to put an end to this, we need those books!"

Mole didn't need to question Badger to know he was right. After all, a Mole and a Badger armed with sticks and rocks would hardly be a match for hundreds of savage batrachians. Instead, he put his head down and tried to keep up with his remarkably spry compatriot. Badger was on a mission. He hadn't moved with such rapidity since the last time the landlord called last orders down at the local tavern... This thought made him grimace. He could have certainly done with a stiff drink right at that moment.

Coming to a sharp stop as they reached the graveyard wall, Badger held his hand up to stop Mole. "Somebody's coming," he whispered, readying his stick.

Mole got into a pugilistic stance, gripping his rock with such force that it drew blood from his palm. Furtive-sounding footsteps approached the wall, followed by frantic scrabbling. Badger prepared to swing when a sleek figure in a black robe hopped over the wall and darted through a gap in the fence. Badger chased the figure to the fence and watched its escape.

WORLDS COLLIDE

"Who the devil was that?" Mole asked.

"I'm not sure... but I think it was a ruddy weasel." Badger scratched his chin thoughtfully. "Hmm... why was he wearing a robe? … I wonder..."

"Come on, Badger. We don't have time for Weasels, we need to get to Toad."

"Quite right, old chap! Let's go!"

With adrenaline coursing through their exhausted bodies, Badger and Mole rushed towards Toad Hall.

***

"Begone you, foul fiends!" Mr Toad's hysterical voice echoed from one of the upper windows of Toad Hall followed by the bang of a shotgun and the splat of an evil toad's head. Mole and Badger were crouched behind a pile of automobile wreckage next to Toad's boathouse. The Hall was under siege from a small army of ravenous toads. They flung themselves at the doors and tried to climb the trellises up to the first-floor windows. It was a good thing that Toad had invested in some top-notch security after his recent Weasel infestation.

"Go away with you... Shoo, shoo!" Toad aimed again, and another monstrosity exploded in a burst of sticky green slime. He didn't seem to be in much peril, but Mole and Badger were completely cut off from him. If they were either to get into Toad Hall or get Toad out of it, they would have to think of something clever.

Badger patted the pockets of his long frock-coat until he heard a faint jingle. Rummaging inside, he pulled out a toad-shaped keyring and grinned. "Come on, Moley... this way. I have a plan." Badger led Mole around to the garage door and removed the enormous padlock on the latch with one of the keys. "Quick, inside!"

Moley squeezed through the gap that Badger held open and nearly collided with a beautiful motor car. "What's this doing here? I thought Toad wasn't driving anymore."

Badger lit an oil lamp with matches from his pocket and closed the door behind them. "He isn't... I made damn sure of that." He jangled the keys triumphantly. "The old rogue had a relapse a couple of months ago but I managed to nip it in the bud."

"Bravo, Badger... I'm surprised that he went along with it. Couldn't he have picked the lock and hotwired the car?"

"Well... technically, yes. But, I promised that I would be checking regularly and if I saw evidence of him tampering with either... I'd beat the little bounder to a pulp!"

Mole chuckled nervously as Badger slapped his stick against his free paw. "Anyway... what's your plan, Badger?"

"It's very simple, my boy." Badger grinned and tapped the bonnet with his paw. "Climb aboard, and put your seatbelt on..."

Toad was fumbling shells into his antique shotgun when his garage door exploded. The roar of an engine and the insistent poop-poop of a car's horn sent his heart doing backflips. Forgetting the toads forming a pyramid of bodies under his window for a second, he looked on as Badger aimed his car at the toads and stamped on the accelerator.

Mole screamed, and Badger roared as the wheels of Toad's motor car spun in the mud before gaining traction and lurching forwards like a pouncing cat. As the glutinous toads gave up on the door and tried to use each other as steps to the window, Badger locked on to their position. One of the top-most toads looked around and let out a croak of alarm. It was too late, however...

Splat!

"Get your thieving green backside down here, pronto!" Badger bellowed as he brought the car to a halt in the pile of squished toad goop. "And, bring the Necronomicon!"

"The what?" Toad asked unconvincingly.

"Don't play dumb with me, you nefarious pond-dweller... just ruddy bring it!"

"And the gun!" Mole added as Toad picked up the worm-eaten book from by his feet. Toad tossed the gun and the box of shells into the back seat of the car followed by the Necronomicon. Finally, using the rose trellis as a ladder, he climbed down to the ground and bolted for the car's back door.

"Look out!" Mole shrieked as a toad hopped out from under the car. One of its legs was mangled, but it was still alive... and incredibly annoyed.

Toad cried out in horror as it lunged for his throat. It was inches away from sinking its fangs into his slimy skin when a blood-smeared rock clattered into its face and sent it spinning to the floor.

"Get in, for God's sake. There's more of them coming!" Mole yelped as he rubbed the arm muscle he had strained with his straight bowl.

Toad flopped into the back seat, and Badger put his foot down, speeding up the driveway and onto the road. "Can I drive?" Toad asked hopefully.

"Not on your nelly, you blasted miscreant," Badger snarled. "I ought to lynch you myself for what you did to Old Rabbit!"

"Old Rabbit? I... I don't understand." Toad's face showed genuine confusion.

"This is all your doing, isn't it?" Badger continued. "Confess! Then we may be able to undo what you've done!"

"But... But... I didn't do anything!

"Then why did you steal the Necronomicon?"

"I didn't steal anything!" Toad implored. "You've got to believe me! I was in the willows reading from this old book when those things appeared."

"Balderdash!" Badger roared.

"Now, now, Badger..." Mole said in soothing tones. "Let's hear him out... If you didn't steal it, Toady, where did you get it?"

"Um... Err..." Toad looked sheepish.

"Come on, Toady. We can't help you if you don't tell us everything."

"Okay," Toad sighed like a deflated balloon. "I was lonely... Spring is coming, and I don't have a ladyfriend... again. So, I went to see Fergus the Ferret... he can get certain kinds of magazines and stuff."

"Oh, Toad..." Mole shook his head.

"I know, I know... Anyway, I'd finished looking at the one I got last week so, I went to see him this morning to get another, but he didn't have any more..."

"Then what?" Badger pressed as he pulled the car

over at a picnic spot on the edge of the Wild Wood.

"Well, we got talking, and he told me about this God in a book he had. He said it could sort me out with a mate... all I had to do was read a certain page..."

"What page?" Badger demanded. "Show me."

Toad picked up the evil tome and flipped it open to a page he had marked with a receipt for a new pair of slippers. "This one." He pointed his webbed finger at it and handed it to Badger.

"Oh, good Heavens... This is a prayer to Tsathoggua, one of the Great Old Ones!" Badger continued to read the scrawling script. "And, you definitely didn't kill Old Rabbit?"

"Heavens no!" Toad was aghast. "I may be a silly ass sometimes, but I'm no killer!"

"I believe him, Badger," Mole added.

"Hmm, so do I," Badger confessed as he continued to scan the page. "If he didn't do it... But why?" Mole could see the gears turning in Badger's bulbous brain... it was a wonder steam didn't shoot out of his ears. "It says here that only amphibian lips may wake the Sleeping God... He who speaks the incantation can command. Got it! You've been set up, my good man!" He yelled in Toad's face. "Those fiends have used you as a key... you silly ass!"

"Who has?" Mole threw up his paws in confusion. "What are you talking about?"

"Fergus the Ferret! He and his weasel gang have orchestrated this whole thing. They stole the Necronomicon, as I first suspected. They killed Old Rabbit to provide the sacrifice to Tsathoggua, unleashing madness on the town... all they needed then was this buffoon," he jabbed a paw at Toad. "To speak the incantation and summon him to earth!"

"What do we do?" Toad asked.

"Load your shotgun... we are going to pay a visit to Fergus the Ferret!"

***

Badger brought the car to a stop by a festering pond deep in the heart of the Wild Wood. Motioning for Toad and Mole to follow, he climbed out of the driver's seat and skirted around its perimeter. Finally coming to a stop next to a blood-spattered black stone altar. "Come out, Fergus... the jig is up!"

A nasal voice snickered from somewhere nearby. "You shouldn't have come here, Badger!"

"Show yourself!" Badger snatched the shotgun from Toad and flipped the safety off.

"What can the three of you do against my coven?" Fergus chuckled again, long and rattling.

Badger was about to make a scathing retort when around twenty weasels and stoats in black hooded robes appeared from the undergrowth clutching wavy sacrificial daggers.

"Um... we're surrounded." Said Toad.

"I can see that you ass," Badger replied.

"Get 'em, boys!"

As Fergus' demented cackle filled the clearing, the cultists attacked. Badger managed to blast two of them before having to reload. Toad walloped one in the snout with Badger's stick, and Mole planted another with a fierce jab. In the end, however, they were overwhelmed.

"Don't kill them yet! Bring them to the sacrificial altar! As his acolytes did as commanded, Fergus finally showed himself. He had been lurking in an old rabbit hole. Stretching his sleek white-furred body, he sloped over to his captives. It was time for a good gloat. "I knew you'd come... I was counting on it. You see, I need to feed Tsathoggua a tribute when he arrives, and who better than you three?"

"Why?" Badger growled. "What's all this for?"

Fergus rubbed his paws together. "With you and the rest of the villagers out of the way, we will be kings here! We will finally get to claim Toad Hall!"

"That's it?" Badger snorted derisively. "No plans for world domination? No demanding masses of wealth from the government? This is all because we kicked your furry backsides out of Toad Hall?"

"Enough!" Badger had clearly struck a nerve. Fergus marched over to the car and snatched the Necronomicon. "It's time to summon a God!"

Striding to the edge of the pool, Fergus tilted his head back and began to chant in a bizarre language that sounded like the babble of a flooded stream. Fierce winds blew the leaves and debris in the clearing into a dizzying cyclone as lightning flashed and thunder rumbled. Fergus' chanting rose in pitch and speed until the water of the pool erupted like a geyser.

The airborne mud and filth hung in the air before coalescing into a big roiling ball. As Mole watched, open-mouthed, it formed itself into the shape of an enormous toad with bat wings and long tufty ears.

"Iä! Iä! Tsathoggua!" Fergus and his minions cried in exultation.

"Take them as a tribute, my Lord!" Fergus yelled over the din of the elements. "Then finish off the villagers.

Tsathoggua opened his sleepy eyes and looked at his offering. Opening his gigantic maw, he licked his fleshy lips with his long rubbery tongue.

"Quick," Mole hissed at Toad. "Say the word."

"Which word?"

"That word. The one you said when I saw you on the riverbank."

"What... Fhtagn?" Said Toad.

Instantly, Tsathoggua retracted his tongue and spoke in Toad's head. "What do you want of me? Why has my slumber been disturbed?"

"I... I... didn't wake you." Toad snivelled. "It was him!" he nodded at Fergus.

Quick as a flash, Tsathoggua's tongue scooped up the fiendish Ferret and swallowed him in one big gulp. The next few moments were pandemonium. The Toad God ate the acolytes one by one before vanishing back into the pool leaving only Toad, Badger, and Mole alive.

"Wh... what happened?" Toad stammered.

"I remembered what Badger said about those who speak the incantation having command. You spoke the incantation, Toad!" Mole smiled.

"But... I didn't command him to eat them."

Badger shrugged. "I guess he took umbrage at being disturbed... a feeling I completely understand."

"So, what now?" Asked Mole.

"We will need to help the town recover... first though, I suggest we have a nice cup of tea and throw this damn book on the fire."

WORLDS COLLIDE

To mutters of agreement, Badger led his friends back to the car. The riverbank was safe once again... for now.

--END--

FAITH AND BEGORE
By Derek Power

First things first: zombies and leprechauns are real.

I know what you're thinking, but just trust me on this one. I've first-hand experience of it all. Now that we've got that out of the way, let me tell you how I know this. More importantly, let me tell you about zombie-leprechauns. I mean, if you think The Leprechaun from that old horror movie was scary, you ain't seen nothing yet when it comes to the walking wish granting undead variety.

How can I make such a ridiculous statement and sound so sure of myself? Easy, I'm living through a Zombie-Leprechaun apocalypse right now. Let me tell you, it's nearly as bad as you see on the shows and somehow worse at the same time. I suppose on one hand we—humans—are lucky that it seems to be contained entirely to Ireland. The only problem is the entire island has been quarantined off from the rest of the world. I mean, who thought all it would take to unite North and South was a humanity ending apocalyptic event? But if one thing can unite people, it is when they have a shared goal of survival.

I'm not talking about just people in Ireland, let's be clear. I'm talking about every other nation on the planet. I think the ring of steel around the island was put together in less than four hours. Nothing in or out by sea or air. I'd say the only reason we haven't been nuked off the face of the Earth is because, as usual, somebody in power wants to see how they can turn a pretty penny from the suffering of millions.

You just know that there is an army general somewhere wondering if they can weaponise zombies in a controlled fashion.

But I'm getting ahead of myself. First, I need to tell you how I came to live in this horrific fantasy lovechild of Disney and Freddy Krueger.

Let's start with the zombies.

It turns out that what the movies have mostly told us about the walking dead isn't true. They rarely, if ever, come from some mad virus or scientific experiment that got out of control. No, zombies have been around for as long as Voodoo has. That's right, in order to wrap your head around this, you need to accept that magic is a thing. I mean, I did mention the leprechauns, right?

But yeah, zombies. Ireland is not known for having

an abundant supply of the walking flesh eating dead. All our myths and legends are greatly lacking in the undead department. We've absolutely loads of stories about magic and shapeshifters, witches and what not. Just no animated corpses chowing down on the grey matter of whoever they shuffle upon. Who knows why that is? Some nerd in a history society is better placed to explain it. The thing is, though, that despite having so many stories riddled with magical and mystical elements, modern day Ireland just doesn't believe in magic anymore. I, for one, blame technology. Once you have a thing in your pocket a little bigger than a cassette tape (kids, if your parents aren't part of a roaming zombie horde, ask them what a cassette is) that can do wonderful things, magic becomes easy to dismiss.

Which is how the zombies first got into Ireland.

Like most countries when goods or people come to the island, there are checks in place. You can't bring in a plant that would possibly throw the ecosystem into disarray or a breed of fox that would be an extinction level event for some hedgehogs. The people in charge of doing such checks are good at their job. But then one day somebody passed through the airport with a large steel box that had several locks on it. During the checks, and I am telling you this based off reliable information, the box was opened. What was inside? Yep, you've guessed it. A zombie head.

A genuine, snapping, snarling, looking to spread its zombie love bite, undead head.

Which is how it always starts, isn't it? Somebody investigates something they shouldn't and boom: infection spreads. The custom checker thought the head was just a prop for a movie. Sure, he had seen it on his phone how all those things are done with robotics and rubber. Without even asking permission of the case owner, he reached inside, got bitten and the rest, as they say, is bloody awful.

They say Patient Zero basically turned most of the airport in the space of an hour. After that it was game over. You see, if you only need to stop one or two zombies, you can contain these things. It is the way of it. Zombies only win in the stories because they have the numbers. That's literally it. A numbers game. Zombies gain upper hand when they hit double digits. You know how many people work in an airport? How many passengers pass through on a daily basis? Neither do I, even though I probably should know. But I can tell you whatever the number is, it is enough to cause problems for an island of about five million people.

We were overrun inside of a week. Zombies don't sleep or need to go to the bathroom.

At least I don't think they do. It's a topic never covered in the movies. Maybe they just pee on the go.

But the leprechauns, you said something about leprechauns. That's what you're probably shouting at me now.

Yes, the leprechauns. You see, it turns out that leprechauns and fairy folk from all the old Celtic tales… they're real as well. Which makes you wonder if all the old stories about fantastical creatures from around the world should be believed, also. Like I said, as humans grew more and more dependent on technology, they just stopped believing in the Old Things. Which seemingly suited the Old Things because they all went into hiding and left humankind to their own devices.

Get it, devices? No… okay.

Anyway, in Ireland, that was the leprechauns. Little wish granting, pot of gold guarding, end of a rainbow living leprechauns. Honestly, nobody saw it coming. As the newsfeeds were all focused on zombies roaming the lands and eating people, making more and more zombies, nobody was paying attention to the conspiracy threads and posts that said leprechauns were now being turned into zombies as well.

After all, it is human nature to only accept one incredible thing at a time. Two is just asking too much. But it was true leprechauns were real, and the zombies were biting them just as indiscriminately as they were humans.

But how? I'm sure you're asking that.

It turns out that zombies see things a bit differently to humans. Something about the transformation, or maybe when your eyes start to decay, they open new spectrums to view in. Obviously, nobody has ever spotted this before because in order to have your eyes decay, you must be… well… dead. Kind of hard to tell the living what you are seeing when you are worm food. But yeah, there you have it. Turns out leprechauns have been walking around in plain sight for centuries and people just could not see them. All it took was a little zombie apocalypse to reveal that to the world.

Every mushroom cloud has a silver lining.

Whatever magic the leprechauns had been using to hide from mortal sight, zombies saw right through it. If they spotted something moving with brains, then the zombies just shuffled after it until it was chow time. It didn't matter whether it was a human or a leprechaun, a brain is a brain at the end of the day.

Of course, one thing people are good at doing is adapting. Even in the End Times some folk figured there was a new job for them. Just as influencers became a thing thanks to social media, zombiologists cropped up in some survivor camps to help people better understand the enemy.

What the zombiologists did learn was interesting though, because for the first time in human history, we had two types of zombies to study. Which led to a morbidly fascinating observation being observed and documented. That last part is important because the zombiologist who observed it only had a few minutes to write it all down before they were bitten. Thankfully, her notes were found a few weeks later when a search party had been sent out to find her.

Which they did. Roaming around the woods of Wicklow, moaning for 'brains'.

Anyway, the discovery was that zombie-humans and zombie-leprechauns are after two vastly different things. The human variety are, just like the movies imply, interested in eating brains. Those zombies whose lower jaw hasn't fallen off from decay just keep mouthing the same word over and over again. They want to eat the brains of humans. Yes, they will nibble on flesh, take a bite out of any exposed skin, but the brains are what they are after. And, as it turns out, this is not just some trait added to the legends so that zombies are scary and gross. There is a reason they do this.

Through all human history, people have only ever wanted to do one thing at the end of the day. Prove they are smarter than everyone else. Turns out this trait is now engrained in our genetic makeup and survives after the transformation from person to undead. Zombies want brains, because on some level, they think eating the brain will make them smarter.

It doesn't, of course. But it did give the zombiologist enough information to come up with a unique distraction technique when they were out in the field. They carried with them human brains in bags. As the hordes of the undead shuffled towards them, the zombiologist just threw three or four brains out on the ground and ran. The zombies fell on the brains like hungry undead hippos and the zombiologist got away.

Wait, didn't you say that the zombiologsit had got bit? I did, but I never said which type of zombie had done the biting. You see, if a human zombie can turn a leprechaun into a zombie-leprechaun, then it stands to reason a zombie-leprechaun can bite a human and have the same effect. Which is exactly what happened. While all the normal zombies were chewing down on their free brains, a zombie-leprechaun that had been nestled in amongst the horde broke free and chased after the zombiologist.

You see, she hated the noise that the zombies made, the constant moaning for 'brains', so while out in the field she used headphones that could cancel out the sound if it got too much. The problem is that one of the best things to use in electronics is gold. It makes conductivity utterly amazing. So, while zombies wanted brains, zombie-leprechauns wanted nothing more than gold. Like grotesque squirrels, they attacked any human with gold, gnawing and biting at them to get the shiny trinkets in their mouth. Literally anything with gold. Jewellry, smartphones, coins. If it was even one caret, a zombie-leprechaun could sniff it out. Tossing away some electronics or jewellry would have had the same effect as tossing a brain towards a human zombie.

Not that the zombiologist thought of this. Which was how she got zombified (yes, that's a verb now) and lost her headphones in the process.

Overall, a bum deal.

She remained human just long enough to scribble down those final findings before the leprechaun had chewed through her left ear and the zombie infection took over completely.

But this information did get me thinking.

Currently, I'm living in the bastard love child of a Celtic Legend and a George A. Romero movie. All the rules have been thrown out the window. Nobody does a nine to five anymore, because you're running away from flesh eating monsters most of the time. Then you must factor in that the world learned about leprechauns and magic being real. This is what bad B-Movie plots are all about. It did give me an idea, though.

See, leprechauns are known for granting wishes. Not like a genie, which would make things so much easier. But still, a wish is a wish at the end of the day. If you're looking to get out of a zombie infected wasteland, how are you going to do it?

With a wish, of course.

All I need to do is capture a leprechaun.

I can hear you judging me right now. But you got to trust me on this. I've had a lot of time to think. See, zombies are real, as I've explained. Leprechauns are real, but they are just like people. Humans have been hiding, sometimes fighting, the walking dead at any given chance. The leprechauns must be doing the same thing. Running, hiding, using their magic when they can. All so their zombified fellow leprechauns don't nibble on their fingers to get them gold rings.

Now, how am I going to do this? Well, that is a great question.

See, while the zombie-leprechauns are chasing after people looking to eat their ears off for earrings, the still living leprechauns are just as greedy. You think the economic crash of 2008 was because of sub-prime lending? It was because leprechauns were stealing gold straight out of the human vaults and topping up their supplies. That is, until the King of the Leprechauns reigned all that in and told them to knock it off. At least that is the going theory I read online. It could, obviously, be a load of shite, but right now it's as good a working theory as any I've heard.

All I need to do is set a trap, lay the bait, and survive the flood of zombies that will come while waiting for a leprechaun to show up.

Sure, what could possibly go wrong?

***

Right, well, let me tell you... I really didn't think that would work.

First things first, I got bitten. That's right, the fearless hero succumbed to the walking dead and was gnawed on.

Entirely my fault if I'm being honest. Can't even blame the zombie, she was only doing what nature told her to.

Anyway, there I was, robbing the National Museum of some golden chalices, lost in thought about how a zombie apocalypse must be a thief's dream situation for capers and heists. I mean, think about it for a second. You've the entire world focused on not being eaten, so all you have to do is not trip any alarms which would draw the attention of the undead and you're golden. Anyway, there I was, opening the display case when she popped out of the shadows and lunged for me. Judging by the uniform, I think she must have been a security guard back during her living days.

We tussled. I fell backwards and instinctively raised my hand up to stop her mouth clamping down on my neck.

Bite. Gnash. Snip. Off with my fingers.

I've no idea how I didn't scream out in pain, but I was able to reach out to a fire extinguisher on the wall nearby and grab it. With a grunt and a swing, I smashed it into her head, knocking said head clean off her body. It went flying across the room like a horrible chattering football of death and decay.

Then I dropped back on the floor, stared up at the ceiling, and groaned.

See, all those years reading comics and watching movies, wasting my life as my now zombified mother used to say, were finally going to pay off now.

If you get bit on most parts of the body, it is game over, but a limb... a limb is like the zombie lottery being won. You've about four minutes to *127 Hours* that bad boy and boom, you don't become a zombie. Now, if I'm being honest, I'd have loved it to be a leg instead of an arm. But beggars can't be choosers.

The only problem… I needed something sharp to hack the arm off and I was already starting to feel tired from the bite kicking in. That's how they get you, you see. Bite, you kill them, then you have a nice little nap and turn.

Which was when the miracle happened.

"You can count your lucky charms, buddy," a cheery voice said to my left.

I managed to move my head and saw the object of all my desires. An honest to God, not just special effects created, magical creature standing there before me. All dapper green suit and bowler hat, complete with shamrock stuck into the band. Even his bright ginger beard was perfection.

"You're a…"

He didn't even bother to answer. Grabbing a sword from one of the nearby museum displays, he ran his thumb along the edge of the blade. Little green stars followed along the metal as he magically sharpened the weapon. Probably the sharpest it had ever been at all, I reckoned. The leprechaun ran over and, without even asking, took a swing and chopped through my bicep.

"MOTHER OF GOD!" I roared.

Well, you would, wouldn't you?

"Be grand," the leprechaun said, tossing the sword away. "You won't even notice. Bit of TCP on it, good as new. Minus the rest of the arm, of course."

He kicked my former forearm over towards the zombie corpse, then offered me his hand.

"Name's Pádraig," he said. "Of the O'Toole clan."

I couldn't believe it. The most Irish of names, but what did that matter? He was a bloody leprechaun.

Which meant I had a chance.

Rolling over, ignoring the intense pain in my missing arm, I reached out with my remaining hand and grabbed the leprechaun's ankle.

"YOU'RE CAUGHT!" I shouted with glee.

Pádraig frowned, looking down at my hand, then back to me.

"Are you kidding me with this?" he asked. "I just saved your arse from turning into a zombie and you pay me back by covering me shoes with blood. Do you have any idea how hard that is to get out?"

I didn't care about his ruined clothes for two particularly important reasons. One, I was bleeding out, and two, I was about to save the entire bloody world from the zombie outbreak.

"Listen up, Paddy, you're caught. You know what that means."

The leprechaun chuckled.

"You haven't caught me, you blithering idiot. You're just holding onto my ankle. That's not how you catch a leprechaun."

He was right, of course, but that wasn't something I was going to let him know. Mainly because I didn't want him trying to make a sudden mad escape attempt. What I hadn't planned on was learning the leprechaun's name without any work on my part.

"Pádraig O'Toole, I name thee," I said, with as firm a tone as I could manage while struggling to not pass out.

The leprechaun's eyes opened wide.

"Oh, Dagda, damn it," he swore.

"Pádraig O'Toole, I bind thee," I said, gritting my teeth a little from the pain.

"Oh, you actually do know what you're doing," Pádraig said.

He was right, I did know. After all, I had had months to read books and plan for this. If you find the same silly entries across multiple legends, it turns out that somebody got it right years ago. How to capture a leprechaun, right there amongst what people used to think were made up fairy tales.

"Pádraig O'Toole, I command thee," I said.

I'm still not sure if magical sparks came out of my hand or if I was just seeing things from the whole 'arm hacked off' thing. But there was a little golden light and bands of magic attached Pádraig's left wrist to my remaining one like magical handcuffs. Two circlets appeared on our wrists before the bands of light vanished from sight.

I let go of his ankle and rolled onto my back.

Pádraig raised up the magical circlet and examined it, then frowned at me.

"Honestly, you humans are the worst!"

I didn't waste any time.

"Pádraig, I wish for my arm to be whole and healed once more."

The leprechaun pinched the bridge of his nose, closed his eyes, and let out a long sigh.

"Are you kidding me? You could have just asked me to do that, you didn't have to do a binding for Dagda's sake. It's the end of the bloody world as we know it, to paraphrase a popular Bangles song. Zombies everywhere. You don't think I would throw out a freebie wish that healed your arm if you'd just asked?"

He wiggled his fingers, and my upper arm tingled

right where the wound was. There was a bright, golden light that flowed down and formed into an arm before growing so intense it was hard to look at. I had to close my eyes, and even then, I could still see the light through my eyelids. But as quickly as it had begun, the light disappeared and when I opened my eyes again, I had two arms once more. Not my original arm, no, that was still on the other side of the room dripping in blood. This was an entirely new arm, fresh from some magical oven. The skin was perfect, missing the several tattoos I had got over the years before Zombie Apocalypse Now.

"Where's my tats?" I asked Pádraig.

"Your exact words were 'whole and healed once more'. That's what mortals never get about wishes. We grant you exactly what you ask for. We're not out to try and trick you for some stupid reason. You all are just too dumb to understand that words have power and meaning. Say exactly what you want, not what you want interpreted. Tattoos are wounds, ergo a 'whole and healed' arm is going to be missing them. Simples."

I moved the fingers on my new hand a few times, made a fist, and nodded. I could always get new tattoos, but bleeding out from a chopped off arm would have made that a little difficult. So, I guess, in the long scheme of things, the leprechaun had done alright. I stood up and smiled at him.

"Alright, tiny," I said. "That's wish number one."

"Like the cartoon says, no wishing for more wishes," Pádraig told me, pointing up at me like a small schoolteacher.

"Oh, don't you worry," I said. "I know the score."

Pádraig arched his left eyebrow and stared at me.

"If you wouldn't mind, given that I just saved your life. Twice, technically. Could I have a wish?"

I frowned.

"You? Who's going to grant it? I'm not a genie. I think you're missing the whole point of being captured. You're meant to grant my wishes."

"No, I will. I will," the leprechaun said, making placating gestures with his hands. "It's just wishes are a unique sort of magic. Sure, leprechauns can grant them. But we can't use them ourselves. All we can do is normal magical stuff. If we want to use a wish for something… well, we have to sort of ask a mortal to make the wish for us so we can grant it."

"Why?"

"Wishes don't just grant things, they warp reality. You wished for a new arm, but that isn't something magic can do. However, a wish can bend the very fabric of the universe so that you have another arm, making you the first human in the world to have three arms if you count that gross paperweight over there."

That, I had to admit, was interesting information. Turns out that even at the end of the world, it was possible to learn new things.

"Okay," I said. "So, you have a wish you'd like made and you want me to request it from you? Is that some sort of magical loophole? Why don't you just get one of your mates to grant you a wish?"

Pádraig sat down on the ground and rested on his elbows.

"It isn't that simple. Leprechauns can only grant the wishes of mortals. If a leprechaun asked for a wish from another leprechaun, nothing happens. I dunno why, I didn't make up the rules of whatever crazy fantasy story we're in. It's why I have been looking for somebody, anybody, that isn't a zombie. The undead generally don't make wishes... or speak using words. I'd spotted you carting all this gold in here and figured you must still be in command of most of your brain. Even though I couldn't figure out what in Dagda's name you were up to."

I looked back over at my Smaug-åsbord gold, my leprechaun bait, and frowned. I had been full sure that had been a great idea. Apparently, I had been mistaken.

"It was a trap? A Smaug-as board of golden trinkets."

"Are you asking or telling?" the leprechaun said. "Also, did you just say Smaug-as board? Like a play on Smaug the Dragon and Smörgåsbord? Doesn't matter. The reason I came in here is because I spotted you doing... whatever you were doing. In the nick of time, too, it seems. So, what do you say? Grant my wish?"

"No," I told him, firmly. "I have two wishes left and I know exactly what I want from both. I need you to bring me back in time so that I can stop this whole nightmare from taking place. I wasn't sure if that was a thing, but you said that wishes bend reality so I'm guessing it shouldn't be an issue."

Pádraig jumped to his feet and held his arms out wide, a big cheesy grin on his face.

"Are you serious? That's what I was going to ask you to wish for. I had a friend, he got bitten. Anyway, he figured this was the best plan to save the world. So, we went looking for a mortal. He found one and the mortal moron just wished for gold, everlasting life, and a big house. Like… seriously. He was the richest idiot in the End Times and he wasn't going to die. Of course, he never thought about putting in a 'non-zombify' clause, so that immortality lasted all of five minutes. Then he nibbled on my mate. Long story. But if you want to go and wish for normality, then let's do it."

I won't lie, I was suspicious of how eager he was to grant the wish.

The Little People were known for trying to make mortals idiots when it came to these games. They would use word play and all manners of other verbal trickery to somehow grant the mortal their wish, while still coming out on top. But I had studied my opponent. This was not a game of draughts. It was chess mixed with monopoly and a dash of Risk, all rolled into one.

Staring down at Pádraig, I smiled, then locked eyes with him.

"Pay close attention," I said to the little fellow before me. "Because my wish is going to be precise, and you are to honour every single word of it. No fairy folk she-nanigans. No making me wish for a nine-inch pianist. I want exactly what I am going to ask for, plain and simple."

The leprechaun nodded his head quickly, rubbing his hands together and licking his lips.

"Oh finally, finally!" he said. "This nightmare will end. Let's do this."

I took a deep breath, then exhaled.

"I wish to be taken back in time to before the Zombie Apocalypse started. I want to be able to intercept the case before it gets to security. I want to be there thirty minutes before it was opened, so that we can avoid a *12*

Monkeys style ending to this tale and be rushing around the place. With you by my side the entire time as support, should I need it."

Pádraig frowned.

"Alright, now listen, I'm not trying…"

I raised my hand and shook my head twice.

"No funny word play," I reminded him.

"No, I get that," he said. "It's just that, well, before this all started, nobody knew leprechauns were real. I can't exactly risk exposing us after we time travel. Is it alright that I am by your side but in disguise?"

I thought about it for a minute. That wasn't the worst idea in the world. Keeping the knowledge that there really were fairy folk living among us would be good.

"Fine," I said. "But that's all, a disguise. Nothing else."

Pádraig nodded his head and clapped his hands together.

"Oh, this will definitely work," he said. "I mean, I had just wanted somebody to say they wanted the apocalypse undone, but your version will work as well. If you don't stop it, I will be there to do it. Of course, I will be there twice, given we're travelling into the past. But let's not worry about that. There are enough genres being mixed up in this mad tale without bringing a sci-fi headache into it."

He held up his hands and bright, golden shamrocks appeared in the air. They spread upwards, fanning out over the pair of his and forming a dome that slowly lowered to the ground. As each shamrock joined its shimmering siblings, the museum became obscured from view, until after a minute there was nothing to be seen but the golden dome around the two of us.

It was quite beautiful to watch.

As the last shamrock slotted into place, the dome touching all points of the ground, I felt like I was on a rollercoaster. Without moving, I moved.

Quickly.

Presumably, it was something to do with how a person travelled backwards in time. The feeling lasted for a minute, then stopped as suddenly as it had begun. There was a blinding flash of light, causing me to close my eyes. When I opened them again, I was no longer in the museum.

"Final boarding call for flight M.C.U. six-one-six," a woman's voice announced over the tannoy.

I looked around and found myself standing in the arrivals lounge of Dublin Airport. About me, travellers went on with their travelling. Some giving me dirty looks as they walked past, others ignoring me completely. Glancing down at my attire, I could see what the attraction was. I was covered in blood, wearing a ripped shirt and probably stank.

Since showering isn't really a huge priority in the Apocalypse.

"Pádraig?" I asked, looking around for the leprechaun.

A small girl ran up to me. She had shamrock hair clips holding two cute pigtails in place and wore a dress that would have made most Irish Dancers jealous.

"Howdy," she said.

"Pádraig?"

"Patrice, I guess now," she said. "But yes, it's me. Your trusty leprechaun."

"Whatever," I said, scanning the crowd. "We need to get that zombie head… there she is!"

I pointed at a woman stepping out of the gangway and turning to the left. She was carrying a rather ornate steel box in one hand and a small, battered suitcase in the other. The suitcase didn't matter, but I knew without a shadow of a doubt that the zombie head was in the box. All that stood between humanity and the walking dead were a few inches of metal and some shoddy locks.

"Come on," I said, running after the woman.

The little pitter patter of feet was all the acknowledgement I needed that the leprechaun was following. All we had to do now was get that box away from the woman and the world would be safe as investing in houses during a boom economic cycle.

Keeping sight of the woman, I saw she turned and went into the toilets. Like any seasoned traveller, I was all too aware that after getting off an airplane the first thing most people wanted to do was use a toilet that did not experience turbulence at the worst possible moment. Following her inside was going to be tricky, given that people generally frowned on males going into female toilets.

But I now had a useful ally.

"Patrice," I said. "Get in there and steal that box."

The leprechaun nodded her head and ran past me, ducking in between two sauntering sixty-year-olds so that she could get into the toilet. Faster than I expected, she came running back out with the box in hand. Without breaking step, Patrice ran up to me and tossed the box up to my arms.

"Meet you on the other side of security," she said, before running on into the crowd.

As she weaved through, the leprechaun caused people to be bumped and jostled out of her way. I spotted the woman formerly known as 'holder of the box of death' coming out of the toilet and looking around, panicked. She spotted Patrice and the chaos the little one was causing and ran after her. Meanwhile, I hid the box behind my back and breathed a sigh of relief.

Moving quickly over to a security door, I reached into my pocket and pulled out my I.D. badge, pressing it up against the scanner on the side and unlocking the door.

Now, I know what you're thinking. "How in hell did he get that? That wasn't mentioned before. Talk about some Deus Ex Machina bullshit."

And you would be right to assume that, except for one important detail. How did I know so much about how the zombie apocalypse started? Well, it's simple really. I was working in the airport the day it all started. How else would I know what the box looked like without having to be told? I had seen it get opened all those months before. Hence knowing what it looked like but also trusting my wealth of comic book knowledge so that when the security guard was bitten, I just high-tailed it out of there before all hell broke loose.

I stepped through the door, closing it tightly behind me, and started walking down the hallway that would lead to an exit on the far side of security. It only took me five minutes. At the other end, I opened the door a crack, peering out to make sure that nobody was waiting for me, then stepped out and merged with the crowd. As I walked along, I caught sight of the woman, talking to several airport personal. No doubt describing Patrice in intricate detail. She would probably find it hard to explain what exactly was in the box, but that hardly mattered now. I had saved the world.

Up ahead, I saw Pádraig, dressed now as a small school boy. I walked over to him and gave him a conspiratorial nod.

"We did it," I said.

"Thank Dagda for that," he said. "It is you, right? The future one?"

"Of course it is," I said, holding up the box. "Why else would I be carrying this?"

"Ah, see, I may have ran into your former self. I didn't know you worked here. I thought it was you, so I went up to you. But you had no idea why I was telling you about leprechauns and boxes with zombie heads in it."

"Doesn't matter," I said. "That guy isn't me and now, thanks to this little time crime, he never will be."

Pádraig smiled.

"I can't believe it's all over," he said. "No more zombies. We did it. Time to relax."

"Well, it isn't completely over," I told him, lowering the box. "I still have one wish left."

-End-

SOCIALLY REVENANT

By Deborah Dubas Groom

Stormy knew two absolute truths. There was never a good time to tell someone they are dying, and it is worse when you have to tell them they are already dead. Her job as a paranormal counsellor, courtesy of the Unveiling, was very different from that of a regular therapist. Her office didn't have ficus trees, soothing colours, lemon water or a swanky reception area. She was licensed to carry a 9mm Glock, holy water, silver bullets and nice pointy stakes. Her business was not only on the other side of the tracks, but about 10 miles past where any respectable woman would work, and that was okay with her.

She was not a hard-living lady, but she had learned

that there were a lot of people, and members of the paranormal community, who did not necessarily want the dead to speak, and they played rough. Her clientele did not mix well with the cucumber sandwich crowd, which included her parents, so she chose an office space on the outskirts of the city, where the paranormal was the norm. She had found a patched-up brick-faced building that had been an old textile warehouse. It had a large office space on the second floor with metal locking shutters, a solid fire escape, security cameras in the back alley, UV night lighting and reinforced floors. The offices were warded, and the furniture was scavenged. It was perfect.

Stormy was not the name given to her by her parents, the Knights. She got tagged with it by some yuckster back in high school, when the glamour that had been hiding the supernatural population for 5,000 years, suddenly stopped working. One minute she was a dreamy-eyed senior writing bad poetry in English class and the next, her thick auburn locks began floating and sparking because the girl next to her was part Fae. Over time she had learned to tamp down its effect, but the moniker kind of stuck. As far as she knew she was human, mostly, and whatever else, that made her just different enough to function in each world.

That rainy morning she parked out front of the small bakery that was two doors down from her office. She got out of her trusty little Honda and raced to the sidewalk to avoid getting splashed by passing cars. She made a quick pastry purchase, then hurried over to hand it to Burt, the gutter troll who, for the cost of a danish a day, kept her car safe. The locals knew to walk on the other side of the street, especially on days like this, as Burt stayed closer to the surface when it rained, and he was an ankle grabber. Stormy considered it money well spent.

Entering through the front door, she felt the light tingle from the protective spells that were keyed to her and her receptionist Siobhan. Stormy usually took the stairs rather than the antiquated, rattling old lift. She preferred, if an unexpected visitor was lurking, to keep from giving them a warning of her arrival. Her soft, dark brown leather, Elven-made boots made no sound on the metal steps. As soon as she pushed through the fire door though, the silence ended, and a loud voice rang out.

"Good morning, Stormy, your 11am is here. She seems pretty tightly wrapped about her mummy issues."

Siobhan burst into hysterical laughter at her own wit, but what could Stormy expect when she had hired a half-price Banshee as her receptionist? Siobhan dabbed at her robin-egg blue eyes and refastened her long dark hair that tended to go into a mad frenzy of lashing tentacles whenever she laughed or screamed. Once she had patted her locks in place, adjusted her cardigan and narrow woolen skirt, she tapped her clasped-hands brooch, and went to get the client from the soundproof waiting room. Stormy shook her head and went into her already opened office.

It still had a lot of the character and feel of its former tenant, a 1940s detective, Sean O'Reilly. He had been a fixture in the mean streets of the city, helping out who-ever he could in the community and enjoying the appreciation of the females from all levels of society. Sean had been larger than life, so much so that he hadn't quite fit through the door when it was time to leave.

She thankfully picked up the fresh brewed coffee waiting for her. Siobhan might be hard on the ears, but she was a gem with a cup of joe. The scent of the fresh ground beans curled around her and the warmth of it seemed to banish the wet and grey weather. Within the hour however, Stormy knew she should have asked for an espresso.

The sharp tap of kitten-heeled shoes rang out as her client walked across the old plank floors. Stormy rose from behind her desk as the grim-faced woman gingerly stepped over her threshold. Normally people would be greeted in the waiting room, but she had found it important to make sure that her clients could enter her office without an invitation. She knew you only got to make that sort of mistake once. She straightened her shirt and plastered on a smile. It was showtime.

"Good morning Mrs. Kent,"

Stormy motioned to the chair. She tried to avoid shaking hands as she liked to keep a safe physical distance until she had assessed a new client.

"Won't you take a seat?"

Mrs. Miranda Kent stared at her with bulging eyes and took a small step backwards. It was not the first time Stormy had elicited that reaction. Whatever had pushed Mrs. Kent to visit must have really tied her pearls in a knot.

Clutching her handbag to her chest like it might be ripped out of her hands, she looked at the mismatched office chairs and draped her raincoat over one before sitting. Stormy sat and leaned back slightly in her banker's chair. She had learned that by leaving a silence, people often felt compelled to take the lead. Miranda, knees pressed together, hands white-knuckled, finally broke.

"Ms. Knight, I will be upfront with you..."

Stormy sat back. This was not going to be a fan girl moment.

"I don't really care for the chaos that has come into the world since the Unveiling. If my husband knew I was here, he would be appalled."

From the intercom screen Stormy could read Siobahn's suggestions for Miranda's husband. She schooled her facial expression to stay passive.

"But this can't go on. I need you to get rid of my mother."

Just to make sure Miranda was not trying to hire some muscle, Stormy decided to clarify just what service Miranda thought she could supply. That's when the tips of Stormy's shoulder length hair began to shimmy. She gave a quick shake of her head to make it appear natural and pressed the red alert button to let Siobhan know they might have uninvited company.

"I see Mrs. Kent... Your mother's ghost needs assistance with moving on?"

Before Miranda could respond, an opaque figure began to materialize on the chair beside her. The woman had blonde, just from the parlour hair, the perfect ladies' lunch country club outfit, and jewelry that would have covered Stormy's rent for a year. She leaned over and tapped through Miranda's hand.

"Miranda Annabelle Scott Kent, I'm you mother, and

I won't be talked about in this way!"

Miranda's face went a deep and unhealthy shade of red. Stormy braced as Miranda first glared at her, and then in a deceptively calm voice spoke to the air.

"Mother, do you remember that time we went to the carnival, and you bought me that huge cotton candy?"

The figure froze for a split second and flicked.

"Of course, sweetheart."

Miranda's eye squeezed shut. Her response was clipped.

"Wrong. You wouldn't have been caught dead at a fair, and if we had, you'd have packed a snack bag with carrot and celery sticks."

A smile flickered onto the figure's face while the rest of her stayed frozen.

"Well, that just shows me as the caring and responsible mother I am."

Miranda snorted.

"It shows that you're a revenant." The figure pixelated.

"That's so prejudicial. Who taught you to use language like that?"

Stormy looked past the doorway to Siobahn who was just out of Miranda's line of sight. Siobahn shook her head as she scanned for the dead. In true banshee style, her jaw had gone slack to her knees, her eyes huge in confusion. Whatever the mother was, Stormy knew she was not a true ghost. Stormy did not like how the figure had floated past her wards. The bickering continued.

"Nice try," Miranda shot back. "You're a memory fragment that was downloaded and did not transition properly. It's time for you to go into the light." The figure shifted into a saintly pose.

"Heaven?"

"No, back into the hard drive you came from."

The mother, or whatever she was, struck a dramatic pose.

"I should've never pushed you out into the world! You're an ungrateful daughter. Your brother would've been thrilled to see me again."

Miranda dropped her head in her hands.

"I never had a brother."

"Well, I meant to have a son, but life happened."

Miranda, not looking up, muttered, "You mean life ceased to happen."

"Why are you like this?!"

The figure became incredibly bright, and then vanished in a burst of sharp light and sparks. Siobahn flitted back to her desk, barely stifling a screech.

Miranda sat blinking, a tremor running along her lips and the crease of her mouth. Words, in monotone began to pour out.

An hour later, a very subdued Miranda Kent, having given Stormy all the information she could, descended the stairs and exited the building. Stormy watched from the window and was glad Miranda was too preoccupied to see the ghoul in the alley checking the rat traps for snacks. When Stormy turned back, her chair was occupied by a man, his shoes up on her desk and a fedora slouched foreword on his head. His shirt sleeves were rolled up, accenting tanned, nicely shaped forearms. His pants, held up with suspenders, had a definite retro flare.

"You know, I kinda liked the broad. She has moxie."

Stormy snorted.

"You always like the women. I can't imagine even in life that Miranda might've been your type."

He grinned, wickedly.

"I was not talking about the daughter, though her type can fool you. I was talking about the mom. She's got a little class and swagger. I bet she…"

Stormy shooed him out from behind her desk.

"I think I get the picture."

He dematerialized and reappeared lounging in a leather club chair that didn't exist, at least in her office. He tilted the hat back, letting her see his sky-blue eyes. Normally they sparkled, set off by his bronzed face, strong jaw, and killer smile, but he was not smiling now. Forearms on thighs, he leaned forward.

"Kid, we've got something weird here. Whatever that was, it was not a ghost. She didn't even know I was in the room."

She pushed her mop of hair off her face and arched an eyebrow.

"Maybe you just weren't her type."

He laughed.

"Sister, I'd have been her type all right, but I'm telling you that there was no one there!"

Sean got up with the lithe ease of a boxer and prowled over to the liquor cabinet that also didn't exist in the office.

"Sean! What have I told you about drinking on the job? We can't do that."

Shortly after Stormy signed the lease on the building and moved into her office, she ended up with an unexpected addition to her staff. For better or worse, Sean, whose former office she had rented, became her de facto associate. When she was out of the office, he was an invisible hitchhiker, unable to materialize outside of the building. But his endless curiosity often took her from strictly counselling to the occasional investigation. Some of the locals who'd been around during his time would consult with Stormy as if she was Sean. The problem with him having a few belts before they went out on a call, was that somehow, Stormy could partially feel the effects. Unsettling as it all was, he did have insights and raw street smarts that made him an asset. Things seemed to be working, at least for now.

Stormy leaned out into the hallway.

"Siobahn?"

A gust of wind ushered a harried looking Banshee into the office, her eyes perfect circles, her body vibrating. "What was that? It weren't no ghost, or demon, or shifter."

Sean went over and put an arm around her shoulders, which caused Siobahn to spontaneously change her outfit to resemble a 40's pinup girl. Stormy stifled a laugh and Sean gulped. It was an open secret that Siobhan had a crush on Sean.

"If we can get on with business. Mrs. Kent said that her mother died over a year ago. Before she died, she had gotten roped into a variation on cryogenics. Instead of them freezing her head, she found a place that uploaded her memories, pictures and personality profile with the hopes that one day a suitable cybernetic body could be created so that she could live eternally."

Sean and Siobhan stared in silence. Sean shook his head.

"So, she was a sucker who fell for a scam, right? I mean, what we saw has got to be your garden-variety demon or something." He looked back and forth between the two.

Stormy pressed her lips.

"Sorry Sean, but this thing went right through my wards and Siobahn didn't even recognize it. Any other thoughts? Siobahn?"

Siobahn got up, pulling up the edge of her black and white striped tube top, smoothing the cherry red hot pants, and tottered over to the bookcase. Her fingers trailed the spines of the books as she chatted away to her supernatural contacts in the ether. Finally, she pointed with a red lacquered fingernail.

"There is only one place that has a history of bringing stories to life, literally, Wolfie Pug Books.

You remember the lovesick, rampaging female Viking incident? Or when that ogress ate that plastic surgeon who offered her a makeover? That was them. I don't know if they are involved but they might have some answers."

Siobahn graced them with a grin that involved far too many pointed teeth.

Stormy grabbed her car keys

"Well, Wolfie Pug seems like a good place to start.".

"Siobahn, regular office attire please." Stormy ignored the low moan.

She looked at Sean.

"Are you coming?" He grinned and flicked his suit jacket over his shoulder.

"Wouldn't miss this for the world."

***

Stormy walked into the beautifully appointed lobby of Wolfie Pug Books. The building was surprisingly corporate, with marble tile floors, large glass windows and a beautiful quartz reception desk. They could hear the faint buzzing of conversations and movement, but no people.

Sean's voice whispered.

"Head's up kid, we've got company."

In her peripheral vision Stormy caught movement.

A bundle of sticks that had been stacked in an alcove, suddenly righted itself and approached her. As it shook itself out, a small wood-grain face appeared, as well as arms and legs, and tiny twig fingers on its hands. Stormy hadn't met this particular creature before but knew that the question, "What are you?" was the height of rudeness in the supernatural community. It stopped in front of her, stared with its shiny, berry-bright eyes, gave a quick nod of its head, and began to hop from foot to foot up the wide staircase to the second floor.

Wolfie Pug Books was not the sort of place where you went unescorted or uninvited. That was doubly true when you were going to the very private offices of the owner, Heather Dawn. Stormy cautiously followed up the stairs and crossed the mosaic floor to the amber-coloured glass doorway, surrounded in passionflower vines. Her escort motioned her through.

Stepping over the threshold was a shock to the senses. Stormy didn't know if she had fallen into some sort of fugue state, but she smelled spring rain, lilacs, lemons, and sun. There were sounds of water washing up on the coast, the call of shorebirds, and the tall dune grasses rustling in the wind. The light poured in from an open Mediterranean blue sky and gave a gentle warmth to the cliffside garden she found herself in. Stormy saw the orchard, the sparkling ocean, the shell-scattered beach, and white-washed terraced palaces all shifting and existing in an impossible landscape. Stormy stayed rooted in place, her hair forming a corona around her head.

Sean spoke sharply.

"Hey sweet cheeks, snap out of it. You're lit like a sparkler. You're scaring the life out of me and I'm already dead!"

Without acknowledging his voice in her head, Stormy walked forward, skirting fountains of sparkling water, and moving towards the woman waiting by the marble benches under the olive trees. There was no question that this was the illusive Heather Dawn. She had a surreal beauty but also the embodiment of a power so ancient you trembled. Her eyes held such depths that an ordinary mortal would drown, never able to come back without their mind being hopelessly scarred. Stormy saw a tall, elegant woman with olive-skin tone, large warm brown eyes, a wide and gracious smile, full lips, and long neck. She wondered if this was her only form. As if by a trick of the light, one moment she was in a long sheath dress held by a clasp and the next it seemed she was in a sophisticated, New York chic business suit. Rapidly images began to flick past Stormy's vision and then stopped with Heather Dawn standing before her, dressed in a long sea foam green halter dress, her thick dark hair loosely pinned up and an unusual seashell suspended from a chain around her neck.

"Little sister, welcome to my home. Please, sit. I see you've brought a visitor with you. Let him know that he may join us."

Stormy's eyebrows shot up. Heather Dawn could sense Sean.

"Thank you so much for being willing to meet with me, I mean us. I would've asked about Sean but he's a ghost and he can only materialize in the place where he died, his old office. I didn't mean to cause any offence." Stormy worried that she had erred.

Heather Dawn tilted her head to the side, seeming to look into Stormy, her eyes impossible to fathom

"Who told you he was a ghost?"

Stormy's face lost colour and she braced herself against a tree trunk to keep from falling.

"He was shot. He died in the 1940s"

"Those two things are not the same." Heather Dawn paused.

"I would prefer to continue this conversation with all the involved parties."

As Heather Dawn lifted long fingers towards the canopy of leaves, a hand reached out from behind the tree and grabbed Stormy. She twisted sideways, ready to fight, and came face to face with a very solid Sean O'Reilly.

Stormy stammered as her hands touched his face, his shoulders, and arms. For the first time she could feel the warmth of his skin, the rasp of his stubble and the texture of his sandy hair. He grinned with an innocence and wonder she hadn't seen before. He seemed unable to speak. Though reluctant to look away from Stormy, he turned and fell to his knees before Heather Dawn. Slowly, he lifted his face and waited for her to say something.

Stormy crouched beside him, her arm around his shoulders, her cheek against the side of his head. She didn't like the look of sadness on Heather Dawn's face as she spoke.

"I am sorry, but you must understand that you can only stay like this, no more than 48 hours, maybe less."

Suddenly animated, his eye's bulging, Sean leapt up. Stormy stood as well, placing a hand on his arm to keep him grounded.

"But you said I'm not a ghost, so if I'm not dead then why do I only have 48 hours!?"

Heather Dawn seemed to expand, her presence taking command of the space.

"When the time comes to address your situation you may speak to me again, but for now, if you stay longer than the 48 hours, the bullets that shot you will finish their work and you'll die. They were interrupted by the Unveiling, and you entered into a state of being that is most… unusual."

She said the last word with a solemn weight. Stormy's face became a maskof confusion.

"Please excuse me, but I don't understand. Sean was killed, I mean shot in the 1940s, long before the Unveiling. How could he be part of it?"

Heather Dawn nodded.

"It was an event that hit different points in history. Sean's role in this is still to be seen, but I have very little time right now. We need to focus on the situation with the revenants. It's more serious than you imagine."

The pair snapped into professional mode and was wise enough not to interrupt. Stormy also noticed she said revenants instead of revenant.

Heather Dawn's face became shuttered, as if the topic brought her pain.

"I believe, with regret, the troubles started here. Before the Unveiling, I developed my company for the purpose of sharing knowledge, fostering creativity, and bringing dreams to life. We have adapted from bards and scribes to graphic books." She gave a fleeting smile. Her passion for knowledge evident.

"At the time of the Unveiling many on staff were already known to me as paranormal and had found a safe home here. It was the ones who came into their identity during the change in reality that caused the most disruption." She paused.

"I think the person you are looking for is named Benjamin Dirk. He was one of our tech team. He was responsible for programming and systems. Once the Unveiling hit, characters, and creatures from some of the stories started coming to life. Often, they could be corralled with a bit of editing and would disappear. The more aggressive ones needed a systems purge."

Stormy leaned forward, tickled by the idea of dancing penguins popping out of the computer screens.

Sean laughed, "Benny must've been a hit with the ladies."

Stormy rolled her eyes, but the corners of her lips quirked up.

"Let's keep it on topic Romeo." Sean gave an unabashed grin.

"I'm afraid it didn't work that way. Benjamin was enamoured with Dena Li, a sweet young junior writer. He was always stopping by her cubicle but couldn't find it in himself to speak to her." Heather Dawn paused. Her eyes closing briefly. Stormy caught the faint scent on lilies.

"Dena was obsessed with unicorns... She had several figurines on her desk. Benjamin decided to make her dreams come true."

Sean ran a hand over his face.

"While Dina was logged into her computer, he sent a replica of an action figure through her screen. She was terrified... Unfortunately, what he had summoned was an avenging unicorn and it trampled her as she tried to flee."

Stormy wrapped her arms around herself. This time it was Sean who put a hand on her shoulder.

"By the time I reached her, she was already gone. Benjamin became hysterical, screaming that he would save her, but there was nothing he could do. The technology in the building lashed out as if sentient, mirroring his pain. Other employees were injured."

Sean, grim-faced, looked at Heather Dawn and started to rise.

"So where can we find this Benjamin?"

Stormy put a cautioning hand on his back and intervened.

"My apologies, I'm so sorry for your loss. If Benjamin is no longer here, how would he go about releasing these revenants? Where would he find them?"

Heather Dawn answered.

"When we shut down his equipment, he left, swearing to bring Dina back and fix things. Benjamin went to work for Meta Life, an organization dedicated to uploading people's memories and personalities in the hopes of transferring them to synthetic bodies. Two days before her funeral Dina's body was stolen from the morgue."

Sean raised his eyebrows. Stormy felt ill.

"Do you think it is possible that Benjamin has become some sort of technological necromancer, a kind of… technomancer?"

Stormy, becoming animated, slapped her hands together.

"It fits! He vows to bring her back and I bet he's been experimenting on the company's uploaded clients."

Heather Dawn did not smile. Her pallor became the colour of marble and her eyes rimmed red.

Sean and Stormy, now standing, took a step back.

"His power is growing and becoming more dangerous. His revenants were prepped with the hope of being transferred to artificial bodies. They are the uploaded personalities and memories of some of the wealthiest and most entitled members of society. They will be ruthless in their search for homes. If these animated digital creations can possess human hosts, within 24 hours the original host will die, and their bodies will be piloted by memory fragments with no souls or morals to act as a restraining hand."

Stormy and Sean's faces were transformed into a rictus of horror. Stormy slung her purse over her shoulder, knowing time was short.

"How do we free people who have already been affected? How do we stop all this?" Heather Dawn looked at them from what seemed like an incredibly distant place.

"Cutting off the heads of the hydra will do nothing. You have to take out the heart. Find Benjamin. We are counting on both of you."

A mist enveloped Stormy and Sean. When it parted, they were standing on the front steps of Wolfie Pug Books. As if in a daze, they walked over to Stormy's little blue car. She pointed it out to him.

"This is my Honda. Someone stole the letter "n" off of it, so now it's my little Hooda."

Stormy stopped talking as Sean looked at her.

"I know. I was here for the ride, but this is the first time I get to drive."

Stormy gave a sharp laugh.

"Show me a current drivers' licence and we'll talk. Now get in. We need our resident wonder Banshee to do some quick research so we can find this guy."

***

As they drove, Stormy couldn't help looking over and wanting to touch Sean to reaffirm that he was not a Heather Dawn induced hallucination, but she could smell his cologne, and feel the warmth of his skin radiating from his body as he leaned close to her.

Her sense of wonder was quickly replaced with a surge of adrenaline when she saw the obstacles on the road. Her wheels screeched as she slammed on the brakes. Wide-eyed both Sean and Stormy stared at what seemed like a street party that blocked the path to her building. An old-fashioned police officer, who bore a striking resemblance to Charlie Chaplin, held up a hand that stopped them while a chorus line of sparkly vam-

pires came dancing across the road, with a pixelated
Bob Fosse shouted directions. On the corner cosplay-
ers surrounded a famous sci-fi princess and her space
smuggler lover. Stormy pointed.

"Wait! Is the smuggler Christopher Walken? That's
so wrong."

Later, Stormy would swear to people she had heard
the faint sound of cowbells. She did her best to explain
it all the Sean, but he was too busy looking at the bizarre circus to listen.

She sat back and watched random wires crackling
and dancing on the end of telephone poles, and people's
phones projecting faces that yelled back at them. Sean
spotted Agatha Christie and Dashiell Hammett sitting
on a bench in a bus shelter, taking notes. The neighbourhood was packed with fictional movie characters
spouting their famous lines in an endless loop and bug-
eyed people walking through them. The street entertainment was not the only source of amazement.

"Benjamin must've found out we'd be looking for
him." She mentally slapped her forehead. "If he's this
hooked into the internet, our searches must have set off
some sort of alarm."

Sean let out a low whistle.

"Well, I don't mean to scare you doll, but have you
checked out the lineup in front of home sweet home?"

Stormy made a small, strangled sound. Stretching
down the block, along the broken pavement of the
derelict sidewalk, were people yelling to get into her
building. Being the only tenant, it was a safe bet they
were looking for her. The only good news was that the
bakery, and the Lebanese pizza place beside it, were

getting some business. From the occasional jumping, it looked like Burt was enjoying himself as well. She could also see the faint shadows of "loved ones" hovering around the frightened and frantic people in line.

Stormy drove past the building, pulled into the back alley, and parked in a space just behind the fire escape. In pulling down the panel behind the car, they were able to hide it and make it up to the office undetected. Within three steps of the office fire escape door, they heard screaming and it was not just Siobhan. Sean grabbed Stormy's gun as they raced in, while she held a stake. The scene that greeted them was one for the record books.

Papers flew everywhere, caught up in the banshee's frenzied energy and shouting. The phone was ringing and there were hundreds of messages circling the room. The opponent seemed to be a wraith, clothed in a long diaphanous, cape, hanging over its face, arms, and hands. She was equally strident and rattled the timbers. Stormy raced towards the two and broke to a halt. The shoes on the wraith, she knew those shoes. They were specially designed with the Knight family crest. She clenched the stake tighter.

"Siobahn, mother, stop this now!"

Sean's mouth flew open and then he burst into peals of laughter. His collared shirt stretched across his chest and grabbed the attention of all three ladies.

"Button it, O'Reilly!"

Sean lifted his hands in a sign of surrender, but his shoulders still shook in merriment, and there was worse to come. Both Siobahn and Lucinda Knight spun towards Stormy. Lucinda started first, her perfectly shaped brows raised.

"Gwendolyn Delphenia Knight, tell this harridan to let me into your office. I have no intention of being locked into a waiting room. My problem is urgent." Pausing suddenly, she eyed Sean appraisingly. "And who is this quaintly dressed gentleman?"

Stormy gave a low groan. Sean gave his most charming smile, stepped up and took Lucinda's hand. Her eyes sparkled and Stormy could have sworn her mother sucked in her stomach and her cheeks. Sean brought Lucinda's hand to his lips.

"Please forgive me for not introducing myself. I now see where Gwendolyn gets her beauty. I'm Sean O'Reilly, and I'm her associate. If there is anything I can do for you, please let myself or Gwendolyn know." Stormy knew that he used "Gwendolyn" a second time just to get to her. Oh yes, those wicked baby blues made it very clear that he intended on getting good mileage out of this. Siobahn now began to rage.

"She waltzed in here ahead of everyone else and demanded to know where you were! She only got past the wards because you share DNA. The crowd is ready to burn the building down. Have you seen this stack of messages?" The pieces of paper previously floating around the room crashed. "The city is a madhouse, it's starting to wake the dead, and not the good kind!" Suddenly, seeing Sean in the flesh registered for Siobahn. Her eyes grew to the size of side plates.

"You're, he's, he's…" and then with a shriek she began flying around the office so quickly it was impossible to track her. Stormy ushered Sean and her mother into her office. Siobahn would need some time before she would be ready for the story.

Lucinda sighed heavily at the flea market decor in the office and sat.

"OK mom, I won't even ask why you were wearing the patio drapery. We're really in the middle of something that is time sensitive. Why are you here?"

Lucinda took a moment readjusting her clothes. Her platinum blonde hair was cut into a flattering angled bob that accentuated her heart-shaped face, high cheekbones, and far too observant eyes. Her looks were money in the real estate business. Her posture would have made any ballet teacher proud. Stormy waited, trying not to click her fingernails on the desk in sheer frustration.

"Gwendolyn you've got to fix this! I have worked too hard as chair of the social committee at the club to have it destroyed by the return of Lupinia Blackthorn! I don't mean to speak ill of the dead, but that woman was a blight. She was loud, and bossy, and never listened to anyone!" Stormy ignored the irony and was pretty sure she knew who the particular 'anyone' was.

"After her passing, her daughter Tia joined the committee, and she was a dear. Suddenly her mother appears and then poof, her daughter starts acting and talking just like her! She has been working like a demon to dismantle every improvement I've made." Lucinda shook but managed to thank Sean and stroke his arm when he brought her some water. Stormy bristled and forced herself to use some of the calming methods she taught her clients.

"Mother, as you can see the city is in chaos." Her mother frowned.

"Gwendolyn, you know I'd rather you called me Lucinda. "Mother" makes me feel old."

She turned to Sean and flashed a perfect smile. "All I'm asking is that you banish that woman back to wherever she came from."

Stormy scrunched her shoulders up tight.

"That's the problem. She's not a ghost and for the record, I'm not a witch and I don't do spells."

Lucinda, snapped into her keen hunter mode.

"Well, if she isn't a ghost, what is she?" She looked quickly between Sean and Stormy. Siobahn entered the office and sat down.

"We're calling them digital revenants. It isn't a ghost. It seems that people who uploaded things about themselves, have had their files "brought to life" via a technological necromancer."

Siobahn whistled.

"A techno necro?!"

Sean gave a bark of laughter.

"That sounds dirty."

Stormy shot him a look.

"We are following a lead on a man named Benjamin Dirk," Siobhan's ear-splitting laughter interrupted Stormy.

"That's great! If we hire him, I could answer the phone, "Hello, Dirk and Stormy Knight." Stormy gave her a death stare.

"Let's pull it together please. Heather Dawn said he developed a sort of cyber wizardry during the Unveiling. He's trying to resurrect a lost crush, Dena, and we think he is using a place called Meta Life as a way to—"

Lucinda leapt out of her seat, upending Siobahn.

"You met with Heather Dawn?! Do you know how hard it is to get to see her? I haven't even been able to get a meeting!" Lucinda began to pace, her eyes shining.

"If Heather Dawn is involved, I want in."

Lucinda motioned everyone to get closer to the desk.

"So, this Benjamin Dirk is causing the problems. Why not call the police and having him arrested?" Sean turned to face her."That would be great ma'am

Lucinda reared up. "I mean… Lucinda… but we haven't found him. No one can seem to locate Meta Life."

Lucinda smiled like she had just scored a ticket to Paris fashion week.

"That's because it changed its name. It is now called…" she began to rummage around in her Birkin handbag and pulled out a pamphlet and slapped it on the desk.

"It is now called Eternally Yours."

Stormy's jaw dropped.

"Mom, you can't be considering this!" Lucinda snorted.

"Don't be ridiculous dear. It was dropped off at the club and Lupinia stuffed it into my purse, the cow." Lucinda unfolded it and began to read. "*Our brain is made up of about 86 billion neurons.*" Sean shook his head.

"Who did the count on that?"

"Shh, let her finish," hissed Siobhan.

Stormy and Sean exchanged surprised looks. It seemed being able to match a banshee in a screaming match had earned Lucinda some respect.

"*The brain turns input, sensory data, into outputs. By*

mapping the brain and the complex connections of all these neurons, we believe we can encode all this info that makes us who we are and upload it. The key to creating life extension technology is mapping the interactions of the neurons.

At Eternally Yours we have several packages available. The most popular are the Cloud, the Avatar, or the deluxe Cyber Life. The last is still in development and is taking a waiting list.

The Cloud stores the information, the Avatar allows you to communicate with your loved ones and the Cyber Life will eventually download your mind into a custom designed cyber body."

Stormy jumped up, ran to her mother, and hugged her.

"Mom, you are a genius. That is what he is planning to do. He is trying to recreate Dina for a cyber body. What's the address?"

Lucinda, at first startled, allowed a brief unguarded moment of relaxing into the embrace, and then pulled back.

"They don't list it. What you must do is phone and book an appointment. Shall I do that now? Also dear, I do hope you'll let Heather Dawn know how helpful I've been and how I'd love to meet her for lunch." Lucinda did her signature Debbie Reynolds grin and Stormy smiled.

"That's perfect. Thanks mom, you're a lifesaver."

This time Lucinda didn't correct her. Of course, her mother was seizing the opportunity, but Stormy had also caught the returned squeeze. Maybe it was time that she did schedule a visit home.

WORLDS COLLIDE

***

Approximately 36 hours later they were cruising through the city in Lucinda's Lexus. It was pointed out that the Stormy's Happy Hooda wouldn't make it through the gates. Siobahn, sitting up front with Lucinda, and Sean and Stormy in the back.

Once they'd driven out of the madhouse of her neighbourhood, they began to get into farmland. Both Sean and Siobhan looked wistful. Stormy left them to their memories. Upon cresting the first hill past the marker in the instructions, they saw the building that housed Eternally Yours. It had an adobe-style front that could be mistaken for a ranch except for the tendrils of electricity that formed patterns in the air from the blue and purple lit rocks that bordered the property. It was obvious that someone was not worried about staying hidden now.

They pulled onto the cobblestone wraparound driveway. There was no one in sight but the front door was open. As they exited the car and stepped into the entrance, a pungent metallic smell of ozone prickled their nostrils. Sparks of turquoise light flitted off Stormy's fingernails and only Lucinda's hair stayed in place due to industrial strength hairspray. Still, no one appeared.

"...Trap?" Stormy whispered to Sean.

Siobahn put her face between the two.

"Big time. I feel a strong urge to keen."

Stormy turned to her mother.

"Okay, thanks mom. Why don't you wait outside until this is over? I'm not sure how this is going to play out and I can't risk you getting hurt." Lucinda straightened to her full height.

"Gwenie, no offence dear, but I am one of the toughest women you've ever met and if you think I'm going to let my poetry-loving daughter go in without me, then you are crazier than that banshee."

Siobahn preened at the acknowledgement and Stormy blinked. Suddenly the doors slammed shut and black, snake-like segmented arms dropped down from the ceiling and wrapped around Sean. He gave a sharp intake of air. Blood started to appear on his shirt. He grimaced at Stormy, regret in his eyes.

"I'm sorry kid, but I think it's started."

Siobahn let out an angry shout. She sliced the restraint and transformed into a paper-thin long fabric, wrapping herself around his torso to stem the bleeding. More arms shot out from the floor and the group barreled down the hall. Suddenly Stormy's hair pulled hard to the right. Sean raised his gun and shot through the locks to an unmarked room. Alarms sounded and they raced inside, only to be greeted by a squirming tangle of wires and dripping oil, resembling some alien spaceship nightmare.

In horror, they watched a figure emerge through the jungle of writhing cords and tubes. They heard the whirring of gears and scraping of metal. The smell of burning copper and plastic made Stormy lightheaded. Jointed rods in silver and teal mimicked the movement of arms and legs, and ball bearing creating a cacophony of clicking and rumbling. The face was difficult to decipher as ports replaced the ears, eyes replaced by blue gel-filled sockets and the skin a synthetic polymer. Tiny lights flashed around the edges of his face. The rest of his body was obscured by an opalescent sheeting. It was Benjamin Dirk.

"I would welcome you all, but only Mrs. Knight had an invitation. Now if you'll excuse me, I don't want to keep my lady waiting." Stormy stepped forward.

"Mr. Dirk, you've been through a horrible trauma, but real life requires more than a cyber body or Avatar. What you're creating is like a sophisticated memorial recording. The revenants you've released are a menace!" Benjamin gave a grotesque imitation of a smile.

"You are right. That program was too shortsighted and didn't have the capacity to do what it promised. I've created a system where the mind can be disassociated from the biological body, allowing the person limitless lifespans. I can then take it back out into the actual world. I've done it all for her." He craned towards Stormy.

"Since you're here, see for yourself."

To his left, wires and tubing parted like a beaded curtain and a female figure, with a torso wrapped in linens, was wheeled out by motorized flashing units. Their flexible arms kept her from falling forward and supported the tubing that entered ports spaced every three inches on her body. Clear silicone pistons extended from her clavicle to her jaw. The face seemed to be a 3D printing of the original Dena Li. It was the most repellent and heartbreaking thing Stormy had ever seen.

"Benjamin, please tell me what you've done." He looked at her, surprised by the question.

"Can't you see? I used my abilities to bring her electronic synapses back to life! I connected her brain and uploaded it and transferred it into this body I've assembled with enhanced electronics. Me! I saved her. Now she'll live forever, and she'll see that I'm more than she realized. She isn't finished of course, but with the help of some of the organs I harvested from her body the adjustment should be easier."

Stormy watched as thick globules of syrup pushed through the tubing, making obscene noises, and causing Dina's body to twitch. She prayed that the real Dina was not in that nightmare. Lucinda spoke.

"Benjamin, there is no denying your work is… impressive, but I've been reading up on the research and I'm not convinced that the mind, as you have reduced it, may have access to all the biochemical information it needs to recreate someone. I'm not sure any of us knows what makes a person real. I looked at this company as a possible investment and decided it was a pile of magic beans."

The orbits that had held Benjamin's eyes flared red.

"You! With more money she could have been back by now!"

Jagged metal-tipped fish line whipped out from the palms of his hands towards Lucinda. Sean leapt to push her out of the way. Siobhan screamed like a Valkyrie and swooped down, carrying the fallen Lucinda out the cargo bay doors. Sean, now the object of Benjamin's ire, collapsed as Benjamin released a shriek of grinding hears. Stormy jumped in.

"Wait, please Benjamin! I've talked to Heather Dawn, and I know you're not a killer. What happened was an accident. Please don't do this. You've talked about being the right man for Dena! Tell me if she could forgive deliberate murder."

Still huffing like a steam engine, Benjamin began to

stand down. The fluid pumping into his neck and torso turned a darker shade of purple.

"Benjamin, no matter how much information you upload, there is no code for enjoying flowers or artwork, the soul or love. No matter what you do, it won't be her."

Benjamin retracted the dangerous filaments.

"She loves me." His tone was soft. The lights in the room seemed to lose their hard edge.

"May I speak to her?"

Benjamin went completely still. Dina's brown eyes glowed with green irises. He nodded.

"Hi Dena, I'm Stormy." Dina wheezed.

"I'm Dina. I love Benjamin. You should go." Stormy slowed her breathing.

"Dina, does Benjamin hold your hand?"

"My hand has its own attachments. It is not required."

Benjamin cocked his head at an odd angle.

"People in love often choose to show affection this way. Do you feel affection for Benjamin?"

Dina went still, as if processing.

"I love Benjamin."

Stormy moved to stand closer to Dina.

"Dina, what does love feel like?"

A low moan came from Benjamin. In a flat voice Dina replied.

"I love Benjamin," and her frame began to shake violently.

The surrounding flashing lights and hissing pipes became still. Stormy looked over and in place of the monstrosity that was Benjamin stood a thin young man with a weak chin and a receding hairline. His soft, sad eyes looked out from wire frame glasses at the still form that was never going to be Dina. He took her hand in his.

"I'm so sorry Dina. I never meant to hurt you or anyone. I wish I'd told you how much I admired you, your laugh and how you always smiled at me."

His hand shook as he opened the panel for her heart and turned off the switch. The room began to flicker and except for Dena, the tubes and machines disappeared. He leaned his head against Dena's shoulder, his eyes closed.

"The revenants are gone Ms. Knight. I've shut it all down."

There was nothing she could say, then she heard Siobahn wailing.

Stormy ran over to where Sean had lain but there was no body, only a trace of blood. As she turned back to Benjamin he was gone too, but she caught the definite scent of lemon, lilacs, sunlight, and rain.

-End-

HUGGY-WUGGIES AND BLOOD SPLATTER

By Patrick Winters

The Sun rose up in the sky, giggling with joy as it brought another fun-shiny day to the land of Weewah!

"Time to wake up, everybody!" it called out. Its voice rang out far and wide in every direction, echoing from the rolling Red Hills down to the Lazy Valley, from Billybum Forest over to Golden Town, where the great and noble BrightBrows lived. Then, all the creatures of Weewah began to wake from their slumber, just as they did every morning when the blazing Sun graced the sky and gave its call. After all, its light and its warmth were a gift, and that gift couldn't be wasted! Not when there was work to be done or fun to be had!

Collywobbles didn't have any work to do today, so she took her time getting up. She stretched and she sighed, feeling well-rested after a good night's sleep. Then she threw off her covers and rolled out of bed, thinking about the fantastic dreams she'd had last night, where she'd flown through clouds and bounced on great big marshmallows with all her friends!

She walked over to her bedroom window and stuck her head outside, waving up to the sky. "Good morning, Mr. Sun!" she called out. And while she knew it couldn't hear her, being so far away, it was the thought that counts!

Collywobbles (or Colly, to her many friends) was a Wuzzylump, and Wuzzylumps were just one of the many creatures that lived in the land of Weewah. They were a delightful group of beings, with big round ears and fuzzy fur of all colours and hues, all living together in a quaint little village on the edge of Billybum Forest. And while most Wuzzlylumps stood only three feet tall, they made up for their short sizes with their incredibly big hearts, which were stuffed with love, care, and a constant yearning for merriment. They enjoyed playing games, tending to gardens—and eating pancakes! And a big, hot stack of those sweet, tasty cakes were exactly what Colly wanted to start her day with.

Colly headed into her kitchen and set to making her breakfast. She gathered all the ingredients she needed and put on an apron and some oven mitts before she started cooking. After all, safety was very important, and she had to protect that lovely lavender fur of hers!

She ended up making just sixteen of the sweet treats, because she wasn't that hungry this morning. But it made for a fine plate of pancakes, all the same, and she wasted no time in scarfing them down.

Colly was starting to get full (having eaten twelve of the sixteen cakes) when she heard a knock on her front door. She cleaned herself with a napkin and then rushed to answer it, eager to see who was visiting her cottage this early in the morning.

It was Widdershins, her greatest friend in the whole village!

"Good morning, bestest buddy!" Colly said, throwing her arms around him in a big huggy-wuggie.

"Good morning, friendliest friend!" Widdershins giggled as he returned the embrace, then he stepped into the cottage. He tripped as he did so, and he came tumbling down onto his big belly! Widdershins was often tripping here and there and being a bit of a bumbler in other ways, too. It had earned him plenty of owie-wowies in the past, but he never let it get him down—even when he was falling down!

Colly helped him back up and brushed off his amber-coloured fur. "Are you okay?"

"Yup!" Widdershins chuckled. He patted his stomach. "Sometimes it helps, being a little tubby-wubby! Extra cushion!"

They laughed at that, and Colly invited him into the kitchen. She offered him some of her pancakes. Widdershins said no thank you, since he'd already eaten two whole plates of them that morning—but he went ahead and finished them off, anyways.

"So, what have you got planned for the day?" Colly asked.

"Well, I was gonna go into the woods to pick some flowers, and I wanted to see if you'd like to join me! My cousin Bibble visited yesterday and said she's been wanting some new ones for her cottage! And I just know how much you love to pick flowers!"

Colly jumped with joy! "It's one of my most favorite things to do! I'd love to join you! Besides, I'd better go along just to keep an eye on you. The last time you went flower-picking, you brought back a whole bunch of scritch blossoms by mistake and wound up giving half the village a rash!"

Widdershins shrugged. "They looked like fizzybuds, to me!"

Colly shook her head and joined Widdershins in another round of laughing. But their fun was cut short when a deep rumbling sound reached their ears.

"That's odd!" Colly said. "That sounds like thunder! But it couldn't be!"

Colly stepped over to her kitchen window, and Widdershins followed. They peeked outside right as another big rumble sounded overhead. It had been a perfectly sunny morning just minutes ago, with hardly a cloud in the sky—but now there was a huge, dark one hanging in the south!

Storm clouds were pretty rare in Weewah, but this one was *really* weird. It was a deep, icky gray, and it was getting bigger and bigger as they watched! It bubbled and spread, taking up more and more of the sky as those rumbly-bumblies continued, and then flashes of purple lightning started to strike inside the gray.

"I've *never* seen a storm like that before!" Colly exclaimed.

"Me neither!" Widdershins said in awe. "Looks mighty bad, to me!"

"How did it start up? Where did it come from?" The more Colly thought about it, the more the questions bothered her. And as the cloud got even bigger, she started to believe that it was no ordinary storm brewing up there. "This smells like something Crookbone would do!"

"Oh, golly," Widdershins said, looking nervous. "I sure hope not!"

Widdershins was right to be nervous. The Wuzzylumps were all-too familiar with the gangly and grumpy sorcerer—and his terrible ways.

Crookbone was a Needlar, and like all Needlars, he was a very unpleasant and mean-spirited creature. He was so very bad, in fact, that all the other Needlars grew tired of him and banished him from their home in Blickblack, far to the west of Weewah. That'd been some years ago, and Crookbone came to their land shortly after, building himself a big stone home out in Billybum Forest. He lived there with his pet and lackey, a talking greez-fox named Sneevly.

Ever since then, Crookbone had been turning his meanness onto the Wuzzylumps, practicing his dark magic and using it to bother their village in all sorts of ways. They'd had plenty of troubles with him before, and Colly and her friends had been forced to put a stop to his mischievous plans several times over. Now, seeing the strange storm, Colly was sure they'd need to do it again.

"I'd bet a year's worth of pancakes that Crookbone has something to do with this!" Colly said, setting her hands on her hips and stomping a foot. "It's probably some new spell of his! And we've got to stop it, before it does any harm! I say we go out to his home and give him a stern talking to!"

Widdershins moaned. "But Colly, we just ate! And you should wait at least thirty minutes after eating before you go swimming—or go after mean sorcerers!"

"Oh, phooey! I'm going out to Crookbone's house to see what he's up to! And I'll do it by myself if I must! So, are you coming with me or not?"

Widdershins looked down and shuffled his feet, thinking about it. "Oh, okay," he finally answered. Then he puffed out his chest in a show of bravery. "I'm going with you! But I think we should ask for some help."

"Way ahead of you!" Colly said, heading straight for the front door. "I know just the Wuzzylump to take along with us! And together, we'll stop whatever that nasty sorcerer has planned! Let's go, bestest buddy!"

Widdershins followed behind Colly as they left her cottage. They were off to investigate!

If they'd stayed awhile longer and kept their eyes on that strange storm, they would have seen the great big meteorite that came falling out of the swirling gray haze, landing somewhere in Billybum Forest—and they would have seen the big, wobbling spaceship that followed after it a moment later, landing elsewhere in the jolly old woods.

***

The trio made their way through Billybum Forest

with heads held high. Well, two heads held high, and another looking all around, taking in the woods with anxious glances.

The strange storm had gone away before they'd even left the village, disappearing just as quickly as it had started—but Colly was as determined as ever to investigate matters. She still had a bad feeling in her tummy about that nasty looking cloud, and she wouldn't be satisfied until her tummy was settled. Widdershins, however, had not been so steadfast.

"Did you guys hear that?" he asked for the twentieth time in their journey. "I thought I heard something over in those trees!"

Colly patted his back. "It's probably just a zoopliff, sniffing around for food!"

"Indeed!" Gubbins agreed, walking a step behind his friends. "Have no fear, Widdershins! All will be well! We will address the shifty Crookbone with our query soon enough, and once things are set right, we shall return home, safe and sound! Chin up, good fellow!"

Widdershins finally calmed down a bit, and Colly smiled at Gubbins in thanks.

Gubbins was a very smart, confident, blue-furred Wuzzylump. He had read many books and knew an awful lot, and he had used that big brain of his to become an inventor! The only problem was, most of his creations didn't work the first couple, few, or even dozen times he tried them out. But he had never let that stop him! After all, it was a very important lesson, learning to finish what you've started!

Colly had asked him to join their mission, certain that he would have some new creation to help protect them, if they encountered trouble. And he'd brought just the thing: a brand-new kind of slingshot, whose strap could be pulled back, secured in place, and then released by pulling a little trigger. Gubbins told them it was easy to reload, that it could shoot stones farther than any other slingshot known to Weewah—and, best of all, he had already tested it, and it worked just fine!

Gubbins had held the slingshot at the ready all through their trek, and when Crookbone's house finally came into view, he gripped it even tighter. "There's the scoundrel's abode!" he warned. "Tread lightly, friends!"

"His front door is wide open!" Colly noted. And that it was.

"Maybe he has guests," Widdershins whispered. "It wouldn't be polite, showing up when he's busy with guests! Let's come back later!"

"We won't do any such thing!" Colly snapped. "Now, come along! And quietly!"

Colly took the lead as they snuck up towards the house. She half-expected Crookbone to burst out at any moment, springing a trap and casting a spell on them. But they made it to the front door without incident.

They peeked inside—and saw a surprising sight.

The house was dim and dark, but they could still see that the place was a mess. Books and papers had been tossed all about. Furniture was overturned. And Crookbone's collection of potions had been smashed across the ground, bits of glass and dried concoctions spread all over.

"Hello?" Colly called out. No one answered.

"Golly, I've got a bad feeling about this!" Widdershins said. Then he pointed at the floor. "What's that?"

He was referring to a big puddle of something or other which lay at the center of the house. The Wuzzy-lumps stepped inside, getting a better look at matters, and Widdershins shuffled over to the puddle.

"It looks like shoogberry syrup! Maybe Crookbone had pancakes for breakfast this morning, too!" Widdershins bent down and stuck his fingers in it. Then he had a taste. It made his face scrunch up. "Ick! That sure isn't shoogberry syrup!"

"So, what is it then?"

Widdershins shrugged and licked another finger. Then another. He grimaced each time. "Not sure, but I don't like it!" But that didn't stop him from licking up the last of it.

"This sure is strange," Colly said, setting her hands to her hips.

Gubbins nodded. "Most peculiar!"

"Maybe we should look for him outside!"

Colly stepped out of the house, and the others followed. They never bothered to look up, towards the rafters overhead. They would have found Crookbone, if they had: viciously mauled and folded over across a beam, half-eaten and forgotten by the thing that'd carried him up there.

The Wuzzylumps spread out a tad, calling out for Crookbone and looking to the ground for a trail to follow, or anything else of note. A moment later, Gubbins shouted out: "Over here, dear friends!"

Colly and Widdershins came running over. They looked down at what Gubbins had found, and they gasped. It was the tail of a greez-fox, with turquoise fur and a fluff of white at the end!

"Is that . . . Sneevly's tail?" Widdershins asked, sounding a little sicky-wicky.

Colly swallowed down a lump in her throat. "I think it is!"

Then, something happened which made the Wuzzylumps jump back. The big, wild bushes in front of them started to rustle and shake—and then something leapt out, landing in front of the three friends as they screamed!

It was Sneevly, pet and lackey of Crookbone! His eyes were wide with excitement, he was trembling all over, and sure enough, his tail was gone.

"*H-h-help me!*" he stammered, glancing back to the bushes. "*Th-th-they're after m-m-m-me!*"

"Who's after you?" Colly asked.

Sneevly was about to give an answer, but then he let out a sharp yelp. Something else in the bushes had grabbed him, and all of a sudden, it pulled him back in!

The bushes shook violently as Sneevly cried for help. Then there was a loud crunching sound—followed by a wet smacking—and the bushes went still once more.

The Wuzzylumps stood there, their breaths caught up in their little lungs. And then something rose up out of the bushes—towering over the scared trio.

It was a huge, bug-like monster! It stood nine feet tall, with eight long, crooked legs supporting a long, spindly body. It had two arms that it was raising up over its head, looking like big, sharp blades, and its shell-like exterior was a glistening yellow colour. Four big eyes jutted out of its oblong head, and a threatening hiss came out of a mouth consisting of tiny, twitching appendages.

Those stalky legs started to creak to life as the thing stepped forward, towards the Wuzzylumps, and the hissing grew louder.

The Wuzzylumps stared up at the creature, too shocked to move—and then a series of quick, loud bangs rang out, accompanied by some wild yelling!

"*Fuck you, bug-dick!*"

The giant monster shrieked and spun around, looking to the source of all the noise. It was a six-foot, hairless creature, which came running out of the woods at full charge! He was covered in a suit of metal and carrying a big, metal thing in his hands, which was causing all the banging. Little pellets were shooting out of the contraption and hitting the towering creature, and they seemed to hurt the monster!

It ran at the metal-suited creature and swung one of those sharp arms at him, but it missed. The monster reared up and swung again, and this time, it hit the metal-being, who fell to the ground, dazed.

Colly moaned and Widdershins bit his nails as Gubbins dashed forward, his courage returned. He leveled his slingshot at the big, shrieking monster. "Over here, vile creature!" he shouted.

The monster whipped its head around, then changed direction, heading for the Wuzzylumps once again. Gubbins aimed for one of its eyes, pulled the trigger—and the slingshot's strap snapped in half, its small stone going nowhere.

Gubbins looked at his invention with dismay. "Oh, drats . . ."

The big mean thing stopped in front of him, and Gubbins looked up at it—right as it swung one of those wicked arms through the air. Gubbins' head popped off, and a spray of that shoogberry syrup-looking stuff went splishing and splashing across the ground.

Gubbins' head bounced and rolled out of sight, into some bushes, while the rest of him fell forward.

Colly gasped and held her hands up to her mouth. But Widdershins was on the ball, dashing over to the bushes and ignoring the shrieking mean thing. It did the same to him, turning its attention back to the metal-being, who was getting back up and shooting again.

Widdershins rifled through the branches and scooped up his friend's head. "Gubbins?" he asked it. "Are you alright?"

Meanwhile, the giant monster and the metal-being shrieked and yelled on. Then they ran at each other. Right as it was about to jump on him, the metal-being dove between the monster's legs, sliding on the ground and shooting pellets up at its gut. The creature's belly popped open in a rain of green gunk, which splashed across the metal-being before he rolled out of the way.

The monster gave one last screech, then it toppled over, falling to the ground and going still.

Colly shambled over to Widdershins' side as the metal-being stood back up. He spat on the monster and hoisted his contraption up onto his shoulder. Then, he looked over to the trembling pair of Wuzzylumps.

"Who are you?" Colly asked him. "*What* are you?"

"The name's Commander Slate," he said. "And I'm a lean, mean, muff-diving machine, on most days. But right now, I'm a soldier, looking to stomp a mudhole in the enemy."

Colly pointed to the big monster. "And what's that?"

"The enemy."

Widdershins moaned, drawing their attention. He was still trying to talk to Gubbins' head. "Say something, buddy!"

"He ain't about to answer ya, fuzz-ball," Commander Slate grumbled. "He's dead as they come."

Colly looked up at Slate with tears in her eyes. "You mean he . . . passed on into Sleepy Land?! Already?!"

"Yeah. He's gone. Bit the dust. Kicked the bucket. Opened a buffet for worms, with his ass as the main course."

Colly shook her head. "But Wuzzylumps *never* go to Sleepy Land until they get really, really old!"

Commander Slate shrugged. "That's gonna change, sister, so long as those fucking insects are running all over the place. Average life expectancy around here is about to go down faster than a smacked-out whore working shore leave, if I don't do something about it."

Widdershins set Gubbins' head down on the ground. "I feel a bit . . . icky . . ."

He turned away, right as his morning pancakes came back up. Colly rubbed a hand on his shoulder as she addressed Slate. "You mean, there are *more* of those big mean things out there?!"

"By now? Probably. But with any luck, most of them—and their eggs—are still around the meteorite they showed up in. I'm going after them, with everything I got." He pulled out a gizmo from the belt around his waist and looked it over. "And according to my scanner, that meteorite is just a mile or so to the west."

Commander Slate turned and started walking away, but Colly and Widdershins ran after him.

"Can we come with you, Commander Slate? Please?" Colly begged, stepping in front of him and barring his way.

"W-w-we're sc-scared!" Widdershins added.

"Negative! You'll slow me down."

"But we need you to protect us! We won't be able to defend ourselves, if any of those big meanies catch us in the forest!"

"Can we stay with you, sir?" Widdershins pleaded. "Pretty please?"

Commander Slate grumbled and rolled his eyes. "Fine, you plushies can stick with me. But when things start going down, be sure to get the hell out of my way! If you don't and fuck things up, I'll use you as a loofah to clean my taint!"

"What's a loofah?" Colly asked.

"What's a taint?" Widdershins added.

"Never mind! Just shut yer mouths and follow me!"

The Wuzzylumps snapped to attention and tried to keep up with Slate, who headed further into Billybum Forest without a moment's hesitation. They would have to see to Gubbins when they got back—and when things were safe again.

***

Colly and Widdershins kept as quiet as they possibly could, per Commander Slate's instructions. But the order didn't seem to apply to him. They hadn't gone very far at all when he started talking. It began as a quick release of his evident frustration, but it evolved into a much greater story—of who he was and how he'd come to Weewah.

"You know, a few weeks ago, this would've all

seemed pretty fucked up to me. The bugs, this fruity place, you stuffed animals. Completely off my radar. But the last few days have widened that radar, the hard way.

"Sure, I expected some weird shit when I joined the space marines, but damn, this is next level! I thought it'd be mostly support and rescue missions. Simpler shit. But, no! Me and my team get orders to drop straight into a clusterfuck! And for what? Natural resources! Things we should have plenty of, if the people calling the shots had their shit together!

"You know, the historical types say humanity used to live on a rock called Earth. But that was centuries ago. People treated it like a whore, and it died like a whore: all used up and nothing left to give. So, we hopped through space, over to Stratos IV. Same sort of planet, same sort of resources—but fully stocked! And guess what? Humanity gives a repeat performance! Then we started looking at other systems, looking for places to mine in the search for more resources. The world government set up an operation on Golmira—some out of the way moon. Shortly after, all contact with the facility was lost. So, me and my team get sent along to look into matters.

"We didn't have a fucking clue what was waiting for us. Every one of those miners was dead before we got there, and my team followed them straight to hell. Those bugs crawled out of the earth and killed them all. But I fought and I survived. I kept low and took them on when I had to. Went down into the tunnels beneath Golmira. As it turns out, the bugs had an operation of their own down there.

"As near as I can tell, they saw our mining facility as a declaration of war. So, they set to launching their offensive. They were gonna send meteors into space, filled with their kind. An army of them, some grown, some still in their eggs, all meant for Stratos IV. I found out about the plan just in time to sneak into their operations. Set explosives. Blew their little set-up straight to kingdom come, along with all the meteors they were gonna launch! Save one, which was sent out before I could reach it. I got into our ship and went after it. No way I was gonna let it reach home! Besides, I had to get some more payback for my people. I was about to catch up to the meteor and shove a missile up those aliens' narrow asses. But then I lost it in some cloud, which had appeared out of nowhere. It surrounded us. Thought it was some kind of magnetic storm or something. But now—seeing how it spit us out here, in this fucking cartoon land—I think it had to be some kind of inter-dimensional rift."

Widdershins raised a hand. "Sir? What's a—"

"Zip yer lips, furburger!" Commander Slate snarled back. "You wanna give away our position?! I'm about to shove my foot up yer ass, turn you into a slipper, and step in a lump of dog shit on purpose, if you don't cut all that chatter!"

Widdershins shrunk under the Commander's gaze. Colly took his hand in hers as soon as Slate looked forward again. The friends inched closer together as they made their way through the woods. After all, it was good to stick close to friends, especially when you were worried or scared.

The Sun had meandered across the sky, still smiling

as it brought the afternoon light, which shone and sparkled through the trees. The forest was quiet all around them, but it seemed like a strange sort of quiet. There was no singing of birds or chittering of other animals, and that was rare in Billybum.

Commander Slate continued to lead the way a while longer, watching the little scanner in his hand and keeping his Banger ready at his side. That's what Colly decided to call the contraption, since she still didn't know what it was. It seemed appropriate, though, given the noise it made.

Eventually, Commander Slate put his scanner away. "There it is!" he said, raising his Banger and hunching forward. "The meteorite's just ahead. Keep your eyes peeled and your sphincters tight, fuzz-balls! The enemy could be anywhere!"

Colly and Widdershins stared in awe as the object of their search came into view.

The meteorite was enormous—every bit as big as one of the Red Hills to the northeast! And only half of it could be seen! The rest was hidden in the earth, buried in its fall from the sky. A big chunk had broken off from the meteorite's top, exposing a hollow space in the tremendous rock, and the broken piece lay on the ground before them. The inner half of the rock was covered in a sticky-looking mass, and some veiny, milky-white eggs were stuck inside it. Most looked intact. Others were cracked open.

"Shit," Slate grumbled. "Looks like a few have already had a happy birthday." He lifted his Banger up and shot a hail of pellets into the rock, destroying the remaining eggs. "Now to see to the rest."

He pulled something off the back of his belt and started pressing its buttons. It looked like a little rolling pin, and some numbers lit up on it. "Get ready to run, you little plushies! I'm setting this bomb for three minutes. It's gonna be one hell of a blast, but that should give us enough time to get clear."

He pressed one more button, and the bomb started to beep. He threw it up high, into the crack of the meteorite. It fell straight in.

"Move it!"

But Colly and Widdershins couldn't move because they were terrified. And they were terrified, because one of those big mean creatures had just appeared, crawling over the other side of the meteorite and looking down at them from on high.

Slate followed their gazes and brought his Banger up to shoot at the creature. But it leapt down with an ear-splitting screech, landing on top of the Commander and digging the sharp point of an arm into his shoulder, straight through his metal suit. Slate cried out and fell onto his back while the monster stood over him, crouching down and snapping its mouth at his face.

"Oh, no!" Colly hollered.

She and Widdershins held onto each other, watching helplessly as the Commander brought his Banger up between him and the monster. Its mouth latched onto it and the creature shook its head, pulling the Banger out of the Commander's grip and tossing it aside. The monster dug its arm deeper into Slate's shoulder, and he screamed in pain.

The creature crouched lower and tried to bite the Commander's face again, but Slate held its head back with one hand, while the other reached down to his belt. He pulled out something that looked like a little Banger, and he shoved it into the monster's mouth. *"Fuck you, you fucking fucker!"*

He shot it—once, twice, three times. The creature gurgled as a spray of green gunk shot out of its mouth, splattering onto Slate's face. Then it reared up, pulling its arm out of the Commander's shoulder. It teetered to and fro, and then it fell onto its back, dead.

Slate groaned as he got to his feet. Then he shouted at the Wuzzylumps. "Run, god damn it! The bomb'll go off any second now!"

His command shoved their fears aside. Colly and Widdershins turned, running as fast as their little legs could carry them, and Commander Slate followed after them.

Colly and Slate pulled further ahead as Widdershins fought to keep up, his bulk slowing him down. Soon, he was several yards behind them. "Colly, wait for me!" he called out.

Colly turned, urging her friend to catch up. But then the worst thing possible happened: Widdershins' clumsiness came swooping in, and he fell down, onto his big belly.

"Widdershins! Get up!"

Slate slowed down and glanced back. "Son of a bitch!" he shouted.

The conflict of a split-decision was apparent on his face—and then he turned back around, going after Widdershins.

He'd taken only a couple of steps when a tremendous *boom* rang out, and the forest exploded into chaos and fire. A wall of flame rose up into the sky, destroying the meteorite and spreading out through the woods in a rapidly approaching wave.

The explosion swept right over Widdershins and struck Commander Slate, knocking him back. Then the concussive force of the blast reached Colly, and she was flung through the air, crashing to the ground and slipping into unconsciousness.

When Colly came back around, she opened her eyes to the sight of a ruined forest, the trees bent and burning from the bomb's reach, while others were simply gone, turned to ash. And worst of all, she knew her bestest buddy had gone with them, and she cried for him, so very hard.

She got back to her feet, swaying as she brushed at her fur, which had been all but singed off in the blast. Her tears kept falling as she searched for Commander Slate. She found him lying a few yards away, his metal suit broken and burnt, his skin pale and his breathing harsh.

Colly knelt at his side, and he handed her the little Banger. She could barely hold it, even with both hands.

"Learn to use this," he said, his voice a weak croak. "Learn to fight. Those fucking things are still out there. They'll breed. Make more of themselves. You gotta stop them. Find my ship. There are more guns like this in it. More ammo, more bombs. Take them. Fight back, fuzz-ball. Fight back . . ."

And then the Commander was gone, off to Sleepy Land.

Colly stood and wiped at her eyes. Then she started the slow, lonesome walk back to her village, keeping an eye out for any of those terribly mean creatures and clutching the Banger tightly in her little hands.

***

Nine months passed, and the land of Weewah had changed a lot in that time.

Many creatures had left the land or been taken from it.

Homes, villages, and towns had been ransacked or abandoned—ruined and silent reminders of those who'd once lived there.

Golden Town had suffered more than any other settlement. Its gilded buildings and its sparkling lanes had burnt down in a great fire, brought on in a sweeping battle against the BrightBrows. As great and wise as they were, they could not hold back the ferocity that was visited upon them. And now, not a single one of their kind remained.

The Sun had stopped rising in the last few months. It had been too scared of the terrible things it saw happening throughout Weewah every day, and it could not take it anymore. It'd been nighttime outside ever since, and the Moon was left alone in the sky, unable to fall if the Sun wouldn't rise—and it was constantly crying, because of it.

The Wuzzylumps (those that remained) had found a new home out in the Red Hills, burrowing into the earth and carving out tunnels to hide in. They'd been forced to leave their village at the edge of Billybum Forest shortly after the invading Meanies arrived. The Meanies, as they'd come to call the creatures, had taken root in the woods, claiming it as their own and attacking any who dared to venture their way.

Indeed, the Wuzzylumps would not have gotten on as well as they did, if not for their leader, Colly. She had warned them of the Meanies' threat and provided them with weapons to defend themselves, taken from Commander Slate's ship and kept safe in their tunnels.

She showed them how to use the Bangers and the bombs. How to fight back. How to survive. Telling them to push on through the hardship they endured and the fears they felt. Reminding them that, one day, they might win back their home.

After all, that's what a good leader was supposed to do.

-End-

HOUSE OF GRIM
By Ella Ann

Grinding and splintering, the grating discord of bone against bone agitated the settled silence of the night-shaded wood. An obscured figure groaned through the dense fog, stiff. With each jarring step, the cloaked silhouette trudged on steadily, and a dilapidated house soon appeared within view of hollowed eyes. Behind the barbed thicket of hawthorn, beyond fractured, spider-webbed windows, a beam of light swept along crumbling drywall and illuminated dust particles, adrift. The shadow heaved a rasping breath when it noticed the intruder.

"No rest for the undead," it murmured in a thick language, ancient as the spattering of stars above its hooded skull.

As the hazy figure moved nearer, it tugged along a heavy, grey mist that swiftly shrouded the dilapidated structure in a suffocating gloom. As its skeletal hand pushed open the arched, mouldering door, the air within the old house began to churn, spoil, and rapidly turn rancid.

The flashing of the intruder's camera was briefly observed from the dim hall and persisted for only a moment before halting abruptly. Stumbling onto his knees, the man gasped and choked on the putrid vapor drifting into the disintegrating library from behind him. Twisting his youthful, startled face, his gaze caught the silvery, sharp edge of a curved blade glinting from the shadows.

"What do you want?" he gargled, black ooze filling his mouth with the taste of rot, bubbling over his cracked lips, dripping from his stubbled chin.

The cloaked stranger's knobby hand gripped its scythe and, with a movement seemingly too swift for its creaking bones, sliced the man in half, snapping his spine with a crack and spilling his unfurled guts upon the filth-covered floor. From depths unseen, a dark smoke rose and reached forth with sharpened claws to clutch, squeeze, and crush the severed body through cracks in the wooden boards, leaving behind a murky pool of sludge swirled with crimson.

"What I want," the cloaked figure answered, "is rest." Allowing his bloody blade to clatter to the floor, he made its way over to the dusty minibar. Pouring himself a full glass of a malt whisky, he collapsed onto his moth-shredded couch.

***

Nightfall nestled comfortably between the twisted, gnarled branches of the Deathwood, from which no sound of the living emerged except for the rhythmic crunch of dry leaves and a rattling breath not far behind. Though when the steps ceased, so did the breathing.

"Hello?" a tentative voice called into the darkness.

At first, only silence followed. Though, as the woman strained to hear through the deep dark that seemed to swallow up sound, a gurgling breath surfaced.

Wide-eyed and pale, the woman backed against the peeling bark of an ancient oak, her gaze glued to the glinting scythe raised high above her head and grasped by the skeletal hand of a towering, hooded figure.

The woman parted her lips and drew in a sharp breath, but a scream did not escape her lungs before a swift, swooping motion sent her raven-haired head tumbling onto the mossy ground.

"Uh, hello?" a voice whispered.

Confused, the cloaked figure glanced into the surrounding darkness and then down at the severed head, giving it a nudge with the rod of its scythe.

"Excuse me?" The voice spoke again in the shape tones of a whisper.

Turning around, the towering shadow spoke.

"All those who enter the forest of the undead—"

"Yoo-hoo!"

With a start, his tired bones creaked as the cloaked figure righted himself on the couch and looked around his den. Before him, as always, was the antiquated minibar full of liquor. In his boney hand, he still grasped an empty glass. Then, out of the corner of his eye socket, he spotted something.

"Hi, there!" a youthful woman said with a beaming smile. "Long day at work?" she asked before plopping down next to him on his ruined couch.

Staring, exasperated, at his unwelcome visitor, he reached lazily for his scythe on the floor.

"Oh, you can't kill me," the woman said.

He studied her for a moment before realising she was right and sitting back with a heavy sigh.

"Well, get out then. I'm not in the mood for intruders." Involuntarily, his gaze flicked to the ooze still puddled on the floor near him.

"I can't. I'm haunting you."

"Haunting me?" he asked indignantly.

"Yeah, you know, 'Oooooohhhh ooooooooeeeoo-hhhh…'" she paused to look around. "Do you have a white sheet? I'll demonstrate."

"I know what a ghost is," he snapped. "My point being that I'm the Grim Reaper. You can't haunt the Reaper."

An exaggerated groan escaped the young woman's slim throat as she rolled her eyes.

"Stop imitating a ghost!"

"I'm not imitating a ghost; I am one. And don't refer to yourself in the third person. That's so gross."

The boney fingers of his hands curled slowly, knuckle for knuckle, as he ground his teeth.

"I swear to Hell I'll kill you," he growled, staring at the woman.

She stared back for a moment, wide-eyed and un-blinking… before a glint played across her dark eyes and her delicate features broke into a toothy grin.

Suddenly stupefied into submission, his anger dissipated, and a reluctant smirk crept onto his boney face.

"Alright, fine," he mumbled, "but I would if I could."

"You already did."

"No, definitely not. I always remember the annoying ones," he replied, roughly cracking his exposed knuckles. "Must have been one of my colleagues."

The pale woman continued to stand before him for a moment, smiling awkwardly, before moving toward and disappearing down the dark corridor. After several moments, her distant voice echoed faintly down the hall, "Death so nice, he tried to kill her twice."

The Grim Reaper laid back his head and, with a rattling breath, slipped swiftly back into the realm of nightmares.

***

"So, what are we doing tonight?"

Roused abruptly from his sleep, he focused his un-blinking sockets from where he laid on the couch. The ghost's pale face and dusky eyes stared back.

"I'm Annalise, but you can call me 'Anna,'" the ghost said in a cheery voice. "What should I call you? 'Captain,' or something? I've never been a ghost before."

"The Grim Reaper," he croaked and rolled over to face the back of the couch.

"I'd rather not call you 'the' anything," Anna replied,

wrinkling her nose.

"Argh, fine, then 'Death.'"

"Hmm, no, that's too impersonal, like calling me 'girl.'" Anna said, furrowing her brow. "What about 'Grim'?"

"Fine," he groaned, "if it'll get you to shut up."

Anna stared at the back of Grim's hooded skull before turning to look out the partially shattered, cob-webbed window.

"So," she ventured after a moment, "do you have to work, or do you have the night off?"

"Oh, for the love of Hell!" Grim wheezed as he rose from the couch and stormed toward the front door.

"Don't forget your, uh… knife on a stick!" Anna called, plopping down on the couch where Grim had been lying.

Without a word, Grim stalked back in, snatched the scythe off the ground, and left, slamming the door behind him.

*** *

That night, as Grim marched through the Deathwood at a clip must quicker than his typical trudge, he cursed under his breath and recklessly hacked at the surrounding foliage with his blade.

"A ghost? This job just gets better all the time," Grim muttered into the darkness. "'Don't go to Earth,' they'd said, 'it's not worth the extra pay.' But did I listen?"

Grim angrily swung his scythe at the nearest tree, severing a heavy limb with a sharp snap.

"Hello?" the timid voice from his last nightmare called.

"Finally," he whispered to himself in an ancient

tongue, strolling toward her through the heavy fog.

***

"Hey. Psst."

"Go away, girl," Grim mumbled without turning over.

Though weightless, he became aware that Anna had plopped down next to him on the bed as the cool of her presence tickled his spine through his lightweight cloak. It had been decades since he'd ventured into the upper rooms of the old manor, preferring to keep to the old study with the endless supply of liquor. But in an effort to give his new house guest the slip, he'd crept up the stairs while she'd been preoccupied in the library.

"I don't get it," Anna said after a moment.

Grim remained facing the wall, hoping if he ignored her, she'd disappear.

"I said, I don't—"

"I heard you," Grim snapped, rolling angrily onto his back. His hood fell away slightly to reveal his pale skull and hollow eyes, now focused on the mouldy ceiling. "What? What is it you have trouble comprehending, except how to leave someone alone?"

"What kind of a haunt would I be if I left you alone?" Anna asked with a broad smile.

Grim could feel her staring at him but refused to avert his gaze from the black fuzz overhead, a mixture of annoyance and embarrassment blooming as heat in his chalky cheekbones. He'd been at the death game a long time. Centuries blended into one muddy blur, and never during that time had anyone smiled at him. Grim shivered at the thought. As far as he'd seen, the human who smiled upon Death did not exist.

"I don't understand why you sleep," Anna finally spoke, her brown eyes flitting from Grim's shaded eye sockets to where they seemed to be focused overhead. "You've, uh, got a mould problem," she offered, scrunching her nose in disgust.

Grim let out a heavy sigh and sat up. "If I tell you, will you go away?"

Anna's face drooped slightly, and she looked down at the dust-laden comforter. "If you tell me, I'll leave this room. But I can't leave the house. I already tried."

Grim felt a strange and sudden pang run down his brittle spine at the mention of this obnoxious ghost leaving and stood from the bed.

"It's how I receive my assignments," Grim said, grabbing his scythe out of the corner and stalking out of the room.

"Wait," Anna called after him and appeared out of nothing at the end of the hall before him.

With the sunlight of early morning streaming in through the windows, Grim noticed for the first time that, at the time of her death, Anna had been wearing a form-fitting, white dress, which tapered off unevenly at the upper thigh. She also had on impractically high heels, and she had braided the upper part of her light hair into a crown. Grim found himself wondering whether humans had found Anna appealing to observe.

"You're supposed to leave me alone now," Grim muttered.

"I just said I'd leave the room," Anna smirked playfully. "Do you mean that if I keep you from sleeping, then you won't be able to kill?"

"I'll be able to, just maybe not the right people.

So, if you want to prevent premature death, I suggest you let me sleep."

As Grim strolled directly through her, he felt the cool sensation of her presence tickle his bones.

"Fine," Anna said, a tinge of sadness edging her voice.

***

Relentless rain battered the muddy grass and made it difficult to hear the steps of the hooded figure behind him. With both hands in his pockets, he kept one gripped firmly around his pistol as he chanced a glance behind him. Filled with funeral arrangements and life insurance paperwork, the long afternoon had finally given way to twilight, and the cemetery outside the mortuary was dark under the stormy sky.

Catching another brief glimpse of the shadow following him, the man squinted in the downpour, wondering if the figure had slipped behind one of the ornate headstones he so despised. *She'll get nothing like that*, he thought, his thin lips involuntarily twitching into a smirk. *An unmarked grave would be too good for her*.

Removing his semi-automatic from his coat, he pointed it at the nearest headstone and approached, his heavy boots squishing against the soupy ground.

"Which is why, my dear, I left you there to rot," he whispered to himself, the hammering of his hardened heart nearly drowning out the rain.

Pausing a moment to ready himself, he peeked quickly behind the first tombstone, seeing nothing but shrivelled up roses lying on the grass. Slowly, he moved toward the next grave when an abrupt, guttural scream erupted from behind a nearby mausoleum, sending a bolt of fear through the man's trembling limbs.

With the barrel pointed toward the horrible sound, he took a deep breath before quickly approaching and easing himself around the corner. The first thing he noticed in the torrential storm was the hooded figure at a significant distance, stalking toward the woods. With his gun at the shadow's back, the man watched until it disappeared into the brush.

It wasn't until then that his gaze refocused with instant revulsion upon a crumpled form near his feet. Gutted from navel to neck, the entrails of the body before him were being washed clean by the rain and had the appearance of a giant, bloated worm in the grass. Unable to look away, the man watched as the concave, bloody torso filled with rainwater. It was then that he recognised the face and immediately retched his own insides onto the grass next to the worm.

***

"Ugh, you sit around here and groan way more than I do, and I'm the ghost of this house!" Anna shouted from the hall.

Grim scoffed, his back to her as he poured himself a whiskey. "Being Death is much more difficult than being the lingering smear of human existence."

"Yeah, well, have you been human before?"

"Not that I recall," he said, taking a sip and relishing in the burning sensation of the liquor trickling down his exposed spine and dripping down his ribs.

"Of course not. You're such a non-human."

"What in Hell is that supposed to mean?" Grim spun around to see Anna standing right behind him, her eyes narrowed. He fought the urge to smile.

"It means exactly that; you act like such a non-human. 'Poor me, I'm the supreme overlord of the underworld.'"

Grim eyed her steadily, but felt the laughter bubbling in his bones.

"You don't know suffering," Anna continued, "until you've worked a 9-to-5 job for a man you hate, living a life you never wanted, so you can get crap you never needed. Every day, running on the rat wheel just to hear it squeak."

Death reached out one boney hand to stroke the space whereabouts he thought her cheek was and opened his creaky jaw to say something semi-kind. Though, instead, a boisterous laugh escaped.

"One day as a human, and you'd be begging for death," she said, furrowing her brow before quickly dissipating from sight.

With a satisfied chuckle, Grim plopped onto the couch and threw back the rest of his whiskey, enjoying the corrosive sting on his ancient bones.

***

A couple of days passed without any sign of the ghost, and Grim relished in the lack of disturbance from her unwelcome presence. He'd forgotten how much he enjoyed the feeling of entering his dilapidated manor at the end of a long work night and drinking on his couch, uninterrupted.

As several more days crept by, Grim settled firmly back into his old routine, telling himself a little too often that it was how he preferred things. But after a full week passed in eerie quiet, Grim's bones ached in an unfamiliar way, and his rib cage felt emptier than he'd remembered. After a week and a half, his beloved whiskey seemed duller, less corrosive, and altogether unsatisfying.

One morning, after a night of particularly ruthless killings that left Grim splattered in crimson and his skull ringing with screams, he trudged begrudgingly into his silent manor.

"The Devil dammit," he muttered under his shallow breath, "I need a loud clock or a leaky faucet or... something."

Allowing his scythe to clatter onto the floor, he headed down the hall toward the back rooms rather than his worn couch and minibar. Tugging his hood off and dropping his bloody cloak to the floor, Grim allowed the chilled, musty air to cool his achy skeleton. Creeping from room to room, he peered in to look for Anna's faint, ghostly figure and whisper her name. Without luck on the first floor, the stairs creaked as he took them by two.

"Anna?" he whispered as he reached the landing and headed down the hall.

Room after room, she did not emerge, and Grim wondered if he'd missed some nooks and crannies on the first floor of the massive house.

"Anna?" He called, louder. "Anna the ghost, are you here?"

"As opposed to... Anna the corpse?"

Relief warmed his bones when he heard her voice from within the room he'd just entered. But in the flash of a moment, that relief turned to confusion and then concern when he finally saw her. Sitting on the bed, her shimmery figure was curled up next to a body. The body of a young woman, wearing a white dress and heels, with a crown of braided hair on her head.

Instantaneously, Grim understood why Anna was haunting his house.

"You… you killed me here and kept my body?" Anna whispered, her eyes with a watery sheen. "Why?"

"Anna, I didn't," Grim spoke quietly.

"How do you explain this?" she asked, her voice fractured and her eyes averted from both Grim and her decaying body.

"You misunderstand," Grim said, approaching the bed slowly to sit. "I don't actually kill people in the way you think. I pull their souls from their bodies, so they aren't animated corpses, but usually, this isn't what causes death to the physical form."

Anna's dark eyes met Grim's hollow socket, but she did not respond.

"I'm there for the murders and the strokes. The suicides, the car crashes, the drownings… I'm there, but my scythe doesn't cut flesh; it rips free the soul. The only time I actually cause the death is when someone dies in their sleep and look…." Grim pointed at the holes in the corpse's chest. "You were shot…"

A soft sob choked its way out of Anna as she hid her face in her hands.

"And I promise you, I wasn't the one to separate your spirit. There are other Reapers. You weren't one of my… assignments."

"Oh, that's right, this is just a job for you," she whispered, lifting her face to his. "Get out."

"Anna, I—"

"Get. *Out.*"

Reluctantly, Grim rose from the bed and retreated toward his minibar with a frown and down-turned eye sockets.

***

For the next several days, the only thoughts ricocheting around in Grim's empty skull involved how to restore Anna to her obnoxious self. Then one day, while he slept, he dreamt of his next job at a cow farm, and a plan began to take form.

"There might be a way to raise her spirit after all," Grim whispered to himself with a slight smile. *It's been a long week*, he thought. *I can allow myself one small joke.*

Barely able to constrain his excitement until nightfall, Grim set out early in search of the dead cow he'd seen in his nightmare.

***

Dairy farmer slashed and mashed? Check.
Cow corpse severed? Check.
Long trudge back home with the goods? Half-check.
Grim smiled as his thoughts circled round and round his head, with Anna at the centre, like the sun powering his mental orbit. Though he was only halfway home, his bones were creaking loudly under the weight of his load, and for a moment, he wondered if his bones could snap.

"Don't fail me now, legs," he murmured in his ancient language, long lost to time. "I don't want to have to carry you too."

When he finally arrived at the manor, he carefully set his surprise for Anna on the porch before entering the front door and heading for the stairs. Though before he could begin his ascent, her soft voice came from behind him.

"Grim?"

Twisting around, Grim saw Anna standing near the library with a soft smile that made his bones hot.

"Oh, hi," he stammered. "And here I thought you went off to haunt some other Reaper." Grim placed a skeletal hand awkwardly on his boney hip before promptly removing it and silently cursing himself. "I– uh, have something for you."

"Oh. Well… I just wanted to tell you I believe you, and so… I'm not upset anymore."

"Then come with me," he said.

Anna raised an eyebrow. "After you…"

Grim nearly sprang to the front door and flung it open, followed closely by his ghost.

"Oh… wow. That's a lot of blood," Anna said, with her head slightly cocked as she stared.

"Do you… well, do you like it?" Grim asked, smiling weakly.

"Like it?" her brow momentarily furrowed. "Oh! That's so nice. But I don't need to eat as a ghost." She offered a polite smile. "And I've also been here over a month now, so if I *did* need to eat, I think I'd already have starved myself to a second death." She chuckled. "But that's really thoughtful."

"What? No, it's not to eat," Grim declared.

"Oh, good!" Anna laughed. "I guess I just thought because my cat used to leave me dead mice on the doormat, so…"

Grim felt his cheekbones flush and averted his eye sockets. "No, no, it's a, uh… skull. Because you said one time that you like skulls and used to collect them, so I brought you one."

Anna looked solemn for a moment before a grin transformed her into the ghost he'd missed.

"Thank you, Grim. It's just, normally, the skulls weren't still in the head when I got them."

"Oh, well… Is there something else I can get you?" Grim asked, hoping to change the subject away from the severed cow's head.

"Yes, actually." Anna glanced down at her translucent feet, and when her eyes fell upon Grim again, they were shimmery with tears. "You can find out who killed me," she whispered.

"You don't remember anything?" he asked.

Anna shook her head, then slowly retreated from the doorway.

***

"How much will you give me for it?" The young man snatched the ring box from the counter as he spoke, glancing quickly over his shoulder toward the door.

"Why so uptight?" the old man behind the register asked, his voice jagged and eyes surveying the customer. "You trying to sell me hot jewellry, boy?"

"No. I inherited this from my mother."

"Sure thing," the old man chuckled joylessly as he dipped into his tobacco tin.

Without another word, the young man pulled up the collar of his pea coat and exited the shop, a brass bell clanking as the door closed.

***

"I love you."

Anna smiled as the words tumbled out of her mouth,

but somehow Grim knew she didn't mean them.

"What's not to love?"

The man with her appeared to be around the same age, but with an arrogant edge Grim immediately disliked.

"You're sure this is how you want to spend the night?" Anna asked, glancing around the dingy room. "All this dust is going to ruin my dress." Smiling playfully, she did a slow spin under the dancing light of a single candle.

"You know how I love haunted houses, babe."

"Yeah. It's just that, I guess I always pictured it someplace beautiful, roses and champagne, that sort of thing…" Her voice trailed off as she looked around the filthy room.

"What happened to my easy-going girl, huh? Don't go all bitchy on me now that we're hitched."

Grim felt his fists tighten, and anger flooded his bones.

"'How did you spend your wedding night?'" Anna asked herself in mock conversation. "'Oh, in typical fashion, contracting tetanus.'" She laughed harshly and walked over to the bed. "And who said a marriage of convenience doesn't have its perks?"

As Anna threw herself down, Grim noticed her husband's expression had gone cold.

"But if you're going to take my money," she went on, her head dramatically thrown back against the pillows, "at least take my body first."

"You fucking bitch."

"What?" Anna asked, sitting up quickly.

In the apparent realisation that the metallic glint in

the dim room was a gun pointing at her, Anna gasped her last breath.

Suddenly jolted awake, the sound of three gunshots faded as Grim emerged from his vision. Though he was still burning with anger.

"Did it work?" Anna asked, her expression hopeful. "Were you able to view my...?"

Re-acclimating to his library, his frayed couch, his minibar, Grim looked at Anna in her present form. Now a wisp of what she had been as a living creature. All vibrant colours, muted; all tangibility, gone. And for the first time, he wished she had a physical form to hold.

"Yes," he replied, more sternly than he'd intended. "I was able to view it." He'd spent all day tracking down the Reaper who'd been assigned her death and now wished he hadn't.

"And?" Anna asked eagerly. "Who was it?"

"Some cretin you married," Grim replied. "Although, it seemed like some sort of well-to-do, family-forced arrangement."

A strange expression darkened Anna's features, and her eyes filled with tears.

"I remember now," she whispered.

"Do you want me to murder him?" Grim asked, rage searing through his bones.

"Please," she said, curling up next to him on the couch.

As Grim allowed the coolness of her touch to calm his anger slightly, he noticed that the wedding ring he'd seen in his vision wasn't on her hand.

***

Although typically on the night shift, Grim waited

until Anna appeared to slip into some sort of sleep-like state before heading out into the stormy morning. Making his way steadily through the damp Deathwood, he reached the nearest town just as a light rain fell. With the same inexplicable sense of knowing that guided him to the location of all his jobs, Grim knew precisely where his victim would be.

Standing next to one of several coffee vendors along the cobbled street, he waited for Anna's murderer to emerge from the Swap Shop, where he was undoubtedly trying to pawn off her wedding ring.

As soon as his target slipped out of the shop, Grim recognised him and felt his anger churn.

***

For a moment, he thought he'd caught a glimpse of the cloaked figure that'd been haunting his mind for weeks. Although he'd insisted to both the police and himself that he hadn't turned his own brother inside out on the grass of the mortuary, his sanity was being tested, and self-doubt edged its way into his mind. The police had looked at him like a psychopath when he'd claimed he had seen Death commit the murder, and he knew he was still their main suspect.

Even more problematic was that it raised suspicion about the disappearance of Anna. His story that she'd accidentally fallen overboard their honeymoon ferry into dark waters was now under scrutiny.

His brother had always been a nuisance, but never more in life than he was now in death.

Shaking off the feeling of being watched, Anna's husband hurried through the rainy morning, away from the last place he might have made a profit off her ring.

Turning quickly down a misty alley, he promptly decided that hanging onto it was too much of a risk.

Just before he reached the dumpster at the far end, he heard a rattling breath and the sound of crunching bones behind him. Fear-stricken, he froze, realising with paralysing panic that he was at a dead end.

***

"Come on, you bastard," Grim grumbled under his breath. "Realise you need to chuck the ring already so I can kill you."

Grim followed at a distance as Anna's husband walked down the deserted street in the rain, abruptly turning down an alleyway.

"Finally." Grim tightened his grip on the scythe and followed him toward the dead end.

Taking a deep, rattling breath, Grim smiled as his victim abruptly halted. He watched, satisfied, as the man began to tremble.

"Turn around," Grim demanded.

The man neither answered nor moved.

"Don't you want to see the face of Death?" Grim asked with a cold chuckle. He towered over Anna's husband, who could not have been much taller than her, and Grim found this particularly satisfying. "Don't die a coward," he goaded. "Turn around."

Slowly, on trembling limbs, the man did as he was told, and Grim saw with disgust that he was crying.

"Please," he begged through trembling lips before breaking into a full sob.

"This is from Anna," Grim stated flatly, and with a swift swing of his blade, severing the man at his waist. His forearms tumbled free, hands and fingers twitching.

ELLA ANN

The scream of agony echoed down the alley as Anna's husband landed in the muck, torso only, gasping.

"This is also from Anna," Grim smiled, slowly dragging the edge of his blade across the man's chest.

Whimpering and crying, his breaths grew increasingly shallow.

Quickly, Grim punched him forcefully in the chest and snapped his ribs with a sharp crack. Reaching through the broken bones, Grim gripped and yanked out his victim's heart. As it stopped beating in his long, boney fingers, Grim watched Anna's husband die with a look of terror etched into his face.

Grim tucked the bloody heart into his cloak pocket and then rummaged through the dead man's clothes.

***

"Hey. Psst."

Anna rolled over and smiled sweetly.

"Oh, hi. I thought maybe you were asleep," Grim said. "That's how you wake a sleeping spirit, isn't it?" Grim grinned and sat down next to Anna on the couch.

"I wasn't asleep," she laughed, "but you nailed it."

"Did you know I was gone?" Grim asked.

"Of course," she answered, placing her small hand on his thigh and sending a cool tingle through him.

"And you knew why?" He asked, taking a deep breath.

"Yes," she smiled.

"In that case, I have something for you," Grim said, reaching into his pocket.

"Oh no," she laughed, "it isn't the severed body part of another animal, is it?"

"Afraid so," Grim replied, pulling out the sticky,

oozing heart of Anna's husband.

"Is that—" Anna gasped, covering her mouth with one hand.

"It is," Grim smiled until he noticed the tears in Anna's eyes. "Do you not like it?" He asked after a moment.

"No," Anna whispered. "It's not that."

"What's wrong?" Grim asked with a gentleness in his voice that surprised him.

"It's… perfect." As tears streamed down her face, Anna's eyes locked adoringly on Grim's shaded eye sockets.

"And there's something else," Grim smiled.

"There's more?" Anna asked, eyebrows raised. "You spoil me."

"This," Grim said, pulling the bloody box out of the centre of the heart, where he'd crammed it as a surprise.

Opening the box, there was a pristine ruby and diamond ring. Grim removed it from its cushion and held it out for Anna to admire.

She stared at it for a long time before speaking.

"I'd forgotten how beautiful it is," she finally said, glancing down at her own, ringless finger. "But I guess I can't wear it now, seeing as I'm no longer married. And, well, also because I'm a ghost."

"Anna," Grim said quietly. "Will you…"

"What?" she asked, placing her hand just over his.

"Marry me?" As Grim croaked out the words, he held up the ruby and diamond ring. "I adore you."

Anna immediately threw her arms around Grim's neck but slipped through him and into the floor behind the couch.

ELLA ANN

An exhilarating tingle spread through Grim's bones, and he took in a sharp breath.

Laughing, Anna reappeared suddenly next to Grim, and for the first time, he noticed she wasn't actually sitting on the couch but hovering just above it.

"Yes! In this afterlife and the next, now and forever," she beamed at him warmly.

And this time, when she said "I love you," he could hear in her voice that she meant it.

***

As night fell upon the old manor, Grim lit candles for the first time in centuries. Standing at the end of the hall, flickering light dancing along the walls as he made his way toward the room of Anna's death.

As he entered, Grim saw Anna standing next to the bed, and he grinned as if he were seeing her beauty for the first time. With the ring in hand, he approached the corpse of Anna, lying next to the spirit of Anna.

"With this ring, I thee wed," Grim said, bending down and placing the ring on the decomposing finger of his lovely corpse bride. Then, turning to the spirit of Anna, he took her light hands in his and drank in the coolness of her touch.

"From this night forward, I am yours. Wholly and completely. Your happiness is mine, and so too is your sadness. Whether it be the head of cow or heart of ex, I will show you my love in every way possible. I will kiss away your tears and slice away your enemies. I love you, Anna."

"I love you, forever and always," Anna whispered through tears.

"With the undead as our witness, I now pronounce

us, Reaper and wife."

Stooping to kiss his bride, Grim smiled as he pulled her into the next room. There, the bed was sprinkled with stinging nettles, and glasses of whiskey awaited them.

"The honeymoon suite, at last," Anna laughed.

"At last," Grim smiled.

-End-

IN THE MOVIES
By Rachael Boucker

Tall posters hung on the side of the building boasting all the big screen had to offer. Colt breezed past the romance set in a war-torn town and latest animated tale. Stopping, he did a double-take of one giant poster and squinted, twisting his head to his shoulder to make sense of the battle scene, cluttered with cocktails and swords. *Are those medieval knights fighting on a cruise ship?* The title didn't give any further clues, so Colt shook his head and carried on into the movie theatre.

The door creaked and slammed with an echo. *I knew it would be quiet, but this place is a ghost town.* His footsteps thudded in the huge foyer. He felt sure there should be an attendant milling around in the dark corners, but found no one there. Colt approached one of the dark order screens and tapped it. It stayed dark, as did the other two. *Guess I'm buying my ticket the old-fashioned way.*

Rubble-like crumbs and food chunks shifted under his feet as Colt ascended the stairs. He stumbled up the last two. *They've really let this place go since I was last here.* It didn't matter that much. He'd wanted to see this film for months, watched the trailer over and over. *I've been so busy.* That wasn't true. He'd been isolating from the world, hardening himself against a painful loss. *Are they even open? I checked the listing.*

The smell of warm popcorn eased Colt's tension, but not as much as the shrill voice cutting through the silence. *I'm not alone.*

A woman with three children stood in front of the kiosk, shrouded in an eerie glow from the subdued lighting. She had dusty-blonde dreadlocks tied in a messy bun. None of them wore shoes.

"This is outrageous!" the woman in a hemp dress yelled.

"I'm sorry, ma'am, this movie isn't age appropriate for your kids." The guy behind the counter tried to assert himself, though the whine in his tone begged her to see reason.

Scrawny teen doesn't look old enough to have seen the film, Colt thought, sidling up behind the woman, *never mind man the counter alone.*

"I am their mother! Who are you..?" She leaned forward and twanged his nametag "... *Reggie*, to dictate what's best for my children."

Colt watched the woman—*new-age hippy,* he thought—lift a child to her hip who couldn't have been older than three.

"There's a gnarly autopsy scene," Reggie said. "Not to mention the jump scares and stuff."

"Do you hear that, Pebble? Reggie doesn't want you to see the film."

The toddler in her arms sobbed and the two older children at her side threw themselves to the floor in a performance fit for panto.

"There's a cartoon showing on screen two. That one's real good," Reggie said with a desperate smile, "I've seen it twice." The wailing from the children got louder and the teary eyed youth behind the counter looked ready to join in. He kept glancing around—*for help,* Colt presumed, but there were no other staff members in sight.

"Fine." The mother stamped her foot and all three children silenced. "But we'll have the tickets half price."

Reggie opened his mouth to argue, but nodded and printed their tickets.

Colt watched them funnel out of the way and approached the counter. "One for *Clawed Abduction,* and a medium salted popcorn please."

"Sure thing, just let me..."

Colt watched the lad count out cash from his own pocket into the till. *Poor bastard's paying for the other half of her tickets.* Reggie scooped the popcorn with a trembling hand. Not wanting to put more pressure on the lad, Colt glanced away and met the steely eyes of the mother leaning on the wall near screen two. Her glare, unblinking, venomous, stayed locked on him like a predator challenging its prey. Colt hid a yawn behind his hand and pricked his ears to the couple walking up behind him.

"Just wait 'til I get you in those back seats."

"Mason, stop," a woman giggled. "People will hear."

"Here, here you go," Reggie said, plastering a smile over a crippling panic attack.

Colt slipped him an extra twenty. "For excellent customer service and I won't take it back." He grabbed his popcorn and walked on to screen four. The mother still fixed her predatory stare on him. Colt looked away as he passed and wasn't surprised to find her sneaking her rabble in after him. *I could say something. Last thing I want is those kids screaming through the movie.* He debated it for a moment longer, but when the lights went out and the curtains pulled across the screen, he decided to take his seat and leave them to it.

Halfway through the first preview, the handsy couple fumbled up the aisle, giggling and talking in squeaky hushed tones.

They can have the back. I have my space. No one fighting me for an armrest. A memory sparked of someone's arm resting against his, occasionally arching over to steal handfuls of his popcorn. He pushed it aside. Now wasn't the time to open old wounds. *I'm doing just fine on my own.*

A long tone droned, increasing in volume over the production logo, and Colt sunk a little deeper in his seat. *This is it.* He waited for the tone to end, but it continued to grow louder and louder. With no end in sight, the note held—deafening, unyielding. Pushing down on his ears, Colt stood and screamed up to the projectionist, not even able to hear his voice over the shrill screeching. It was like an air-raid siren going off next to his head. "Turn it down!" he screamed. Then a bright light whited out everything and the noise stopped.

Colt squinted and watched a shape floating down in the spotlight, bathing him in blinding light. The light faded, or Colt's eyes adjusted to it, he wasn't sure which. As the silhouette in slow motion freefall crept nearer, Colt reached for the chair's headrest for stability. His hand slipped through air and he crashed onto hard ground. *Tarmac?* He stroked the flat stone beneath him and stretched out his legs to feel for the theatre seats. Empty space surrounded him.

The shape—no figure, was almost upon him. *Did I die? Is this an angel coming for me?* He patted all over his body, expecting his hands to phase through, feeling disconnected from it even though he was solid. *What makes* me, *someone who's never believed in God, worthy of going to heaven?* Another thought struck in the moment before the figure touched down and gained clarity. *How the hell did I die? Was it the popcorn? Did I choke?* It was all so unclear, so bitterly unfair.

Then through the light he saw him. A boy, wearing jeans and a t-shirt with Area 51 printed above a cartoon alien head and an open chequered shirt over that. His hair was shaggy and a single gold stud pierced his left ear. *This is my angel? This kid is going to guide me into the afterlife?* The words, *judge not, lest ye be judged,* popped into Colt's head, but he couldn't keep judgement at bay. He wanted answers, wanted an explanation, and he'd been sent a scruffy preteen. *What the fuck is this?*

"S'up, Pops," the boy said.

"I'm not your *pops,* I'm no one's pops!" He wasn't some old man meeting an expected end. *I'm in my thirties, struck down in my prime.* The boy looked at Colt like he was no one, like he was nothing. "I'm a young man, with so much life ahead of me," Colt continued to protest, scrambling to his feet. He wasn't in the habit of yelling at children, but that derisive look? It crept into his soul, igniting an inexplicable rage. Then he looked up. Beyond the light, something blotted out much of the night sky. Slick metal with a purple aura hung above them. It looked to have the size and weight to crush a town.

"Huh," the boy said, staring at the retracting beam of light and the huge airborne craft hovering overhead. "Seriously, again?" He let out a long sigh. *Of boredom, disappointment?* The emotions were clear to read in the boy's posture, but his dismissal confused Colt, and shocked him further when the boy apathetically said, "Guess I got abducted."

"Abducted?" The theatre was gone. Colt stood on a highway surrounded by smashed cars. Fire-licked buildings marked a smouldering city in the distance. "What's going on?"

"Come on. We need to get moving before one of their scouts catches our scent."

Before Colt could ask more, this child of the apocalypse grabbed his arm and dragged him. The craft let out a hissing whistle and zipped away in a blink. *Spaceship?* Colt thought. Then it struck him. *I'm asleep in the theatre.* Clawed Abduction *is playing and I'm so tired, I've fallen asleep.* It made perfect sense. His unconscious mind was absorbing the movie sounds and translating them in his dreams. He wanted to laugh. He'd wake up covered in popcorn, cursing fatigue for missing the first movie he'd made time for in almost a year of reclusiveness.

"Move faster," the strange boy with a pierced ear yelled.

Colt chuckled and picked up pace. *Sure. I'll play along.* Then doubt crept over his skin like icy fingers. *Why can I smell burning? Feel the boy's grip on my sleeve, the ache in my muscles?* He'd heard things in dreams, seen things, but never in this clarity, and he'd never felt, smelt and tasted things before.

"The army base is just over here." The lad—a good head and a half shorter than Colt—led the way. His feet slapped the road, kicking up smaller debris and ash. The boy let go of his arm and Colt tried to keep up, vaulting over and weaving around obstacles. *Bodies,* his mind tried to tell him, but he refused to look at them. *No, luggage. Seats ripped from cars. There aren't any bodies.*

A howl, a mixture between an injured fox and sparking gears, sucked all other sounds from Colt's ears. It reverberated through his skin and froze him to the spot. His vision swam. Disoriented, no breath he sucked in seemed to sit in his lungs. In the black voids between the streetlights, Colt's imagination ran riot, imagining movement where there was none.

"Hey, look at me." The lad was snapping his fingers in front of Colt's face. "I'm Jay, and I'm in this with you, but we need to keep moving."

"Towards the noise?"

"Sounds like it's coming from the base. They only scream like that when they're hurt bad. Army guy probably shot it."

Colt looked at him incredulously.

"Loud ones are safer than the quiet ones. The ones stalking you never make a sound until they're tearing you apart."

Colt held his ground.

"Whatever, come or don't, but the only people surviving these days are those on the base."

Jay started away, and Colt watched him go. His conscience begged him to follow—*he's a child. I can't just abandon him*—but he couldn't seem to uproot his feet. It was the rain that swayed him. Gentle, barely spitting. The icy drops pricked his skin. Jay's shrinking figure looked so vulnerable. *If, and it's a big if, this is real, I can't let that boy go off on his own.*

The howl came again. Colt questioned his intelligence more than his sanity as he rushed to catch Jay up. He couldn't just abandon him. The kid was putting on a good front, but he knew a scared child lay underneath. That's how he'd been at that age—*eleven? Twelve at a push*—all front, all mouth.

The two travelled in twilight, past wrecked cars, a still life of carnage. After jumping over the barrier, they left the highway, made their way across field and country lane until they came to a chain-link fence encircling the military base.

"Looks deserted," Jay said, then with a shrug he rolled back a corner of torn fence and squeezed through. Reluctantly, Colt followed. The sheared wires scraped his shoulders. One penetrated his clothing and snagged his skin. *Shit, I'm not dreaming. The sting, moist blood, it's too real.*

Tent fabric flapped in the breeze and empty water bottles caught by the wind tapped and scuffed their percussive rolls. Colt felt the word *'hello'* catch in his throat, but he stayed quiet as he meandered past the tents covering the forecourt. A carton of smokes, dealt cards and a Zippo lighter sat abandoned on a drum. Colt picked up the carton and slipped the lighter in next to the three remaining cigarettes. "I quit, before, before..."

"Before what?" Jay asked, watching him stuff the pack into his pocket.

Colt hadn't realised he'd spoken aloud. "I lost someone, and those first days after, all I could do to keep going was smoke." *One after another, down to the butt.* The acrid taste, the burn in his throat, hacking cough. He craved that now.

"Who'd you lose?"

Colt wasn't ready to go there. Carefully walling the loss was the only way he'd kept going. "Never mind. Where would they go?"

Jay pointed to the main building. It seemed as deserted as the forecourt. No one stood guarding this warehouse-like structure. No windows to peer through, just a solid concrete container. *Of survivors? Aliens? The dead?* They approached the door.

Colt kept glancing back at the fence through the drizzling rain. "There's no cars, no trucks." He looked over at an empty helipad. "No vehicles at all." *They've abandoned this place.*

Jay didn't seem to be paying attention. He was too

busy staring at the thick door and the keypad embedded in the wall next to it. "You look like the kind of dick that works in IT." Colt stood dumbfounded, but Jay continued, "So? Can you get us in?"

"I didn't have to come with you, you know." Colt glared, leaving a beat of silence for an apology that didn't come. As it happened, he was a security engineer. Before this madness, he'd spent his days installing and fixing these sorts of things, and his nights on call. *I could've worked less hours, should've been home more.* Colt looked at the keypad and frowned. He knew this model, knew the override code. He didn't know what they'd find inside. After another moment of hesitation he said, "Yeah, I can get us in." Colt recited the code in his mind over and over, testing his recollection, before keying the first number.

"Can't you hurry that shit up?" Jay asked and leaned into Colt.

"I'm going as fast as I can," Colt said and miss-keyed the code in for a second time. "And mind your language."

Jay snorted. Then Colt felt him stiffen at his side. A glance behind showed a huge figure at the fence. Four well defined arms clutched the fence it towered over. Colt put the code in, carefully pressing each number in the eleven digit sequence. Metal links snapped, causing Colt to sweat, and the thrown section of fence crashing near him almost made him key in a nine instead of eight.

"Help!" A woman raced towards them from one of the far tents, arms outstretched. The huge bipedal nightmare took to all sixes charging towards them. Colt froze, watching helplessly as the creature caught the woman. Rearing up, it took her legs and arms in each of its four hands and yanked them. Colt covered his mouth as the woman's limbs tore free. The gushing fountains of blood slowed to short spurts, then drizzles.

"Fuck." Colt let the word hiss out of his mouth in a long breath. The monster—*Alien,* Colt reminded himself—chewed on a bloody stump like it was a roasted chicken leg. *Chicken leg with a shoe.*

"The door!" Jay screamed, slapping Colt hard across his cheek. It was enough to snap him out of it, and Colt turned back to the keypad.

Heavy thudding footfalls advanced, dull beats alternated heavy ones as though the thing was limping at speed. The screen flashed up with the word, **enter**, and Colt pulled Jay inside. A second later, the alien smacked into the closed door. The thick metal held, and Jay dragged Colt down the corridor.

Dim red lights framed the ceiling, faded illumination that didn't reach the floor. "Not a good sign," Colt said. "Their main power must be out."

Some of the wall panels had come away, exposing frayed wires and pipes. Things scraped underfoot and the odd crack and squish made Colt grateful for the poor light.

"This way," Jay said, pulling him around a corner into another dingy corridor. "Survivors will be holed up somewhere deeper. If not, there's another exit further along."

The signs of destruction were everywhere. Colt couldn't ignore the blood anymore. His mind kept flashing back to that woman. *If I'd called hello when we first arrived, would she have joined us?*

The electrical buzzing, his breathing, the boy's breathing weren't the only sounds pricking his ears. Satisfied moans and smacking lips came from a door to his left.

"Mason," a woman crooned, "Someone will hear."

"But, Grace..."

The couple from the back seats! Colt's theory of dreaming reignited. He hadn't got a good look at the couple from the back row, but he swore these were the same voices. *If I can hear them, and the movie, then this is all me.* He ripped open the door to find the couple in a small cupboard. *There was no woman to save. None of this is real.*

"Hey!" Grace hastily positioned her top to cover her bra.

"What the hell?" the man she'd called Mason yelled. "Can't a guy get an end-of-the-world lay in peace? Get lost!"

"If you can hear me, I'm in the middle row and need you to wake me up."

"Who are you talking to?" Jay asked.

Colt spun around to look at him. "The kissing couple. They're—" The cupboard was empty. "They were right..." His voice trailed off. He slapped around inside, feeling for a panel or a false wall.

"You're losing it, Pops."

Colt dry swallowed. *I saw them. They were here, although...* He tried to picture their faces, the colour of Grace's top, and found he couldn't.

"Aliens scrambled your brain." Jay didn't wait for Colt to follow this time. He took off, almost at a jog.

"Hey, I'm not crazy," Colt called after him. When he caught Jay up, Colt found him murmuring to himself.

"As the bearded man approached the quarantine room, he realised deep down what horrors would lie within."

"What are you doing?" Colt hissed. They'd reached the end of the corridor and the only way to go lay through the dark room ahead.

"Narrating," Jay said nonchalantly.

"Why?"

"It helps to observe the world from a distance when I'm nervous."

"Pretty sure that makes you a sociopath." Colt lifted the plastic sheeting marked **Bio Hazard** and peered through. A smell in the air churned his empty stomach. He wasn't sure what death smelt like, but this must be it. *Soured meat and sewage.*

"The man with a beard—"

"Colt, my name's Colt, and I don't have a beard."

Jay scrunched up his face and raised an eyebrow. "That's a pretty bold claim, but ok. What do you call it then? Furry mask, chin bush, face pubes?"

"Will you just be quiet?" Colt rubbed the stubble on his chin, probing for a beard that had never been there.

"Scattered around the floor, scalpels, bone saws and other tools..." Colt shot Jay a glare and rammed his finger to his lips, but the boy finished the sentence with a whisper "... swam in blood."

The fluorescent lighting pulsed on for a flash in between breath-long stretches of darkness. In these blinks of illumination, Colt saw more and more horror. Men and women, some dressed in lab coats, others in military uniforms, lay dead. One blink showed him a woman's glassy-eyed stare, the next, the slick blood trail from her ear to the pool under her mouth.

Then he saw figures gathered around one of the two metal tables, examining a dead alien. *Is that..?* Her clothes were torn and dirty, her face streaked with finger dragged mud. Her dreadlocks, a dirtier blonde than before, were frizzier than when she was screeching at that teen at the kiosk. *What the hell?*

"Now, Puddle," the dreadlocked mother said, "what do you see?"

"Two hearts," one of her children said, aiming a flashlight into the alien's open chest cavity.

"And the arm we removed?"

"It's growing back."

Colt approached with caution. "What are you doing?"

The woman shot him a look of disgust. "Do you mind? You're interrupting our anatomy lesson."

Jay punched him in the arm. "You're doing it again. There's no one there." And the mother and children vanished.

Colt turned to the other table. The alien on this one was a patchwork mess of limbs. Colt leaned in closer. There was no torso showing through. Legs and arms covered every inch of this creature. He'd seen one of these things rip a woman limb from limb, but he couldn't help empathising with the sorry mess that lay before him.

Its eyes were giant black mirrors reflecting Colt's terrified gape. He was sure it was dead until it spoke in a clear, disarming voice. "Help me up there, would ya?" It leaned over, pulled the pack of smokes from Colt's jacket and tapped one out. "You got a light?"

Colt stood frozen, brain struggling to process what he was seeing. He up ended the pack and sparked the Zippo.

"You humans are a bunch of jack-asses, am I saying that right?" It reached out one of its many three-fingered hands and Colt didn't resist as it took the lighter from him, placing the flame next to the cigarette. "Yes, my species regenerate and can integrate the body parts of others, but I'm not related to half the sloshmoids they stitched to me. Fourteen dead legs and eight useless arms." It lifted some stiff, discoloured limbs and let them fall. "Don't you know anything about genetic compatibility?"

Colt wasn't sure what to say, but found words tumbling from his mouth all the same. "Never put any thought into stitching aliens together."

The alien choked out smoke and laughed. "It shows too."

It looked painful, all that mottled flesh rotting on the creature. "Can't you cut off the dead limbs?"

"While I'm awake? What kind of sadist are you?"

"You're doing it again," Jay hissed, trying to drag Colt back, but the talking alien didn't vanish like the movie goers had.

"I suppose there is one way..." A constipated look spread across the alien and all the surplus limbs sucked in, leaving it engorged, flesh quivering as though it would explode at any minute. Then it dislocated its mouth. The limbs spewed out, leg after foot, after arm after hand; a long stream of appendages like a never ending decaying rope. Colt cupped his hand over his mouth and swallowed burning vomit back down.

The alien let out a long burp and wiped one of his four remaining arms across his mouth. "This is the part where I kill you. Nothing personal. After all, we can't carry out a post mortem on humanity while you're alive."

It stopped talking, and looking at the strange vertical mouth, Colt decided it couldn't have spoken in the first place. Jay's fingers dug in hard, pulling him away from the looming alien.

The immense creature took one look at the mutilated corpse on the other table and screeched. It lunged for them, blocking them off from the exit.

Colt turned and pounded on the huge viewing window, only, he realised with a gulp, it wasn't a window, it was the screen and on the other side he could see his body slumped in the movie theatre seat. The alien reared up behind him, a snarling, toothy monstrosity. Colt pounded all the harder on the glass, screaming himself hoarse.

The surface of the glass liquefied. Colt's fist slipped through, then his whole body was sucked into the clear syrup.

Colt landed hard. Light hurt his eyes, only this time it was from the sun. He looked up at blue skies and smelt the salty wind of the sea. *Where am I?* He eased up, rubbing his head.

"What do you mean, my children can't drink alcohol? I'm their mother. Do you hear that, Simple? This woman doesn't want you to have tequila."

Colt drifted his head towards the voice. He was on the deck of a cruise ship, and standing at the poolside bar in a bikini was the dreadlocked mother and her children. *Christ,* Colt thought, massaging his pounding temples, *I'm still dreaming.*

"Where'd the aliens send us this time?" Jay said, standing up and offering his hand to Colt.

"Aliens? You think the aliens that just tried to eat us sent us on a cruise?"

Jay shrugged. "There's the eating aliens and the abducting aliens. Reckon this was the abducting ones."

"What are you even doing here?"

"I came through the window like you did." He pointed to the other side of the ship. "Like they are."

A vortex had opened up, a swirling disc like haze, and through it came five medieval knights riding horseback. The hooves clipped across the deck, and the lead knight lifted his visor and called out to Colt. "Pray tell, good sir, why is there a scantily clad brothel atop the waves?"

Colt didn't have to find words. A plump woman in a one-piece sprung up from her sun-lounger, armed with an empty glass that had fallen next to the horse's hoof. "He knocked over my margarita."

The knight dismounted and regarded her with disgust. "Silence, boat wench, or I shall run you through." He unsheathed his sword, holding it high so it glinted in the sun.

"Me and my George paid good money to come on this cruise, and I sharn't be spoken to like this by the bleeding *entertainment.*" The middle-aged woman shoved the knight's shoulder and thrust her empty glass into his gauntlet. "You owe me a drink. Nothing 'bout this in the brochure neither, was there, George."

A balding man in the sun-lounger next to her lifted his sunglasses, shook his head, then went back to nursing his pint.

"Is this the part where you tell me I'm doing it again?" Colt whispered to Jay.

"Nope, this seems legit."

"We're in search of the Holy Grail," the knight continued, ignoring the woman's glare.

"In the Caribbean?" the woman screeched. "This is the worst play I've ever seen."

"This is where the wizard sent us." The knight tossed the glass behind him. "He said danger would plague our quest, but never did I expect to see such wanton moral abandonment." He glanced at the woman, but only addressed Colt.

"My drink," the woman said. Hands on hips, she squared up to the towering knight. "And an apology. I know people, I have influence. Don't I, George?"

The balding man gave a noncommittal, "Mm hm."

The knight pushed the tip of his blade against her sunburnt chest. "You will not address me again, whore. Men are speaking things of import. Be gone."

She stood her ground. "Have your job for this, I will. See you go to prison too. Threatening innocent—"

The knight pulled the sword back and thrust it through the woman's throat. Blood gushed all over her pale blue swimsuit as the blade slid back out. There was a lone scream from someone on the far deck. Then all hell broke loose. The five knights broke off, diving into the crowd with weapons drawn. A knight still seated on his horse jousted a man trying to defend himself with a parasol. An older gentleman fended off a sword wielder with his walking stick.

"Yeah, we should probably go," Jay said coolly, like this was a perfectly rational turn of events.

"Go where?" Colt said, diving behind a deck chair.

Jay grabbed his sleeve and dragged Colt to the edge of the pool. Only it wasn't a pool, it was another screen, and once again Colt could see himself slumped in the theatre chair. He dived in feet first, slowly sinking into the thick, syrupy water. It enveloped him inch by inch. Colt had never experienced such fear as his legs disappeared into the unknown and his body and head stayed trapped, vulnerable to the carnage sweeping across the deck. When only his head remained above the surface, he sucked in greedy breaths, tilting his nose skywards. *I'm going to drown!* He held his breath and closed his eyes. The thick water that had folded him in its embrace vanished and a brief rush of air assaulted him before crashing onto something hard.

"Shoulda belly flopped," Jay said, dusting himself off. "Come through much quicker that way."

Colt coughed and looked around the smoggy street they'd landed in. It looked like a preserved piece of history, the brick houses, cobbled street, only with the fire damage and crumbling walls, it wasn't that well preserved. A noisy engine flying low spluttered and spat as smoke streamed from its tail. It looked like a spitfire, an old fighter plane.

"Quick, someone's coming." Jay moved behind the remains of an anti-tank gun.

Colt recognised the voices. *Mason and Grace.*

"You have to marry me, make an honest woman outta me."

Mason sprinted out of a side road first, with Grace right on his heels. Over his shoulder, he yelled, "An honest woman? Your profile said you were five-nine and a *natural* blonde!"

Colt turned to Jay, wondering if he'd seen them this time, but the boy was looking at something else. Dislodged bricks clacked across the road and a couple hurried out arm in arm over a rubble heap, eyes darting wildly.

"I know her, that's that actress, the one in all the chick flicks and period dramas," Colt whispered.

"Highly doubt you know any famous people, but ok."

This kid. Never known anyone so disrespectful. Colt peered around the metal shield. The wilted turret, cracked and melted, framed the lovers. The actress he recognised was wearing an old style army nurse getup, and the man, vaguely familiar, was in a corporal's uniform.

"I have to, for queen and country," the corporal said.

"But I couldn't bear to live without you, Charles." The actress draped her arms around his shoulders, tears running down her cheeks.

"Now you listen here, Mary-Anne. I'm coming back for you. When all the fighting's done, it'll be you and me against the world."

"Against the world," she repeated, swooning in his arms.

As they kissed, Colt jumped up and shouted, "That's the movie poster! Right there, them kissing, the street all blown apart, and a plane going down in the sky. This is a goddamn movie!" *The aliens, the knights on a cruise ship, they're all playing in the theatre. Have I actually been sucked into a film?*

Corporal Charles slipped the strap of his rifle from his shoulder and took aim, tucking the actress behind him. "Identify yourself!"

Colt stuttered out his name, torn between a firm belief that all this was imagined and the paralysing dread that maybe it wasn't. Maybe he was one false word from a bullet tunnelling into him. And that's exactly what Colt thought had happened as he heard the whistling of something speeding through the air. *He fired the gun!* Only there had been no shot, no bang. The rifle barrel, aimed with steady hands, tilted as the corporal glanced up. A bullet wasn't speeding through the air. Something much bigger hurtled towards them. The corporal and actress fled as the bomb landed. Colt curled up, knowing that the explosion would mean his doom. *Die in a dream, die in real life.* He wanted to wake so badly, but that fraction of a second stretched out. No boom. No fiery ball of death and destruction. Unfurling, Colt found the huge bomb unexploded in the road. The film stars were gone, but in their place stood four familiar figures examining the unexploded weapon.

"I want to hit it," said the child the mother had previously called Dimple, holding up a shovel.

"Very well, an experiment. What do you predict will happen when you strike it, Pimple?" asked the dreadlocked mother.

"You'll blow us the fuck up!" Colt shouted in disbelief.

"I was asking Wimple," the mother said, glaring at him like an unruly child interrupting her lesson.

"Wimple, Dimple, Pimple, you don't even know your

kid's name."

Jay had hold of him again, trying to pull him back, but Colt carried on striding to the mother.

"I remember my children's names perfectly, Mr Shelton, it is you who keeps forgetting them."

Colt was about to ask how she knew *his* name when the child struck the bomb and the blast thrust him through the air. He saw the screen looming towards him and prayed that this would be what woke him, this would put him back in his chair. Jay still had hold of him, and as they slipped through the clear syrup, he wondered if he could take him with him, if this child could be made as real in his world as every other they'd seen together.

This time he landed without pain and though gravity seemed to tether him the way it always had, the ground didn't seem as hard. Bright colours assaulted his eyes. The forest looked plastic, the grass a sea of green with little definition. *I'm still real,* Colt thought, staring at his hands, but the world looked computer generated.

"I saw this movie," Jay said.

Colt didn't remember the last time he'd seen an animation, but there was something familiar about the world he now stood in. "So you admit it, this is a film. I'm not crazy."

"I wouldn't go that far, but yeah. See that bear?" Jay pointed to an animated bear skipping along with a smile plastered on its face. "That's Coby. He's searching for other bears, but he's the only one left. Deforestation and shit killed the rest. Don't think he knows that yet though."

The Bear spotted them and waddled over. "Howdy,

friends. Have you seen any bears 'round here? I've been sleeping all winter and now I can't find anyone." He let out a chuckle. "Silly me, always losing things."

Losing things. Alone. If I could turn back time, like the bear does... Colt knew how this movie ended. How the bear would travel back, helping the people to live with nature, saving his friends. *Because I've seen it before.* He held his head, tears and grief begging for release. *No! I know how it ends because this is my dream.*

A shrill battle cry erupted, and from the trees darted the mother, now dressed in furs, and her children. They pounced on the bear. In a flurried attack they drove sharpened sticks into him. No blood came out, but the bear met Colt's eyes for a second with a look of surprise and anguish. Then he was still.

"What the hell is wrong with you?" Colt stormed over wrenching the mother's stick from her hand and tossing it to the ground. "He had a chance. His story was going to end the right way."

"The children wanted to hunt." The dreadlocked mother took a knife from her fur boots. "Now either help us skin it, or stay out of our way."

"Fine! Give the kids nightmares, I don't care. Get them blown up, teach them to maim, and steal, and murder, I don't give a fuck, just—"

"Mummy, I want to murder." The youngest child grinned and poked his stubby finger at Colt. "I want to murder him."

"Well of course you do, my sweet cherub."

"It's a bloody kids film." Colt scowled at the child. "No murder allowed!"

"No sex either," Mason's voice came from the trees.

"I look like a doll down there."

Jay sighed. "See what you keep getting us into?"

"Me? What *I* keep..!" Colt threw his hands in the air. "Why are you even here?"

"You know why I'm here," Jay said.

"No, I don't. I don't even know where here is. How here is. Why here is!"

"Pops, I can see you're upset. Why don't you try—"

The mother and children surrounded him. Somewhere in the trees Grace and Mason giggled, and Colt finally snapped. "Enough! All of you just leave me alone."

"Calm down, Pops, everything is ok."

Colt had been consumed by the heartbreak of loneliness, the crippling hole it left, but no one here was going to fill that hole. "I'm done with all of you. I don't care what world I'm thrust into next as long as none of you are there." He wrenched Jay's hand off his sleeve. "Especially you!"

"Think I want to be with you?" Jay shoved him hard. "You're such a fucking cock!"

Colt felt more than rage, he felt wounded. That wall of grief cracked, and he screamed at the boy. "Jason Mathew Shelton, your mother and I didn't raise you to—" Colt clasped his hand to his mouth, falling hard to his knees. "Jason?"

"S'up, Pops."

A giant screen appeared below them and Colt's knees sunk. "No, I didn't mean it." Jay wasn't sinking. His feet stayed planted. Colt reached out pawing at his ankles, trying to get a grip. "Come with me."

"I can't."

"Then please, let me stay. I can take the monsters and the knights, war and madness, I can't take losing you." He regretted reaching for him. His torso, flat on the screen sunk in another inch. Colt kept his head arched staring longingly at his son.

"Sorry, Pops. That's the way it has to be."

"No, I can't." Colt bawled. Huge tears and stringy snot flooded his face. He slipped through deeper, his fingertips barely touching Jay's trainers.

"You need to remember me this time, Pops." Jay's words grew quieter, as the syrup reached Colt's ears. "There's no one else left to, and if you don't accept reality, you'll never break free of the fantasy."

Colt didn't fall this time. He opened his eyes, finding himself back in the theatre. A patch of sunlight poured through a large hole in the roof. Below it, in dust and rubble covered seats, sat four skeletons. *The mother and three children.* Twisting around in the seat, Colt saw another two sat at the back. *The kissing couple.*

"No! *This* isn't real. I don't want this to be real." Colt's hair and beard were long and matted, his clothes oily with grime and bodily fluids. He placed his hand on the armrest and startled as he brushed cold, hard bone. Even in the dim light, he recognised the tattered remains of the alien t-shirt draped over the small skeleton. "The movie, the one about the bear, we were at the credits when they burst in." Lifting his hand to his shoulder, he fingered the scar of a bullet wound, wincing as though it was still an open wound. "They shot us." He remembered grabbing Jay's hand, remembered people screaming, fleeing the masked gunmen. *I was still holding your hand when...* The shot rang out in his head as clearly as the day the bullet pierced Jay's neck. *I should have reacted sooner, should've got you out.*

There'd been civil unrest for some time. The up rise of militia wasn't unexpected, but it quickly devolved into a slaughter. They'd evacuated the city so long ago. Colt was the only person left to wander its streets. In some of his more lucid moments, he wondered if there were places out there, untouched by the horrors he'd lived through, but he couldn't leave Jay. His boy needed him.

Colt got up and stumbled out of the dilapidated cinema that sat amidst the destroyed city. He glanced at the slumped behind the kiosk a skeleton had the nametag *Reggie* pinned to its uniform. Rubble sprinkled the carpet and the second from last stair was destroyed.

The streets were deathly quiet save for the odd bird and fighting strays. He walked in a daze for three blocks then fumbled the keys to his apartment. He was already rebuilding the wall that kept back all the memories of Jay. The good, the bad, the first time he'd held him, a tiny baby in his arms, the last time he'd held him, a child with blood in his mouth and terror in his eyes.

In his apartment, his food stash was untouched. He choked down a meal before things began to look as they once had. He knew he was grieving, knew he'd lost something precious, but he couldn't for the life of him remember what it was.

I've been moping too long. I need to get back out there. He suddenly remembered that film he'd been dying to see. Colt locked his apartment behind him and wandered the streets again, his mind retouching any sign of bombs and guns, leaving him with a version of how the world should've looked. How it looked when Jay still lived.

Colt strolled past the unreadable posters: the wartime romance, the animation, but like always the third one gave him pause. The faded image encased in the charred and grimy plastic frame itched in his brain. He could never remember what that one had been. *Zombie pirates dancing the flamenco with flowers raining down?* The title didn't give any further clues to the film's content, so Colt walked on shaking his head and entered the movie theatre.

-End-

THE CASE OF THE MISSING DRAGON

By Michael D Nadeau

Strange meetings

He opened the drawer to his desk and pulled out the bottle hidden under the piles of parchment, savouring the quiet that pervaded his normally chaotic office. He leaned forward and slid a glass over, pouring himself some of the ancient, and very expensive, elven spiced wine that he kept for just such an occasion. He enjoyed finishing a case and celebrating in the quiet of his tower office, especially when he got paid as much as he just did. Sniffing the contents of the glass before bringing it to his lips, he was just about to take his first sip when his intercom buzzed, shattering the peaceful afternoon.

"Caer, you have a client out here," the squeaky voice of his diminutive secretary said over the intercom.

Caer sighed and set down his glass, running his hand through his bone white hair as he narrowed his violet eyes. He hit the button and tried not to sound irritated. "Thank you, Swin, send them in." He shook his head and replaced the bottle under the pile of parchment, shutting the drawer. It wasn't Swin's fault, she was just doing her job, and, as one of the Ling, it was a miracle that she stayed as focused on that job as she did.

"Well, Caer, that's the problem. I can't."

Caer closed his eyes and rubbed his forehead in exasperation; he didn't need this today, that last case had pushed his limits of restraint far enough. His slender fingers hit the button again as he sat up straight. "Why can't you send them in?"

"They won't fit in the tower so I told them you would come to them," Swin said with a giggle.

"Get in here, Swin," Caer said with that tone that told her he wasn't having fun. He sat back once more and downed his glass, upset that he couldn't take the time and enjoy the drink he had earned. "Aliant, oen," he said, whispering the words of magic to unlock the door.

Swin strode in, her long, curly, auburn hair hanging down to her thin waist. She was all of three feet tall, average for the ling, and her piercing green eyes held a mirth that he didn't feel at the moment. "Sorry, boss, but I figured you would want this one."

"Why would you think that after the last case?" he asked, standing up and walking to his wardrobe. "I just got back and haven't even had time to rest."

"Because it's Sendrilian'ar." Her words hit the room like a mountain, causing him to stop mid step and hold it there, letting his foot down slowly.

"You're joking..."

"Normally I would be, but not today," she said with a bright smile; Swin could really light up a room when she wanted to. "He really is outside waiting to see if you will help him."

Caer cursed and opened his wardrobe, selecting his best longcoat and sword. *What does Sendrilian'ar want with me?* he thought making sure his trinkets were in his inside pockets; he didn't go anywhere without his trinkets. He strapped his sword on and spun, looking at himself in the full-length mirror. Caerlanavyn Shaelara was a private investigator, as well as an elf, and looked very good for being well over two hundred years old, despite the stress these last twenty years had put on him; being branded a rogue wizard had that effect on you.

"Handsome as ever, boss," Swin said, batting her eyes and flashing him a smile.

"Thanks, Swin. You really know how to make an elf feel better," Caer said with a wink as he walked by her.

She slapped his ass as he did and laughed. "You know I do, sexy," Swin said. "I'll work up some papers for him to sign just in case he doesn't eat you."

"You're the best!" Caer walked down the hallway and leapt down the hole in the floor, feeling the magic take hold of him and arrest his fall. He set down lightly and walked to the foyer, grabbing his phone on the way. The first thing he noticed, besides the client waiting for him, was the absence of animal sounds in the dense forest. That would usually trouble him, but he knew exactly why all the birds and other creatures had fled; having a dragon sitting on your front lawn would do that.

"About time," the deep booming voice said, echoing around the small glade.

"Sorry, wasn't in a rush to get eaten this afternoon," Caer said with a heavy dose of sarcasm, which, of course, went right over the dragon's head.

"If I was going to eat you, I wouldn't have sent your secretary a message." The dragon shifted his bulk and swivelled his massive head around so he could stare at Caer with those ancient eyes; eyes that narrowed as he looked at the elf leaning against the tower.

Caer examined his fingers and yawned, feigning boredom; a dangerous game considering the size of the dragon he was trying to irritate. The beast was over seventy feet long, from head to tail, and was covered in golden red scales that were tougher than any metal. His teeth were the size of short swords and the fire breath the dragon could summon could roast an entire town, magic wards or not. "Well, now that the pleasantries are over with, Sendrilian'ar, what can I do for one so impressive this day?"

"I should've killed you the last time we met," Sendrilian'ar said with a snort, flicking his tail and thudding into the ground hard enough to make Caer stand for balance.

"I saved your mates egg..." Caer started, knowing that it was futile. That was one of his worse cases, successful or not; her screams still gave him nightmares and elves didn't sleep.

"You let her die!" the dragon roared as he lurched to his feet, small flames licking the edge of his snout.

"I tried, Sen... you know I did." Caer walked forward, knowing that the vow that was made that day would hold out against any anger the dragon still had in its heart. "It was her or the egg and Verendil said to save the egg." The silence that filled the glade stretched on and was only broken by the heavy breathing of the enraged dragon.

After a long pause the dragon's head lowered and a single tear fell to the grass, causing a flower to bloom on the spot. Dragon's tears were one of the more potent magical sources in the world. "I know...I just miss her."

Caer didn't want to go there anymore, so he tried to get back on track. "So, seriously, Sen. What do you want to hire me for?"

"The egg you saved that day, my son Xandren'il, is missing."

The Search

Caer shifted gears and thrilled to the sound of the engine whining as he sped towards the cave where Sendrilian'ar last saw his son. He couldn't believe that someone would be stupid enough to kidnap a baby dragon, never mind one that belonged to Sendrilian'ar; he was the most feared dragon in all of Tavar. Pulling up to the cave he saw that there was a crowd gathered around the entrance, no doubt dragon hunters looking for an easy bounty; word had spread quickly of the missing baby.

"Oh, great another one searching for a quick gold

note," a burly dwarf said, brandishing an axe to block Caerlanavyn's way.

"Has uth awar," Caer said, ripping the axe out of the dwarf's hand and sending it flying away with magic. When the dwarf drew another weapon, this time a dagger, Caer drew his slim sword and smiled, dropping into a defensive stance.

"I wouldn't do that, Avar," a husky female voice said. "That's Caerlanavyn Shaelara." An attractive female orc with grey skin and long braids stepped out from the crowd, her skimpy outfit showing off her voluptuous curves and muscled physique.

Caer laughed and put away his sword as the dwarf fell back, fear washing over his scruffy face. "Kith, how have you?" he started to ask, but her slap stopped him from talking any further.

"You son of a bitch!" Kith said, advancing on him as he fell back. "You never called me after our romantic getaway."

"Kith, wait..." he tried, but she was on him again. he ducked this time and spun, getting under her reach, and grabbing her tusks that protruded from her mouth. He lifted up, forcing her head back and held her there. He smiled when she moaned loudly, her arms going around him softly and holding him close. He knew what really turned her on and made her forget her anger; orcs were tricky like that when they were angry. "I'm sorry, Kith. Let's talk about it over coffee."

"Oh Caer," Kith said as he let go. She kissed him deeply and lifted him off the ground. After the kiss she let him go and slapped him on the back. "So why are you here anyway?"

"I'm on a case," he said, knowing that the arguments would start soon from everyone else.

"Who is this guy anyway?" one of the other bounty hunters asked. the kid was human and only about twenty years old; he wouldn't even remember the events of that time.

"That's the rogue wizard that helped the dragons," another hunter said with obvious disdain. "The elven highmages banished him from their floating towers and branded him twenty years ago.

"Ignore them, Caer," Kith said, sneering at the crowd as they walked to the cave entrance. "They can't find any trace of the dragon, so they're upset."

"Well, I have a lead I need to check out," Caer said as they made their way into the cave. "Sendrilian'ar said the kid was coming here to test his might against a Knight of the Star."

"No."

"As crazy as that sounds it's true." Caer bent down and grabbed a small handful of dirt. "Ses on tor," he said softly. His magic made the dirt glow and soon footprints could be seen leading into the cave; footprints that resembled the metal shoes of the Knights of the Star. He took out his phone and snapped a couple of pictures of the glowing prints for his case files and then sent the pictures to Swin in a text.

"If that was the case then there would be a body, one way or another right?" Kith asked as they came to a large cavern.

Caer put away his phone and patted her on the shoulder. "One would assume that, yes." Torches lit the edges of the high ceiling and a scuffle could be seen, yet no blood had been shed. "This way," Caerlanavyn said as they walked the path of glowing prints and saw that there were obvious dragon prints that simply stopped near the back of the cave; yet the metal imprints kept going. "Now we just have to find the secret door," Caer said as they reached a dead-end tunnel seeing one half of a print next to the wall.

"Oh, that's easy," Kith said pushing him aside and lashing out with a massive kick against the wall. The stone shuddered and fell in, the mechanism shattered under the powerful blow.

"I had forgotten how subtle you could be, Kith."

"It's one of my charms," she replied with a tusky grin.

They followed the secret corridor for a ways and exited on the south side of the cave to find a single tire track in the dirt heading towards the eastern province of Jalys. "I would bet my very long life that those tracks belong to a Cappadocia 22," he said with confidence.

"That's oddly specific," Kith said, bending down and inspecting the tracks herself. "Why that model?"

"Because that is the type of bikes the Knights of the Star ride." Caer bent down with her, wondering what she was looking for. When she grunted and stood back up, he peered at her with interest. "What did you find?" Caer knew she was a damned good bounty hunter and tracker so she may have learned something he had missed.

"Well, I can tell you that it wasn't just one knight on that bike. The tracks are deep, like he had a very heavy passenger," Kith said, smiling at him with that look.

"Well, I think it's time to pay a visit to Star Tower."

Knock, Knock

The capitol city of the Jalys province loomed before them like the glass marvel that it was. The high-rise buildings soared to the sky, only matched by the floating island towers of the elves far above. Reise was a bustling city, filled with shops, corporations, busy streets, and of course its share of crime. To combat this crime, the local police enlisted the aid of the Knights of the Star. These armoured knights rode on bikes of gleaming chrome and patrolled the streets with an iron fist; sometimes literally.

Caer shifted down and pulled up to the light, his sleek, white, sports car sparkling in the high sun. He hadn't been to the city in years and the excuse to visit the Lord of Star Tower came as an unexpected bonus to a hectic day.

"Tell me again why we didn't just let Sendrilian'ar know where his kid was?" Kith asked as the light turned and Caer sped off again.

"Because he would come here and raze the entire city in flame."

"Oh, yeah."

"Besides, I owe you that coffee, remember?" Caer spun the wheel, screeching around a corner and narrowly missing a wagon full of fruit, its gnomish owner screaming obscenities as they took off.

"Oh, you owe me more than just coffee," Kith said, squeezing his thigh.

"Work, work, work," he replied. They took the ramp to head downtown and immediately saw their target;

Star Tower.

The gleaming tower of the most successful corporation in all of Tavar, Star Tower was the bane of wizards. Built to dampen their powers, it was the home of the Knights of the Star, an organization of valiant knights that worked to protect the innocent and uphold justice; it helped that they got paid by the truckload as well. Run by the enigmatic, Lord Aris Silverblade, The Star Tower was one of the most fortified buildings in all of Riese, next to the castle of Highlord Jalys himself, that is.

As they pulled into the parking garage Kith turned to Caer with a serious look on her face, her tusks sticking out menacingly. "So, tell me again how they are going to just let you walk in there and ask questions?"

"Oh, they're not," Caer said as he parked the car and shut down the engine. He got out and waited for her to join him before hitting the alarm. "I'm just going to sneak in, find the kid, then break out and run for the sun."

"Well, that answers that question," Kith said rolling her eyes.

They walked to the iron bound door near the back of the garage, a huge lock hanging off of a large chain. Before Kith could even try to break it, Caer took out a small pouch from his longcoat and opened it, producing a small metal-looking sliver.

"That doesn't look like any kind of lock pick I've seen," Kith said as she scrutinized the tiny stick.

"Nope, it's a special trinket that has no magic what-so-ever." Caer set it into the lock and smashed it in deep, the seemingly solid metal melding like clay. Once it was in good, he took out a lighter and a small candle, sticking in and lighting it. The wick flared to life like it was soaked in oil, and he grabbed Kith's hand and ran back around a stone column.

"What..." Kith started, but the rest of what she was going to say was drowned out in an explosion that sent pieces of iron and oak door flying past them.

"Compact cinder causing clay—or C4," Caer said as he ran for another stone column, this time hiding down behind a small wall. No sooner than they concealed themselves did another door open in the far wall, as if invisible to the naked eye. Security men in dark cloaks and sunglasses came pouring out, small lightning wands ready for action, led by a massive man in full gleaming platemail armour. They surveyed the damage, heedless of the two sneaking back they way they had come

"You knew they had a secret elevator, didn't you?" Kith accused as they ran as quietly as they could for the newly visible security entrance.

"The obvious door is never the one you want," Caer said as they got in and hit the button that read 'up'.

"Is that an elven proverb?"

"No, it was in one of my fortune cookies last month. Ironic that it fits the situation so well though huh?" Caer pulled out another trinket and set it on the panel as the door opened. This thing looked like a red and white U and stuck to the metal wall with a small thud.

"You own a magic magnet?"

"This priest owed me a favour and I took it in trade," Caer said as he scanned the hallway. "This will keep the elevator here until we have to leave."

"I thought magic was dampened in the tower?" Kith asked as they walked quickly down the hallway.

"It is, but not items made by magic. The thing doesn't emit anything but natural forces...magic just made it really strong." Caer got to the end of the hallway and opened the door that read 'stairs' and ran up two at a time. "Now come on, that diversion won't keep them busy all day." They ran up four more floors and opened into a carpeted hall lined with suits of armour.

The Prisoner

"Now what?" Kith asked as they closed the door behind them.

"Now I try a direction spell." This high up the magic dampening field should be lessened as most wizards use magic to get this far. *At least in theory,* Caer thought as he closed his eyes and pictured chains and a holding cell. "Fin bind," he whispered and breathed a sigh of relief when a tiny red arrow appeared in the air pointing to the fourth door on the right.

Caerlanavyn and Kith ran for the door, anxious to get the dragon and be gone before the knights were alerted to their presence. The locked door was huge—easily built for a small dragon—and was nothing to Kith's shoulder. The door splintered inward and Caer strolled in like the hero he felt he was, only to stop short at what greeted him. "Who the hell are you?" the wizard asked as his mouth hit the floor.

Sitting on the floor of the massive room wasn't any sort of dragon, but a rather well-muscled man in chains. The man had red hair hanging down to his shoulders and he looked like he had been defeated. He looked up with defiance though, as if his spirit was trying to regain some bit of purpose. "I am... was, Second Knight Marcus Syll. Who are you to break into a protected cell?"

"He doesn't look like a dragon, Caer..." Kith stood at the broken door, keeping an eye out for incoming knights.

Caerlanavyn ignored her and walked forward, taking out another trinket. This one looked like a small sword with very serrated edges. "Well, Marcus, I came for the dragon. If I release you, could you take us to him?"

"I would. The order stripped me of my title and rank for adhering to the code I was raised on. Yet how are you going to break these chains with that tiny sword?" Marcus stood, his muscles flexing against the steel chains to show how strong they were.

Caer smiled and set the tiny weapon to one of the links of the chain. "This is a Hard as Knives saw—H.A.K saw—and was enchanted to eat through metal quickly." Caer ran the blade back and forth quickly and cut through a single link, breaking the chain in minutes. "Why did they imprison you?"

"Because I didn't kill the dragon. It surrendered and I was forced to take it prisoner. It is unlawful to kill any that have given themselves to you willingly."

"Persecuted for saving a dragon...rings a bell," Caer said with a frown. He had been thrown out of the ranks of wizards years ago for that very thing, branded a rogue for his actions; actions he would repeat again given the chance. "Do you think the dragon still lives then?" If that child were dead, the whole city was in jeopardy from Sendrilian'ar and his wrath.

"Last I heard they were taking it to the high tower for questioning. Since it surrendered, the final judgement was left to Lord Silverblade." Marcus looked Kith up and down, nodding his approval of her worth.

"You knights, always size everyone up, don't you?" Kith asked with a dangerous tone to her voice.

"Only the sexy ones," Caer answered for the fallen knight as he pushed them both out of the room. "You said the dragon surrendered to you?" This case was getting stranger and stranger by the minute. "Sendrilian'ar said he last saw his son at the cave because he was going to challenge a knight to single combat."

Marcus took the lead as they went, guiding them down the hall towards the far end and the main elevators. "I received a message saying that there was a dragon holding a maiden hostage and to head to that cave to save her. Once I got there the little guy was in the middle of the cave waiting for me."

"And no damsel in distress?" Kith asked sarcastically.

Marcus shot her a scornful look as the elevator door opened. "No. Just him with his tiny arms in the air. He said he surrendered before I could even swing my sword." He hit the top button labelled 'T' and the doors closed.

Caer went over these details in his head as the light bardic music came over the speakers, the sound of the harp and females voice soothing despite the danger they had rushed into. He couldn't believe they hadn't been found yet, nor had even run into any knights as they traversed the tower. *I'm missing something,* he thought as they shot upwards. *This is too easy.* Kith answered his own nagging doubts with her own observations as the doors opened to an empty corridor.

"Why isn't there any knights patrolling these hallways?" she asked out loud as they walked cautiously down the empty hall. Portraits of lord knights of years gone by decorated the walls and pedestals held large gemstones and other treasures, yet no guards could be seen.

As if her words were the catalyst to the final act of a grand play, the double doors at the end of the hall opened and a booming voice greeted their arrival. "Because we've been expecting you, of course."

Caer looked at his companions and shrugged, knowing that they were in the belly of the beast—so to speak. *Well, at least I know what I was missing.*

Welcome

Caerlanavyn walked into the grand room hesitantly, the words to a spell ready on his lips. His eyes took in the whole room as he entered, from the grand oaken desk and the double wide bay window behind it, to the couches to the right complete with trays of wine and cheeses. The setting sun casting vivid colours across the deep red carpet as they entered, and a hearth blazed in the corner.

The man behind the desk stood slowly and seemed like a story book character come to life. He had long flowing blond hair and piercing blue eyes that followed their every move as they approached him. He was wearing ornate chainmail armour and an elegantly worked blade lay on the desk in front of him. He walked around his desk, his sweeping cloak billowing out behind him as he did; this man knew how to look the part.

"Lord Silverblade, I presume?" Caer asked as he bowed low, his long white hair brushing the carpet as he did.

"Yes, and to who do I owe the pleasure of addressing, besides you of course dear Caerlanavyn?" the lord knight asked, stopping in front of the group.

"To whom," Kith corrected with a tusky grin that held no mirth whatsoever.

"Ignore my friend's friendly disposition, she hasn't had her pills this morning," Caer said before it got ugly. "This is Kithandra Skarr, dragon hunter. She has three degrees, two in warfare and one in mathematics."

"Killing is all in the numbers," she interjected.

"And I believe you know your own fallen knight, Marcus?" Caerlanavyn continued before Kith kept going. He noticed that Marcus was keeping his mouth shut but was quietly seething; it was written all over his face.

"Oh yes, the young man that started this whole debacle." Lord Aris paced and motioned them over to the couches. As they sat, he took out his phone and hit a button. "Send in our guest."

"I have to ask, Lord Silverblade, why kidnap a dragon and bring it to the city. Surely you have the knights to take any dragon, but you risk the deaths of the people by leading one to your doorstep." Caerlanavyn sat back, his feet propped up on a marble coffee table earning a disdaining look from their host. He took a glass of wine and sipped it, giving an approving nod.

"That's the whole problem with this situation, dear

dragon lover," Aris said as the double doors opened once more. "We didn't kidnap him."

"Then why is he still here?" Kith asked as the baby dragon as led in by three knights, weapons drawn but not threatening the creature. The dragon was only a baby, yet he was the size of a full-grown horse. With a wingspan of nearly ten feet and a tail that stretched for days, the little thing was still a force to be reckoned with; luckily, they had no fire breath until their fiftieth year.

"Because I asked them for sanctuary," the dragon said, flipping his tail slightly as he walked over.

"You what?!" Caer was on his feet now, his wine sloshing out onto the carpet. "Why?"

"I just don't want to kill anyone, Caer; it's not in me." Xandren'il said, lowering his head in shame. "Father would never understand, and I couldn't live with him hating me."

Caer shook his head in disbelief; a dragon that didn't want to kill people. *About as rare as an elf that wants to help one, I guess,* he thought. He turned to the lord with a frown. "But why did you accept?"

"He asked for sanctuary, and as Knights of the Star, we *had* to accept." Lord Aris waved the accompanying knights away and put his own feet up. "Hence my dilemma, dear Caerlanavyn." Aris took a big sip of his own drink as the dragon made its way over. "You see, we are at war with the dragons and if Highlord Jalys finds out we are harbouring one, code or not, we will be thrown down."

"So why *are* you giving him sanctuary?" Kith asked, narrowing her deep brown eyes. "I've seen you knights bend your ethics before—been on the receiving end of at least three such instances, as a matter-of-fact—so I know you *could* slay the kid and still sleep at night."

Instead of answering, Lord Silverblade looked at Caer and raised his eyebrow. He smiled and took another deep sip.

Caer closed his eyes and wondered what he was missing. That was happening more and more lately, and it was getting tiring; he was sharper than this usually. It must be something huge since they obviously can't afford to lose the highlord's support...Then it hit him, the ultimate victory over the dragons and the biggest payout at the same time. "He wants to use Xandren'il as a bargaining chip to draw up a truce."

The Cost of a Bargain

"Well done, Caerlanavyn. I knew you would do well on this case," Lord Aris said. "That's why we let you in here once we knew it was you following the case. Anyone else and we would have shut them down quickly."

"Why him?" Marcus asked, finally breaking his silence. He had sat forward now, intrigued at the conversation.

Xandren'il snorted grey fumes, the tendrils of smoke drifting up towards the high ceiling. "Because of his past. He saved me when I was just an egg and was branded a rogue wizard by the elven council."

"You're the elf that sided with the dragons?" Marcus asked, his eyes going wide.

"I didn't *side* with the dragons, Marcus. I did what I thought was right and without being paid for it." He looked right at Lord Silverblade when he said this last part, then lowered his head. "I still couldn't save Verendil though..."

"What matters now is that Xandren'il wants to help, and you are the perfect elf to help him," Aris said, standing and smoothing out his cloak. You will be paid handsomely for your part, do not fear."

"Well, that's the worst part then," Caer said as his head came up. He was holding a white tube in his hand and had uncorked it while unobserved. "Because I'm still going to do the right thing, no matter what." He held the tube up and blew, leaping to his feet as he did. A fine white powder burst into Lord Aris's face and the man tripped backwards, coughing, and trying to call for help; he was snoring before he hit the couch.

"Quick, we don't have long," Caer said as he raced to the window.

"You planned this all along, didn't you?" Kith asked, trying not to laugh.

"Once I saw the bay window I did, yes." Caer pushed the heavy oaken desk out of the way and waved Xandren'il over. "Ok Xan, it's up to you now."

"I don't think I can carry all of you down that far," the dragon said, looking worried. "My wings are strong but not that strong." He looked at Kith when he said this and immediately cringed as she scowled at him.

"Did you just call me fat?"

"Not now, Kith. Look, Xan, it's not that far and you just have to get us down slower than falling." Caer went to the window and took out his dagger, rapping the glass in the corner with the hilt. The pane shattered and wind rushed in, blowing them back a bit.

"I'm staying," Marcus said, walking back to Lord Silverblade and propping him up. "Without the dragon they have no case against me."

"Won't they still charge you with treason since you were with us?" Kith asked with a note of compassion in her usually gruff voice.

"Don't worry about me," he said laughing. "My father is on the council, and I plan on leaving the order anyway after this." He turned to Caer and gave a bow. "Mayhap I may even look for employment with your firm in the future."

"You're hired," Caer said as he pushed Xan towards the broken window. "Now let's go before the other knights get in here."

The dragon grabbed them in its claws, and leapt off the sill, beating his wings as hard as he could. Their fall was arrested, but they were far from flying. Spiralling down slowly, they heard shouts from above and whistling as arrows zipped past them. The dragon rocked back and forth as it tried to swerve in the arrow storm, almost dropping his cargo.

"Grab Caer with both claws!" Kith shouted to Xandren'il as she climbed her way onto the dragon's back. She covered the dragon with her body, taking an arrow in her leg and back.

"Kith!" Caer screamed. Before he could do anything else they were out of range and almost to the pavement.

"Hold on," Xan warned as he swooped down fast, trying to avoid a direct collision. They slammed into the street, horns blaring as tires screeching around them. Caer got up and grabbed Kith, hefting her over his shoulder with a strength he didn't know he had.

"Fly home, Xan. I'll be right behind you." He struggled to the garage, getting Kith into his car as the knights came pouring out. He hit the gas and flew off, squealing through the city as the bikes came after him.

"Must you hit every bump?" Kith asked weakly.

"Save your strength," he said as he made a hairpin turn down a one-way street. "Smos clo ara!" he shouted, causing a cloud of fog to roll in behind him, obscuring him from the bikes. "Why did you go and do that anyway, you foolish orc?"

"I still want my coffee...and maybe a bit more than coffee..." she sputtered, coughing up blood.

Caer pushed the car to the limits of its speed, using magic to help evade the knights. He had lost them once he passed the borders of Riese and out into the highway, but he still wouldn't make it back in time to save Kith. He had a scroll in his office that he kept for emergencies, and he prayed that Swin was still at work. He hit the speed dial on his phone and prayed that the diminutive, little Ling picked up.

"Shaelara P.I., how can I help you?" Swin said as she answered the phone.

"Swin, it's me. I need help."

"Boss! Xan said you were in trouble. Help is already on the way."

"It is?" Before Caer could even wonder what that meant a huge shadow washed over the car. He looked up to see Sendrilian'ar's huge claws coming down gently, wrapping around the car. "Hold on, Kith, we're going to make it after all."

Epilogue

WORLDS COLLIDE

Caerlanavyn sat back and downed another glass of spiced wine. He was trying not to worry too much about Kith, but she had been sleeping for almost three days. They had arrived just in time for him to use his emergency healing scroll on the female orc, and then Swin cleaned her up some more. He should really look into hiring a priest to stay on site for things like that.

A loud roar pulled him out of his contemplation, and he turned to look out his tower window. Sendrilian'ar landed outside with a grace that still shocked Caer to this day. How something that big could touch down and not make a racket he would never understand. His intercom buzzed before he even stood up.

"Boss, Sendrilian'ar is here," Swin's voice said crackling over the tiny box on his desk.

He ignored her and went to his couch, pulling a blanket from the shelf and covering the sleeping orc before he grabbed his longcoat and sword. He knew why the dragon was here and quite frankly he was just as blown away at that as well.

Sendrilian'ar had taken the news of his son not wanting to kill people with a grimace and a nod, just thankful that he was safe. Once they had filled in the great dragon about what had happened, Sendrilian'ar admitted that the dragons on the council had talked about a truce as well. The catch? They would only talk to the elves if Caerlanavyn was the mediator.

Messages were sent and texts responded; the elves were sending someone later this evening to discuss the formalities on where and when, but he needed to talk with the dragon first, just to know where they stood.

All in all, it was a successful case, and one that earned him a good-sized bag of gold, but this was only the beginning, and he was pretty sure it was going to give him a big headache.

"Hold all my calls, Swin. I'm going flying."

-End-

PLUTO'S GATE
By L. T. Emery

It was a mild autumn on the flood plains of the Alcantara river. Enjoying the peace and beauty of my farm, I watched the sun god Helios and his horse drawn chariot begin its quickening descent across the sky. Sparks sprayed as I worked at my grinding wheel. I admired the glistening shine coming from the blade of my sword and placed it reverently next to my spear and dagger.

Rumors abounded on Sicily that the new emperor, Gaius Caesar, otherwise known as Caligula—but call him that at your peril—had landed on the island the previous day with a legion of five thousand men. Gaius was the toast of Rome; I'd heard the town folk call him 'our baby' and 'our star', and it was said that he was admired by all the world, from the rising to the setting sun. Even the beauty of this evening couldn't pull me from my melancholy though. I didn't need the oracle to tell me the new emperor was there for me.

Six months peace. Rome could only give me six months.

"Marcus," I called. "My son, have you checked the flock?"

"Yes, Papa. All present and accounted for."

"Good-good," I nodded and patted him on the shoulder. "No more missing?"

"No, Papa."

"Good boy. Put these away," I said, pointing to my weapons. "Be quick though, we'll be having guests tonight. Tell your mother to ready the oven."

"Okay, Papa." Marcus said, and carefully lifted my sword and spear.

"Leave the dagger," I said as he reached for it.

"Once you're done polish my armor."

"Papa?"

"You heard me. In all likelihood I'll be gone on the morrow."

"But you only just got home."

"I know, son," I said. "But Rome calls. Your job is to protect your mother and our farm now."

He was only ten—the poor kid—and he looked scared. I could see it in his eyes. I had to be hard with him, as much as it hurt my soul, but the world is hard, and he'll need steel running through his veins as he grows into adulthood. Joy filled my heart when he looked to my sword for a moment, straightened himself, lifted his chin and nodded.

"I will, Papa."

"Good boy," I said and ruffled his hair before he marched away.

I slowly stood, wiping my tired hands clean on an old rag, and walked the twenty feet to the river. My joints ached; my scars burnt in anticipation of what was to come. I looked at my reflection in the water and saw someone I didn't recognize. A man grown old. I'd hit my fortieth year in summer just gone and wanted only one thing; to live out my last days in the company of my family. Not with stinking, sweaty centurions.

I washed my hands and splashed my face with the frigid water. It revitalized me and I walked to the fields to find my best sheep. Only the best for the emperor.

**

"Phemonoe, it's good to see you," I said.

"Antonius, it's been too long."

The oracle stood at center of her temple, surrounded by twenty marble columns. Between all, save one, stood marble statues of gods. Standing stock still garbed from head to toe in a red cloak, the hood hanging over her head, masking most of her features, she exuded an almost god like confidence and ease.

"Not long enough," I said, smiling at her.

She pulled back her hood, revealing a round face, hair and lips as red as her cloak. Piercing green eyes seemed to gaze into my soul. I came to her temple with two tasks in mind. First, in the hope the oracle would tell me my worries were wrong, even though I knew they were right. She saw right through me.

"You wish to know your future, yet know you already do. Why come to me?"

"Please don't talk to me in prophecy. We've been through too much together."

"Ahh, yes. That hell hole west of Dacia. We saved each other that day."

"Yes. I fear what is about to come more. Do you see a future where I'm retired and happy with my family?"

Phemonoe gave me a mournful smile. "I see a day to come when the hidden will be revealed. I see a door being closed and a shut door opened. I see pain and loss and victory. I see much, Antonious."

"I just want to farm and be happy with my family. I've fought enough for ten lifetimes"

"We must fight for what we want."

"Fight, fight, fight. Is that all life is?" I asked.

"You already know the answer to that one," she said, chuckling. "Tell me, Antonius, has there not been a small part of you expecting this day to happen since we were sent here, to keep watch?"

I shook my head in in sheer, stubborn disbelief. "Yes! But not when the bloody emperor of Rome is visiting!"

"Maybe there is a reason for his presence too?"

I raised an eyebrow. I hadn't thought of that, but quickly dismissed it. Not everything was thanks to the Parcae.

"I'm sorry I don't have the answers you seek."

I waved a hand at her, "You merely say what you see, you need not be sorry."

I looked to the statue of Virtus, God of bravery and strength, and whispered a prayer to him. I then completed my second task.

I slit the sheep's neck at the temple. I made it an of-fering to the gods, even though I knew it would do me no good but leaving a haunch in futile hope.

As I left the oracle, she called to me, "Antonius, you should ready your blade."

"One step ahead of you Phemonoe," I shouted over my shoulder.

"Not that one," she said, and my blood ran cold.

***

I took a knee, my wife next to me, as Gaius and his entourage came up the long entrance way to the farm's villa. His retinue was relatively small; the emperor rode out front, closely followed by who I assumed was his second, a hulking man. Behind them sixteen more fol-lowed, all in the red garb of the Praetorian Guard.

"Gaius Caesar," I said, nodding as he pulled up, keeping my voice even.

"Primus Pilus Antonius Maxima," he boomed, slid-ing off his horse and handing the bridle to his second. "Stand. Let me get a good look at you. It's an honor to meet the man who single-handedly fought off a whole Germanic tribe. You'll need to regale me with the story over dinner."

Images of the battle flickered in my mind. The beau-tiful rainbow that born it all in that hellhole west of Dacia. The clash of blades. The screams. The silence. The blood and gore. My men all dead. I felt my knees weaken at the memory but pushed them back compos-ing myself. I nodded, "I have never spoken of that day, your majesty."

"Well, this is the perfect opportunity to tell your story. And please, call me Gaius."

"Thank you, your- Gaius," I said and bowed my head once more.

"And who is this shining goddess next to you?"

My wife, blushed, and nodded. He wasn't wrong though; she was a vision. Hair the color of the sun hung to her waist. Her eyes shone like opals, while her thin pink lips often hid her feelings. She was from the far north: a Geat. She was lithe, toned and only a few inches smaller than me—and I stood an inch over six foot—but her femininity still shone through. She was warrior woman with a soft soul. She and Marcus were my life.

"This is my wife, Estrid."

"Your majesty," she said, smiling. "Welcome to our home."

"And what a home Rome has allowed you both, if I do say so myself."

I ground my teeth, and said, "And very grateful to Rome am I."

Gaius chuckled at this, turned back to me and said, "Don't get me wrong Antonius, you have earned this and much more. Rome owes you for your services."

"But here you are anyway," I slipped, and my stomach dropped at the disrespect I'd just shown the Emperor of Rome.

Out of the corner of my eye I noticed the second's hand lower to the hilt of his sword.

The emperor lifted a finger; the smallest of motions, no one else would have noticed, but I did and so did the second, and he relaxed. Gaius showed no anger in his expression, on the contrary, he looked almost sad.

"I fear we have gotten off on the wrong foot. Tiberius

always spoke so highly of you. He told me you liked a drink. Shall we?" he said pointing to my home.

I chuckled, "I did. Now, I'm a just humble farmer."

Emperor Tiberius had been the one to grant me this land. I had worked my way up from a humble Centurion, all the way through the ranks to Primus Pilus, the ninth most senior officer in the Roman army and a close confidante to Tiberius. I had a knack for knowing how foes would act during war, it gave my men an advantage. I'm lucky enough to have been able to save many lives in my time as Primus Pilus. It all ended in that hellhole west of Dacia, I lost hundreds of good men and lost the taste for wine that day too. If I'd carried on, I'd be in six feet under by now.

"Come Estrid, show me around this beautiful home of yours," Gaius said, linking his arm with Estrid's and leading her to our home.

I let him lead her off and fell in with his number two.

I called to Tarsos—only a mite smaller than Gaius's number two and the best farm hand you might wish to have—and asked him to show the men to the stables and then onto the summer quarters to feast.

"Sure, boss," he said.

I eyed the hulking number two, he stood a good six inches taller than me, his shoulders near nearly as wide as his horse's.

"Antonius Maxima," I said, by way of welcome.

"I know who you are, farmer," he growled. "You're a storyteller. You're weak. Too weak to defeat a tribe of Germanics."

I chuckled, and squared off, looking up at him, showing no signs of fear or submission, and narrowed my eyes. "You don't know me very well then, do you?" I may have been old, but I didn't take kindly to people like this. I could tell he was a bully. He might've been able to fight, but at the end of the day, all he was was a bully. A dog at the end of Gaius's leash. I'd knock him down a peg or two if he pushed me.

"Come, Cassius," Gaius called."

"Quick," I whispered, "Daddy's calling."

***

"So, Maximus, tell us the story of your victory against the Germanics?" Gaius said between gulps of wine.

The meal was going well. Gaius sat at the head of the table, with Estrid opposite. Cassius—who it turned out was the lead Praetorian Guard—kept his eyes on me the whole meal. I grew tired of the small talk, I wanted to know what Gaius wanted with me.

"Forgive me, Gaius, but first, what are you here for exactly?"

"Watch your tongue, farmer," Cassius spat.

I eyed him straight-faced. "Are you okay in here with us civilized people? Are you sure you wouldn't be more comfortable outside with the dogs?"

Cassisus's chair flew backwards, toppling to the floor as he stood and reached across the table for me. I'd already eyed up his size and the distance from me; I knew he couldn't reach me, no matter how hard he tried. Still though, I felt the air as his hand swished in front of my nose. His face burned as red as his uniform.

"Cassius!" Gaius boomed.

His voice of authority surprised me. Up until that point Gaius had been all joviality and jokes. Cassius stood to attention in an instant.

"Enough."

Cassius blanched, pulled up his chair and sat. I saw his knuckles whiten as his grip on the chair tightened, but he followed orders and quietened down. He still couldn't stop staring daggers at me, but I could've care less.

"My apologies, for the unpleasantness of my right-hand man here, Estrid," Gaius said to my wife.

"No apologies necessary, Gaius. My husband's tongue can get away from him on occasion." And then she struck me with another stare of daggers.

"Yes, well, I think I do owe you an explanation," Gaius said, turning to me. "I'll get right to the point. As you know, any emperor of worth expands Rome's empire, and I'm no different. Antonius, I want you to lead our armies and conquer Germania once and for all."

Goosebumps bloomed all over my body and I glanced to Estrid. She sat straight-faced, knowing I couldn't refuse, but I saw the muscle in her jaw twitch just that miniscule bit.

"I know you have given your all for Rome already, and I hate to ask, but your experiences with the Germanic tribes will be imperative to our victory," Gaius continued. "This is why I want to hear your story."

I sighed, organizing my thoughts, when Marcus burst into the room, sweating profusely, breathless and white as a sheet.

"Papa!" he panted.

Tarsos bundled in shortly after. I looked to him in confusion.

"Sorry, boss," he said, "I tried to stop him, but he's

not talking any sense."

"Marcus, what is it?" I said rising from the table, without leave from Gaius, and grabbed my son by his shoulders.

"The-they got them, P-Papa. All of them this time."

"Who got what?" I pressed.

"The flock. They're all gone. I went to lay in the fields, it's peaceful at this time. The blood. There was so much blood."

"Raiders?"

"I-I don't know. I think so. Thank Jupiter they didn't see me."

My head dropped, and my blood ran cold.

Head down, I whispered to myself, "Virtus give me strength." I had wished this day would never come. Looking back up to Marcus, I said, "Did you see where they went?"

"Pluto's Gate," he said.

"The gorge?"

"Yes, they retreated into the gorge."

A million thoughts buzzed through my head. Pluto's Gate was long rumored to be the entrance to hell. I had to act quick. I turned to Gaius, "I'll lead your armies, Gaius. We'll take Germania. But first, I need your men to help me stop these raiders. I won't leave until my family are safe."

Gaius grinned. His cheeks reddened by the wine rose, and his teeth shone. "Raiders! We'll kill them all! Boy, how many were there?"

Marcus looked to me for guidance. If it was possible, he whitened even further upon realization the Emperor of Rome was addressing him. I nodded to him, and he

L T EMERY

turned back to Gaius.

"I-I don't know, your majesty. Half a dozen, maybe more."

"No matter. We have sixteen of the most elite fighters, we'll cut them to shreds!"

"Marcus," I said, turning him back to me. "Go, take a horse and get the oracle."

"The witch?" Marcus said, confused.

"The oracle," I corrected. "Bring her. Tell her what you saw and wait for us at the entrance to Pluto's Gate. Do not, under any circumstances, enter it. Am I understood?"

"Yes, Papa." Marcus said and left, running.

"Cassius! Fetch the men," Gaius shouted, raising his glass.

"No!" I cried. "Tomorrow, we'll go at first light."

"Antonius! Come now, let's strike while the iron's hot!" Gaius pushed.

"Your Majesty," I said, showing my respect. "You want my skills, my expertise. It starts now. I lead the men. We go at sunrise."

"Never!" Cassius boomed. "He will not lead my men."

Gaius looked from Cassius to me and back again.

"Cassius, these men are yours and by rights you should lead them into battle. But this is Antonius's land, he knows it best. He will lead us on the morrow."

Cassius's eyes darted to me and then up to the heavens in thought. I could see it was hard for him. I knew what was going through his head. He could protect his ego, fight for his command tomorrow, or he could fight for the safety of his emperor. It was no contest.

"Your Majesty," Cassius began, "You cannot join us in this fight. It is far too dangerous. You have Rome to think of first."

"I have to agree to Cassius, here. You cannot join us in this battle. These... raiders will be far too dangerous for you to join us."

Gaius was swilling two bottles of wine around his stomach by this point, and there was no reasoning with him.

"I am bored with all the politics," Gaius said to both of us. "Cassius, are you not the best of the best? Are you not Rome's greatest fighter?"

Cassius could only nod.

"Then you shall protect me with your life. You shall see me through this battle. And I will have a bit of bloody fun!"

***

"You know what you're going to find out there," Estrid said to me, as we lay in bed. Sleep alluded us. There would be blood on the morrow, and I hoped it would not be mine.

"I know, my love."

"I'm coming with you, you know."

"Never in life," I said calmly. I knew if I put up too much of a fight, she would dig in her heels and come anyway. The coming battle would be too dangerous though. I couldn't allow it. "You must stay, wait for Marcus to return with the oracle. One of us must be here when he returns. I have to go, so you must remain, my love."

She furrowed her brow, but soon smiled, knowing I was right.

"Why must you go at all?" Estrid asked.

"You know why."

"I hope the men manage."

"They're Praetorian Guard, they'll cope. I just wish that-" in a whisper, "Caligula, had not insisted on joining us. But nothing can be done about that now. Meet us at the gate with the oracle when Marcus returns. It's our only hope."

***

I slept little, feeling the battle lust already wrapping its wicked tentacles around me. I thought back to the day Tiberius decreed the land to me, given for my services to Rome. I also remembered real reason he stationed me on the isle of Sicily, the warning from Delphi.

The weight I felt on my shoulders was more them just the armor. It was the knowing that this would be my last morning with my wife for a long time, maybe ever. I wished I could wait a little longer, just to see the sun rise over my farm once more.

It crushed me knowing the sun had already set on my quiet retirement.

We left before dawn, riding for the sandy beach of the Alcantara river. Sixteen Praetorian Guards, Cassius, Gaius and I arrived as the sun crested the horizon. We stood on the shore looking into the gorge. The men sat astride their mounts—spears pointed towards the heavens in one hand, while the other held the reins of their horses, shields tied to their forearms. The formal armor and red crested helmets shone as bright as the sun.

Sheer cliffs of layered black rock rose vertically from the waters ahead of us. We were silent as we looked into the darkness, the only sound being that of the river running into the gorge.

"Gaius," I started, "I beg you to rethink. Please take a man and ride back to my farm. Do not join us in this battle."

"Antonius, I am surrounded by the best of men and the strongest or warriors. I have no worries about my safety."

I gave my head the merest of shakes and continued.

"The river is not deep," I said to the men. "The horses can get through in single file."

"Gaius," Cassius said. "You stay behind me at all times."

"When we get through, Felix, your Contubernium stay together, and stay in formation on our left flank. Atticus, likewise, but your men take our right. I will lead, and Cassius, you take the rear. Be sure to keep an eye out behind us."

Felix and Atticus lead their respective Contuberniums. They were good men. Solid fighters. I could tell by the way they led their men.

"Nothing can get behind us in there, we're a gorge barely wide enough for a horse," Cassius spat. The condescending bastard.

"Keep your eyes open on our rear," I calmly repeated.

I gave my horse a kick, and we were off. The horses splashed into the cyan waters and we started our way through Pluto's Gate.

It didn't take long for the rock faces on either side of us to change. The black stripes straightened into vertical striations. They looked like the scorched fingers of giants trying to claw their way out of hell.

Bangs echoed all around us—falling scree bouncing off the rock walls. Tensions mounted, and the men started to murmur. A horse neighed its discomfort.

"Easy," I grumbled to them, and they settled down.

The further in we went the more the sunlight seemed to be sucked out of the gorge. In the gloom, the rock walls started to look more like leeches, sucking the light from us.

The river took a wicked right turn into a series of rocky rapids. To the left of the turn, a cave had been dug out of the rocks, by the running water, and there it was, the rainbow. The very same I'd seen west of Dacia. My breath caught and my stomach felt as if it had dropped to the ground. The rainbow film swam in front of the cave entrance that stood only eight feet high. Reds, purples, greens all danced in front of the black emptiness of the cave behind it. Its beauty hiding the terror that stood behind it.

I lifted a hand for the men to stop.

"What is it?" Felix whispered behind me.

"No good," I simply said, drawing my sword. "Follow me and be on guard."

"Should we not light some torches?" Felix asked.

I looked over my shoulder at him, giving him a mournful smile. "You're going to need your hands free for sword and shield soon enough."

My idyllic life as a farmer was now truly over. There was no going back from this.

***

I kicked my horse on once more, this time a little harder, to fight her mounting anxieties.

As I ducked my head down and went through the rainbow film my ears popped. I opened my jaws wide, getting my hearing back to normal, and looked around. I was in no cave.

I looked back over my shoulder and saw more horses appear from thin air. The cave entrance and gorge were nowhere to be seen.

The horses trotted up onto the bank of the river, which was now merely a stream. The stream, however, ran purple as the water trickled over rocks of mauve, violet and lilac.

No further than ten yards in, I looked around to see we were in a rainforest. The monolith trees' bark was a deep grey, while their leaves were the bright blue of the ocean. High pitched squeaks echoed from the treetops and a low hiss seemed to come from all around us. This was no forest any of the men had ever seen, but I had. Once before.

"The hell have you taken us, Antonius?" Gaius shouted from somewhere behind me.

"We won't be here for long, fear not," I told Gaius, but really, I was addressing all the men. "I have brought us here to show you what we will be fighting. What has been terrorizing my land of late. Growing stronger, more confident. That all stops today."

The men looked around; their jaws hung agape looking at this alien land. The hiss started to get louder from my right, and I glanced that way, seeing nothing.

"This is not what I agreed to," growled Gaius.

"Your majesty," Cassius said. "Let me take his head for this traitorous act."

I stared Gaius down. "You agreed to help me stop the

raiders, did you not?"

Gaius ground his teeth. I could see the rage in his eyes at being tricked, but he relented and gave me a nod.

"Good," I said, dismounting my horse. "Did you ever question how the story of me singlehandedly beating a whole Germanic tribe ever got out, considering I've never spoken of it?"

The rage began to subside in Gaius's eyes and interest took ahold instead.

I walked to Felix and handed him my horse's reins. The hissing from my right continued to rise. I needed to wrap this up.

"I have never spoken of it before. That is true. The stories all came from someone else who was there-"

It was too late; they had come too quickly. Two of them from my right. The hissing grew so loud it felt like a cat was scratching the inside of my skull. They seemed to appear as if from nowhere, thanks to their coloration matching the tress so well. I lifted my shield, drew my sword and set my feet.

They were insectile beings, standing at least seven feet tall. A long fat abdomen sat between six strong skittering legs. Their upper body was armored like the rest of it, a pair of useless wings fluttered from their backs, making the hissing noise we all heard.

They looked much like the mantis insects that flitter around the farm in mid-summer. Each arm ended with eye-wateringly sharp scythe blades. I felt like I could cut myself just by looking at them.

Their heads were terrifying beyond comprehension. Two bulbous compound eyes made up the majority of its head. A pair of huge mandibles snapped open and closed; they sounded like a miniature hammer hitting an anvil over and over. Most disconcerting of all were the tentacles that swirled below its chin. Covered in hair they undulated from side to side, as if seeking something.

They were fast. They came like lightning and I was waiting to meet them.

They attacked at the same time, suggesting a rudimentary intelligence. I raised my shield to the one on the left, its blade digging in at least six inches, catching onto my shield and ducked the arc of scythe on my right. As I ducked its swing, I brought my sword down with an almighty swing, aiming for the joint at one of its knees—one of the few points on the foul creature that wasn't armored.

With an audible pop the leg stayed in the ground as the rest of it passed. White blood oozed from the leg.

Wasting no time, I swung my sword back up into the creature's arm whose scythe was impaled on my shield, removing it with my sword and another audible pop.

They didn't make any noise, but the hiss of their wings seemed to change in tone.

The creature with five legs recovered quickly and was upon me as soon as I turned back to it. I rolled away from another slice of its scythe and jumped up. In an instant I had slashed at its face, relieving the hell spawn of its tentacles. The monster writhed in confusion, if not pain, raising its mandibles to the sky, giving me a target. I swung my sword once more and took its head off. One down.

I heard the whistle of blade before I saw it coming

and dived to the ground rolling as the last creature came for me. It swung its last scythed arm at me once, twice, thrice. I parried each but lost my sword on its last swing. The creatures were huge and strong, and I could barely keep up with it. It had cornered me, my back to a tree. It swung its bladed arm in what it thought was the death blow, but I ducked at the last minute and the scythe crunched into the tree, holding fast.

As it tried to pull free, I pulled my dagger and drove it into its mouth, and out the back of its alien skull.

White blood oozed and the hissing faded as the creature died.

I took a deep breath and turned to the men. If they looked surprised when we walked into this world, then upon seeing these beasts they looked... well, completely terrified. Even Cassius.

I threw my useless shield to the floor, the imbedded scythe went with, and slowly started walking back to my horse.

Silence from the men. Silence from even Gaius and Cassius.

"These things are what have been attacking my farm. My family. These monsters are what we fight today. They're full now from all my Pluto-damned sheep last night. We need to hold them until help arrives. It won't be long."

I looked to each man as I spoke, and saw only fear, until I got to Felix and Atticus. All the men were battle-hardened, but these two more so.

"What are they?" Felix said, still holding my horse's reins.

"I don't know." It was the truth, I still don't. "But

you saw they can be beaten. They have soft spots."

"We can't stay here," Cassius said. "I don't care what you and Gaius agreed too. I can't let the emperor of Rome remain here." He had steely eyes. A warrior's eyes. I knew he wanted to stay and fight, but he was right.

"I know. I told you not to come," I said to Gaius, and then to the rest of the men. "Besides, we won't be here much longer."

"Oh, thank Jupiter," I heard Gaius say.

"I never defeated a Germanic tribe in that damned hellhole west of Dacia. It was another pack these devils. This is why Tiberius sent me here. The oracle at Delphi warned another attack may come from this end of the empire. I never thought it would happen; only half of what she says comes true. I thought I'd live out my days in peace, but it's not to be. So now, I only bring you all here to show you all what we'll be up against. I wanted you to see they can be killed, and now you know how. You know where their soft spots are."

"We'll hold them." Atticus said. "Won't we men."

The men stammered at first, but soon the battle roar grew, as did their confidence. They needed it.

"Good. We'll go back through the rainbow. We'll use that as a bottle neck. Two-line formation. Seven and seven. Spears to push them back. We kill them or drive them down the rapids. In that they'll be cracked open by the rocks, like your morning egg."

Felix and Atticus nodded. Their experience told them it was a good plan.

I turned to Cassius, once more. "Cassius, I know Gaius cannot remain, but he can go back to my farm with two men. My wife waits at the entrance to the gorge, she'll protect him. I need you here. Me and you are the last line of defense, should any make it past the men."

His eyes narrowed and he turned to Gaius, it was his decision to make.

Gaius looked as white as a sheet. He began to say something, but it came out as nonsense. Instead, he just nodded his assent.

"Good, then let's get back to our side of the rainbow," I said and reached up to Felix to take the reins of my horse back.

"Antonius," Felix said. "Your shoulder. Are you okay?"

It was only then did I feel the dull burning in my shoulder and felt a warmth trickle down my back. I put a finger to my shoulder, pulling it back to see the crimson red of blood. The bastard had found a gap in my armor. It was only then I heard the knowing hiss creeping back up. One small mistake and my plan was out the window before it started.

***

Like sharks to blood, my cut drew the monsters to us in legion. We didn't have long.

"Everybody dismount now," I roared, and lifted the blanket that laid under my horse's saddle.

I pulled out the blade to audible gasps. It was a sword made from the scythe of one of the creatures. I had retrieved it from my last battle and brought it home fashioning it into the sword I held. I had no shield, but this sword wouldn't be stopped by their armor. I could have used this weapon all along. It would have made dispatching the first monsters easy work, but I wanted the men to see that they could kill them with their weapons too. Now, it gave me an advantage, and I needed every advantage I could get.

"Stop watching and dismount!" I screamed, but it was too late.

What happened next happened fast, and there's much I missed, what with trying to stay alive. The mantis creatures swarmed. Thanks to their camouflage it was as if they appeared from nowhere, instantly surrounding us.

They ran with alarming speed, their tentacles whipping wildly, smelling the blood in the air. The horses reared up, whinnied and bolted. Soldiers fell; some were crushed by their own horses, others were sent flying toward the creatures, impaled on their scythed arms. For a couple of minutes, it was utter chaos.

There must have been at least twenty of the creatures, if not more. In those first few moments I think we lost at least half of our men. Gaius had been thrown off his horse and into a tree, he looked dazed but otherwise unharmed. Cassius was the only man to retain his horse and was fighting to regain control of it as it circled surrounded by three of the creatures.

The rest of the men found their feet and started to fight. The lucky ones held onto their shields; others were struck down quickly.

In close quarters like this, without formation spears were useless, I shouted to the men as much, but I'm not sure if any heard.

I saw one man eviscerated, his guts spilling to the floor. All the blood was a gift from Jupiter for me. The hell-spawns' tentacles whipped wildly smelling the blood all around, working them into a frenzy. If I had still been the only one to have shed blood, I'd already have fallen.

Another had his head taken off, like a knife through butter. The helmet rolled to a stop at my feet; dead, uncomprehending eyes stared up at me.

This brought me out of my temporary stupor in time to fight off two more creatures. I managed to duck one as it skittered past. I swiped the scythe in a flashing arc, taking all six legs with it. The second I parried each of its blades; first with the scythe, then my sword. It gave me an opening and with the scythe I swung in an upward motion; spilling guts and Jupiter knows what. Finally, I put the legless beast out of its misery as it still tried dragging itself to me.

This gave me a moment to take in the battlefield. Felix still fought alongside three more guards. Cassius had got his horse under control and now fought his way to Gaius with immense power, but also with a grace so unexpected it made me chuckle.

Lastly, I looked to Gaius, still dazed at the foot of a tree. Prone. I think Cassius and I saw the creature at the same time. It scuttled toward the emperor of Rome, tentacles swaying. A small cut to Gaius's forehead gave him away.

"No!" Cassius and I shouted in unison, as we both raced to save the leader of the empire.

Realization dawned in Gaius's eyes, all too late, as two scythed arms crashed down, one either side of his head, missing him by mere inches.

The mantis waved its tentacles over Gaius's face, stroking him almost tenderly. Tasting him.

Gaius obviously could take no more of this insanity and screamed a high-pitched womanly cry. It was an action that probably saved his life.

The creature started back in shock. It quickly regained its composure, opening its mandibles, aiming for Gaius's neck.

Gaius had already started to roll away, so it crunched down on his shoulder rather than his neck. The scream redoubled, this time in pain.

Then Cassius rode through the beast, knocking it off Gaius. I reached them a moment later and found the weak spot at its neck with my blade.

Gaius writhed on the floor, clawing at his shoulder, throwing obscenities my way at every opportunity. I ignored them and cut off a strip of my tunic, sheathed my weapons and tied off the wound to another round of screams.

By then Cassius arrived with a welcoming boot to my guts, sending me sprawling.

I looked up to see pure rage burning in his eyes, as hot as the sun. Tending the emperor of Rome was the only thing that kept me alive at this point.

"You stupid man," was all Cassius said. "You'll pay for this."

By the time I had caught my breath another mantis was attacking. It was all I could do to fight it off as I watched Cassius ride back through the rainbow with Gaius slumped, riding double.

The mantis cut my left forearm, right calf and left thigh in the fight, before I was able to dispatch the thing. I was all but crippled when I realized I was the only man left alive.

I could barely lift my arms as I pushed myself up against the tree Gaius sat at and eyed my doom. Three of the creatures remained.

It was almost as if they were toying with me, slowly making their insectile way toward me. Their tentacles seemed to mock me as they smelt their next meal.

"Virtus give me strength," I screamed to the heavens and set my feet once more.

***

As they came, I heard a shriek coming from the rainbow. It was like someone screaming underwater, until it wasn't. Until it was the guttural war cry of my wife as she emerged from the rainbow, axe and shield held aloft, dressed in the war-garb of her people.

She was a goddess, appearing from the heavens to save my life.

She ran the ten yards to the monsters in a second. Her axe swung through one of their necks before it could even turn. Its head rolled to a stop at my feet.

The other two monsters turned on my wife, and she smiled a toothy grin.

"Come, you vile hell-spawn. Meet your doom," she growled.

One took off, scythes raised, eyes only for Estrid. It swiped a bladed arm for her. She ducked it, swinging her axe above her head, taking its arm off at the shoulder. The beast seemed disinterested with the loss and swung its other scythe. Estrid met it with her war axe. A deafening clang rang out around the forest. Estrid pinned its arm between her axe arm and waist. With her other hand she brought her shield down on its elbow joint. Once, twice, thrice, until finally there was a pop of dislocation. One more swing of the shield took its arm off too.

The other creature ran for her, but I didn't need to give her warning. She knew what she was doing.

Estrid turned and threw the axe. It tumbled end over end, through the air with a death whistle. The axe embedded in the weak spot at the center of its chest.

She looked to me, smiling. Then she looked around at her prey. The armless beast yet lived.

A moment later, axe back in hand, she chopped its head clean in half. White blood and blue brain matter sprayed the ground.

Finally, blessedly, the hissing ceased. Silence was golden.

I broke it by saying, "I fucking love you, Estrid."

She strolled over and kissed me long and hard. "I love you too, Antonious."

I stumbled, but Estrid caught me. I'd lost a lot of blood.

"Come, husband. We need to vacate this hell. The oracle has arrived."

"Good," I said.

Estrid bared a lot of my weight as we walked to the rainbow and away from this place.

***

Back on our side of the rainbow, the oracle waited.

"Antonius," she regarded me.

"Thank you for coming, Phemonoe. I wish I didn't have need of you again."

"I told you the day would come when the hidden would be revealed."

"And you think this is it?"

"That's for you to decide, Antonious," she purred, r

her voice soft as a cloud.

"I'm too tired for all this prophetic nonsense."

"You'll need to face this one-day Antonious," Phemonoe said.

"Can we save this and close the bloody gates to hell before more of those monsters emerge?" Estrid scolded.

"As you wish," Phemonoe said. She raised her hands to the rainbow and spoke beneath her breath, just like she had in that hell hole west of Dacia. At her command, the rainbow shrunk until the gate was closed.

I breathed a huge sigh of relief. My family and my land were safe once more. My safety was another matter, and I'd need to leave to join Gaius and his forces as soon as I was able. I would have to face the consequences for putting the emperor of Rome's life in danger like I had.

My retirement was over. But that could wait. I looked to my wife, full of pride, knowing that with this battle, her life and Marcus's life would be a little safer, and that was good enough for me.

For now, it was over.

***

Epilogue

Estrid and I rode double back up through the gorge to the beach. Phemonoe was just behind us on her pure white mare.

My strength waned as we traveled. Estrid knew our plan, she knew we shouldn't be in the rainbow when the oracle arrived, and she had used her intuition and initiative to come in and save my life in the process. I was grateful and lucky to have a wife like her.

We came to the beach to find Tarsos pacing.

"Boss!" he exclaimed.

"I'm okay," I said. "Estrid will sew me up at the house. I'll be as good as new in a couple of days.

"No, boss," Tarsos said, and it was then I noticed his bloody nose, cut lip and swelling eye.

"Good god, Tarsos. What happened to you?" I said.

"I'm sorry boss, I tried to stop him. But he got me with a cheap shot."

"Who? What's going on, Tarsos? Tell me now," I commanded, even as my consciousness threatened to give out.

"It's Marcus. The emperor took him prisoner. He wants you in Rome in one week. To pay for your crimes."

-End-

ENTRA NELLA PISTOLLERA A JOYFUL VENTURE

By Jasiah Witkofsky

This is the tale of an orphan girl from the principality of Catalonia, during that flamboyant era known as the Baroque, a time of nobility, artists, explorers, and pirates, nestled between the innovative Renaissance and the calculating period of the Enlightenment. Raised in a nunnery within the municipality of Barcelona, the young Dolores Llorenc learned her letters from Scripture and obfuscation, avoiding the punitive lashings of mentors in habits. At the dawning of womanhood, the diminutive maiden found a way to escape the cloister, spending the nights roaming the streets and docksides of Catalonia's majestic capital, the City of Counts.

It was during these moonlit sojourns that Dolores became aware of the seedier side of humanity.
The haggling, brawls, seductions, thefts, and briberies
did not pass unnoticed before the golden-brown eyes of
the innocent. This led to a crisis of belief, a dichotomy
between the ordered sanctity revealed by the sun, and
the dirty underbelly concealed by the darkness.

The lure of the night was too enticing for the
orphan, too enthralling to contain in one miniscule
being, so she invited from amongst her sheltered peers
a handful of her closest confidants to temporarily break
free from the confines of the nunnery. The infinitude
of the outside world held the ability to bewitch all, and
the girls took to the open air, and their own proclivities
towards temptation. One became fond of the intoxica-
tion of the vine, another enamoured by strapping young
lads, one longed to dance, but Dolores's inclination was
to watch and learn from the gambler, the sneak, and the
sailor. Men of skill, of action, who lived a life of freedom and adventure, so vastly different from her own
routine, which she felt was not much better than the
dreary existence of a prisoner, caged and bound.

When it became apparent that one of the tru-
ant girls had grown plump with child, the deflowered
maiden was beaten so ferociously she lost the precious
content of her fecund belly. It was on that pivotal day
the young orphan named Llorenc pilfered what food
and cutlery she could from the kitchens and departed
the white walls of the Virgin, never to return.

Despite an intimate knowledge of the alleyways
of Barcelona, the fact that Dolores could no longer find

refuge within the monastery left her vulnerable to exposure in all its gruelling forms. After barely escaping abduction and an attempt at rapine, she made her way to the boatyard, more specifically, *L'aventure Joyeuse*. The sleek caravel was not the most luxurious of ships that came and went from the docks, but it was kept relatively clean due to a diligent crew who radiated a most jolly disposition. Hiding away between the bulkheads, she made herself comfortable and scarce amidst the spare riggings. It was after a sleep deeper and more relaxing than she had been allowed for nearly a week that she arose to find herself adrift upon the Tyrrhenian Sea, with Barcelona but a shining sliver fading along the horizon.

***

During a salt pork raid spurred on by a groaning stomach, Dolores's presence was abruptly discovered by one of the crewmates. Hoisted aloft and gut-punched by a brawny stevedore, the crafty stowaway was unceremoniously hauled above deck to await her punishment. The ship's men circled to the sounds of the commotion beneath the guiding stars that shone more brilliantly than any night the city could reveal.

In due time, a fur-robed and yawning figure emerged from the captain's quarters to perch in mock nonchalance before the dangling captive. His blond hair was cropped close to his scalp and a powder burn speckled the flesh beneath his right eye. Her captor deposited his catch upon the planked floor to be jeered and gawked at by the entirety of the crew. The extravagant leader smirked, seeming to take a perverse pleasure listening to the descriptive tortures his men spouted towards their squirming captive. He mulled over the variety of extraction procedures raucously shouted about, but his heart changed when he beheld her defiant and fearless stare. In a gracious, genteel manner, he lifted the shaken girl to her feet and introduced himself as Brim Jorge, former privateer of the French Monarchy and current head of *L'aventure Joyeuse.*

Taking her under his wing, or fur-lined cloak to be more accurate, Brim Jorge set the lithe girl to the crow's nest where she learned to scurry the ropes like a lemur, and the intricacies of knotwork necessary for any boat's man. The sailors swiftly grew fond of the bold orphan's refreshing naivete and youthful exuberance. They taught her games of chance, the ability to read the stars, and the vulgar, yet witty lingo that seamen are so well known for. Despite the stench of man sweat, soured sustenance, and crude habits of the ale-guzzling ruffians, Dolores found the freedom of the sea, paradoxically exhilarating and tranquil.

Her open and juvenile adaptability shaped instantaneous sea legs and buffered the abrupt change to her diet, environment, and company. The world changed, yet the malleable, inquisitive mind kept pace through calm waters and tempestuous seas. The men were as diverse as the waters; the boisterous, rotund Sicilian cook, the swarthy, academic navigator from Morocco, a stern, moustachioed cannoneer of Hunnic descent, the flame-haired carpenter who everyone called the Nord. Yet it was the cloaked Frenchman that most intrigued her, with his panache and sense of novelty towards whatever may come his way.

The gregarious Jorge DuPonte doted upon his young

ward as a father would, swathing her in foreign silks and linens... purple was her preferred hue. He made the attempt to train her wee arms in the use of the foil, but it was the pistol he kept tucked into his vermillion sash that best suited her innate proclivities. Brim Jorge allowed his sophomoric protégé to spend his musket shot discharging into the saltwater fishes as *L'aventure Joyeuse* traversed ever northward. The budding woman was a deadeye, a sure shot who managed to deliver a belly-up result nine out of ten times. But when the captain and his men partook too highly of the hops-water and fired heavy metal into the sleek bodies of the striped dolphins, with eyes so much like that of a fellow man, Dolores snuck her way to the Vieux-Port of Marseille when the ship docked. The first mate offered to haul the girl back aboard, but Jorge dismissed him, smiling ruefully towards the back of the fleeing Spaniard who captured his heart like none other.

***

Dolores Llorenc scurried through the bustling streets of Marseille in a bewildered frenzy of adrenaline, not knowing where her next steps would lead her. Without a coin she could call her own, the young lass was unable to satiate the emptiness of her stomach. So, she begged, and her sweet face, large eyes, and innocent demeanour worked for a span, but her pidgin French and Catalonian dialect would get her kicked and spit upon by those who held a deep-seated hatred towards the kingdom across the southern border. This led to her swiping from the edges of food vendors and fruit carts. Thievery sufficed for a handful of days until she made the unwise decision to return to a previous mark. The

WORLDS COLLIDE

turnip-seller's son witnessed the sneak's fingers make purchase and gave chase down the alleys of France's most ancient city. His longer legs quickly overtook the teenage thief, and he unleashed such a beating that most of her face was left mottled and swollen.

The pain, shame, and trauma caused from the thrashing horrified Dolores enough to leave the city, deciding to take her chances in the rural countryside, an environment wholly unfamiliar to her limited range of experience. The initial outreaches of Marseille were tamed and sculpted enough to allow easy access to grapes and apples. Animal pens provided shelter and one generous family graciously fed her mutton and housed her for an evening, regaling her with tales of heredity and the countless generations that tended the acreage for centuries. That night she wept bitterly into wool sheets, for she never knew the caress of a mother or the embrace of a father. She had no heritage, knew no siblings, possessed absolutely nothing but the tattered threads that clung to her small frame. At dawn, she quietly departed the cosy domicile before any of its inhabitants arose to begin another day.

The landscape became more rugged, less manicured, as the weather grew harsh, bleak, and cold. Dolores swiped a horse blanket from a stable to subdue her shivering and teeth chattering. She moved ever eastward, using the sun's rise and the astronomy the Moroccan taught her to guide her steps. Civilisation was now days away and when any cart or horseman came clopping down the trail, she dashed to the trees to hide in the woods. She knew well enough the dangers of being a lone woman in an unknown world.

JASIAH WITKOFSKY

The rains came and the thick cloth she wrapped
herself in grew drenched and heavy with biting mois-
ture. She scavenged what flower petals and blades of
grass she could digest until she retched, purging herself painfully of all inedible material. Fear and despair
kept her up all night despite debilitating weakness and
severe exhaustion. She could feel her ribs through her
shredded blanket as she stumbled across the forest in a
hallucinatory state, unable to determine up from down.
This addled mindset lasted for an unknown length of
time until she collapsed in a pathetic heap beneath dead
shrubbery.

***

Dolores awoke in a haze atop a luxurious four-post
bed the likes of which she had never experienced before, but the severe belly cramps and throbbing in her
temples forced her to take no comfort from the down
bedding that bore her frail body. Concerned voices
rattled through her traumatised brain as she was spoon
fed broth.

'Yellow fever.'

'Syphilis.'

'The plague.'

The time was lost to Dolores as she slipped in and
out of consciousness. Fever dreams of abusive nuns,
being hounded by gangs of hostile men, monsters in
the sea, and dragons in the woods haunted her delirium.
The day finally came when she could raise her head
from the fragrant pillows, a little at first, but enough
strength returned to make her way to the toilet and
intake solid food.

As she recovered, she learned she had been residing

north of Cannes, in the resplendent villa of a Duchess with an unpronounceable name, and was nursed back to health by the noblewoman's youngest daughter. Some weeks earlier, she had been discovered by the young woman's paramour and the stableboy, Pierre. The household took kindly to the tiny Catalonian, giggling at her lilting accent and rejoicing in her foreign mannerisms. The ladies-in-waiting pleated her luxuriant raven locks and garbed her in the current fashions of France's aristocracy.

It was during this time that Dolores was schooled in the courtly ways, perfecting her curtsey and gruelling through the tedious process of hosting dinner parties for distinguished merchants and pampered nobles. Still, the exotic beauty could not help but feel stifled by the boring routines of shallow popinjays and stuffy traditionalists.

Whenever the opportunity arose, the girl from Barcelona sought the stables to find solace upon the sturdy backs of the Andalusians that swept her across the pastures in a union of speed and exhilaration. The marriage of rider and mount provided a rise and crest that transcended speciation into a oneness that could not be denied, as the whipping wind tore through her brunette braids. The sleek and beautiful colorations of the majestic creatures housed intricate and intelligent souls, and Dolores marvelled at their individual personalities and the deepening bonds she forged with the herd.

Horsemanship also gave Dolores an opportunity to spend time with Pierre, who shared an appreciation for her company as revealed by his blushes instigated by her toothsome smile. The young man had a humble and down-to-earth demeanour lacking amongst the intrigues and fineries of the hoity-toity. She found herself growing heated at his nearness and his touch stiffened the fine hairs of her forearms and nape of the neck. A day came when they ascended the barn's loft and atop a spilling of hay, she revealed herself for the first time to a male. She received him in awkward embraces... playful, fumbling, and thrilling. Their romantic tryst a shared secret kept hidden from the high-born, a clandestine meeting for the two alone.

Meanwhile, the Duchess's daughter, who was a wee bit older than Madame Llorenc, had begun to receive suitors for her hand in matrimony. The young woman of nobility had been caught by an untrustworthy confidante in the arms of her lover, and gossip circled of her illicit affair. The most jealous and hot-tempered of the competitors for the lady's hand caught wind of these rumours and appeared one climactic day with a horde of drunken supporters and bullies. He challenged the quaking paramour to a pistol duel and dishonourably unleashed a shot into the back of the ousted lover before he could finalise his tenth step.

Chaos ensued as the lover's corpse was desecrated with a beheading delivered by one of the inebriated infiltrators. This was followed by a savage takeover of the Duchess's estate with the intoxicated trespassers forcing their way inside, raiding the pantries and tormenting the women as the manservants were beaten or chased away. When a fire was ignited within the villa, Pierre scooped up a stunned and horrified Dolores, riding hard with the inferno lighting their way into the night.

***

WORLDS COLLIDE

Dolores Llorenc entered the territory of Genoa a fully bloomed woman. Still petite in stature; her musculature, self-sufficiency, and confidence had reached an excelled potential she never would have envisioned during her sheltered childhood amongst the nuns. It was pleasant to smell the faint tinge of the sea breeze as she hopped off a merchant's wagon that graciously delivered her to the port-city as daylight neared its closure.

The young woman had fared well for herself along her escapades despite the obstacles and hardships that arose to hinder her path. Dolores and Pierre had ingratiated themselves with a pack of Roma nomads who allowed them to perform horse tricks for their travelling circus, Pierre taking the lead of the horse as his spry companion enacted handstands and cartwheels she learned from the tribe's acrobat. They parted ways with the caravan, who steered their ornately painted carriages northward as the duo continued ever easterly, towards the uppermost edges of the gulf.

When their meagre finances dwindled, desperation took root, and Dolores concocted a scheme both brilliant and foolhardy. Portraying the part of damsel in distress as Pierre played the role of the nefarious assailant, the pair caught the attention of a mercantile cart with their antics. Their plan to waylay the unsuspecting transport went horribly awry when the coachman grazed Pierre's midriff with the edge of his rapier. Adrenaline and animal instinct took control as Dolores shattered a fallen branch across the teamster's skull, rendering him unconscious along the side of the roadway. With a strength born of primal despair, Dolores managed to drag her friend to the wagon and guide it to the nearest farmstead.

When Pierre regained consciousness, bandaged and weary upon a stranger's bed, he would not look his partner in the eye. He regretfully informed Dolores that he would not continue their journey and would remain in France, the only home he had ever known. She pleaded, sobbed, and promised the world, but alas, she could not sway her recalcitrant lover to budge his position. So, she gave her farewells and with a heavy heart, crossed the border towards the hub of Catholicism and birthland of the romantic languages.

Despite the loss of a boon companion, her first love and gentle friend, she entered this new realm, this new chapter of her story, with an openness and freedom that left no room for the fear and trepidation that had marked her juvenile years with such heightened uncertainty. So, she brushed the past aside, tipped the driver, and sauntered the Genoese streets with the sea to the south and the mountains framing her view to the north. As the sun set behind her, she made her way into the heart of the city by streetlight and the crescent moon smiling down from above.

***

After grounding herself with a hearty beef stew from a quaint little establishment, Dolores resumed her stroll through the city by night, too enamoured with the bustling seaside array to think of bedding down. Her studies in Latin made the Italian dialect less of a challenge than the flow of the French, and she ascertained she could easily call a place such as this her home. An abode both comfortable, yet exciting, with its constant sea traffic importing an endless array of exotic goods and people from around the globe.

Meandering through the cobbles and wagon ruts, Dolores became aware of a raucous commotion from above. On a rooftop balcony four-stories high, she made out a small revelry alit with lanterns and braziers. There was no stairway or ladder to access the merriment, just a drainpipe bolted to the wall, so, strapping her satchel securely over her shoulder, she began the ascent. As she reached the top and hopped the rail, she saw a dozen rascals, ruffians, and rapscallions of various sorts. Their only commonality was the bright red scarves wrapped around heads, waists, or limbs.

The party did not detect her presence at first, but as she boldly approached, they sprang to their feet, brandishing wide-bladed daggers in her direction. When they realised the intruder was nothing more than a petite, unarmed woman, the man nearest to her motioned the gang to lower their weaponry. The flickering lights shone against the man's deeply bronzed flesh and stringy chin beard as he eyed the newcomer up and down. His attire was a hodge-podge of faded rags and flamboyant sashes that secured an ornate sabre to his side, but the surrounding members of the gathering seemed to hold this eccentric character in some regard, so they allowed him to speak for them.

"How did you get up here, *ragazza*?"

With open-mouthed, wide-eyed honesty, Dolores responded. "I climbed."

The conglomeration of rogues nodded and chuckled, impressed by the fearless audacity of the uninvited guest. Taking the queue, the man continued, "And can we have the Madame's name?"

"Dolores Llorenc," she stammered. "I am new here. I just arrived from the west today."

The man responded with a flourishing bow, "Madame Llorenc, I am Signore Jerome, and we are the Crimson Cinquedeas. Cavaliers unranked and currently dismounted. Men of novel virtue and particular skills." This final remark brought hearty guffaws from the scoundrels behind him. Grabbing a bottle from a stool, the swarthy man handed it to her. "If you are to grace us with your beautiful presence, then you must drink with us."

Not wanting to be rude, she took a swig and immediately coughed out the sour and rancid-tasting liquid, the worst wine she had ever tasted. The party exploded in laughter at her response, but not wishing to be humiliated, she took a three-gulp swill and managed to swallow it down before handing it back, swiping drops from her chin and giving Jerome a steely glance. He offered the young woman his seat and a bowl of pistachios as the men introduced themselves and questioned her lightly about her history.

Jerome, who the scoundrels teasingly labelled 'the Moor' for his deep skin tone, narrow eyes, and beaked nose, took interest in the orphan's curious tale and when he learned of her brief nautical stint, his wine-addled mind brewed a scheme to recruit her into their numbers.

"*Ragazza*, we like your spirit. It would be an honour if you were to join our company. Would you like to wear the crimson?"

Taken aback by the request, she blurted out a response before thinking, "Ye... Yes... " not realising the predicament she stepped into.

He raised a brow flirtatiously. "We are a loyal and leaderless organisation, but to bear the red requires proof of your mettle and acumen. Would you take it upon yourself to perform a quest for us?"

Not wishing to disappoint the first people she met in this coastal city, and possibly emboldened by the strong vintage, she attempted a response to match the wits of this overdressed freebooter. "It depends on what said mission requires. I do have standards and as a follower of Christ, I will not harm another."

Stroking his dark chin scruff, Jerome turned towards the docks, easily visible from their rooftop vantage, and pointed to a particular merchant's vessel. "You see that ship yonder, fair Madame? Being a man of fine tastes and high aesthetics, I would consider it a noteworthy gift if you were to return to us with that purple flag upon the mast. Since you snuck upon us so silently and have worked the nest previously, such an endeavour should be no problem for one of your talents. Am I correct in this estimation?"

She internally debated the proposition, the risks versus rewards, then nodded her agreement to Jerome's weather-beaten face.

"One more thing, Madame." He handed her a broad-bladed dagger, the namesake of their gang. "Do not get caught... and do not name us."

***

In a narrow crevice between two building, Dolores removed her skirts and donned her dark stockings and black corset, stuffing her bag in a large crack in the plaster. She tied her hair tightly behind her, then made her way through the winding streets. She reached the docks and surveyed both sides of the ship, *L'orgoglio del Seno*. She made out one guard upon the vessel resting amidst an amalgamation of sacks. His cap was low on his face, but she could make out a pistol strapped to his rotund midriff.

The midnight hour was approaching, and the waxing moon was now low in the sky. She took advantage of the low visibility to crawl hand over hand on the connecting rope that secured the vessel to the dock. As silently as she could be, she slipped over the rail and scurried to the shadows of the stern.

The guard did not move at all, so Dolores assumed he was asleep. She made sure the wide blade was attached firmly to the lacings of her corset, then climbed the rigging at the back of the ship. She was calm and sure in her movements, keeping the bundled sails between her and the sleeping man, obfuscating her presence as much as possible. She attained the mizzenmast but did not think she had the strength to scurry the line between her current position and the mainmast which bore the lightly billowing flag the bandit gang desired.

Dolores mustered all her courage and began to slowly saw the rope with the dagger gifted to her. When a few threads were the only thing holding the rope in place, she drew in a deep breath and lunged, gripping the twined cordage for dear life as her weight severed the rope and sent her swinging straight towards the largest beam of the ship. She used her feet to cushion the impact of collision into the wooden pillar, and froze in position, terrified and breathless.

Her straining palms and fading strength signalled she

had limited time to pull off this caper. Risking a glance, she blew a sigh of relief to find that she had not been observed yet, so with frog-like bounds, she scaled the mast to the top. With a few savage hacks, she freed the purple flag, which fluttered away from her. In desperation, she dropped the blade to clutch the flag, which almost escaped her swift grasp.

The clatter of the steel cinquedea upon the deck woke the guard as Dolores slid down the mainmast to hide amidst the gathered sails. As the man waddled beneath her to pick up the object that roused him from his slumber, she dropped, using the folds of the sail-cloth to soften her descent. When the dark-clad female thudded amidship by his side, the surprised ship's guard was so startled he dropped the dagger. She took advantage of his momentary paralysis to pull the pistol from the man's shoulder strap, cock the device, and aim it straight at his heart.

"Not one word," she exhaled, both infiltrator and guard wide-eyed with fear. Never had she been in the position of a standoff, gun in one hand, flag in the other. She took careful steps backwards till she made the ship's edge, then scurried down the plank to the dock below, running as fast as her feet allowed.

The man's cries for help turned the few heads that were about at this late hour. The frightened thief wrapped the flag around the firearm, then plunged into the sea. She awkwardly paddled one-armed towards the shore and clutched the rocky edge, catching her breath beneath the dock as shipmen and patrols scurried about looking for the burglar. Since swimming was not a skill that she had developed well, she hugged the shoreline and quietly drifted away from the scene of the crime.

When the Barcelonan thought she had an opportunity, she scurried to dry ground and bolted towards the city. She knew she had been spotted as screams followed her through the streets. Exhausted and unable to catch her breath, she searched desperately for dark and unoccupied regions of this foreign land she knew nothing about. She thanked the Angels and the Virgin when she discovered a covered cart—the perfect place to hide. She dived inside, stilled her breathing, and prayed that no one heard her thundering heart as the hurried steps of several pursuers ran past her place of concealment.

She recited twenty Hail Marys and the Lord's Prayer thrice before braving a glimpse outside the cart. With the street empty, she slid out and tried to retrace her steps as best she could in this strange, urban maze. She stayed in the shadows whenever possible and avoided human contact, knowing that a lone, half-dressed female, nervously walking the night would be a suspicious and scandalous affair.

Tired, scared, and frustrated, Dolores found herself lost and backtracking for what must have been hours before luck or divine providence brought her back to the tight alley that concealed her satchel and clothing. She dressed herself and tucked the waterlogged pistol into her tote bag before pacing back to the rooftop hideout of the Crimson Cinquedeas.

She nearly screamed her heart out when she was muffled and pulled into an alley by a burlap-laden assailant. The man, who was garbed as a leper, hissed for her to remain silent before releasing her as he instructed Dolores to don the rags he shoved into her arms. He then led her into a broad thoroughfare, motioning for her to follow closely. Terrified, but with nowhere else to turn, she had no choice but to trust this stranger. Tears streamed down her cheeks as she sought some option, some means of escape, for she had no idea where her abductor was taking her.

When marching steps were heard coming towards their direction, the man pulled her roughly to a sitting position against a brick wall. He pulled a bowl from his rags and held it out like a beggar would as a patrol of armed guardsmen stomped into view. The constabulary steered clear from the two, one spitting in disgust at their general direction. When the guards passed by, her mysterious saviour pulled her to her feet and continued leading her to some unknown destination.

***

"You thought we would abandon you, *ragazza*?"

Jerome's exuberant voice startled Dolores as he called down to her from a window above. "You sure ran Raphael there on a wild chase." The man who had brought her here withdrew a key from his shredded attire and opened a door before her. Ushering Dolores inside, she found herself within what appeared to be an unoccupied warehouse. The man called Raphael, who she now recognised as one of the rooftop revellers, led her up a stairwell to a gutted room where Jerome sat on an array of rugs with other Cinquedeas, smoking New World tobacco from a pipe.

"Do you bear gifts for us, Madame Llorenc?" Jerome smirked, offering a small pillow for her to sit upon.

Rifling through her satchel, she dropped the purple cloth and captured pistol upon the pile of strewn carpets. Whistling in amazement, Jerome examined the firearm before passing it on to a companion. "Well done, very well done Madame. Regale us with your escapade, for we love nothing more than a good retelling of an adventure."

She told of her endeavours, too breathless to add flourishes and embellishments. The Cinquedeas eyed her with a newfound respect as they popped open another jug of deep red wine. The drunken rogues related some of their own tales of initiation as they fed her skewered chicken and vegetables.

Jerome withdrew a crimson bandana, and with exaggerated fluttering, offered it to the Spaniard. "You exceeded all expectations, and you are now one of us, Madame Llorenc."

She swiped the cloth and retorted, "And how do I know you would do for me what I just risked for you? I placed my very existence in jeopardy to please your whims. How do I know you would do likewise?"

Jerome rose, placing his hand over his heart, feigning wounded pride. "Why, upon my honour, my dear. I am ever at your service... Madame Pistollera. I think that is what I will call you. If you need anything, and it is within my power to give... then it shall be yours. You have my word, and you have my sword." He drew his sabre with a flourish, slashing at the air before him.

The others joined in their praises and promises, each trying to outdo their fellows in pomp and gallantry. She found herself growing fond of their jovial, immature antics. Jerome hung the captured flag outside the window as the bottle was passed about until its contents were completely emptied. When Dolores gave a deep yawn, Jerome ushered his inebriated compatriots towards the door. "You can have this room, for this night is yours, my pretty Pistollera... unless you wish me to stay and keep you company?" He raised an eyebrow in anticipation.

"Is that a proposal? Do you have a ring for me, Jerome?" she countered.

He chuckled as he reached the doorway. "There will be more nights, more opportunities, more chances for you to change your mind. But tomorrow, the day is yours. We shall await your presence, Madame." With a sweeping bow, he closed the door behind him.

As she blew out the assortment of candles that lit the room, she tucked the crimson cloth beneath her weary head as she lay herself down upon the pile of rugs. The last thing she saw before shutting her eyes was the purple merchant's flag fluttering outside the window. It was nice to be a part of something larger than herself, but there would soon come a day when she would fly her own colours. The faint aftertaste of the wine upon her lips was bittersweet... a fitting metaphor for existence. Life held pain, its deep tragedies and heart-rending losses, but it was also a wondrous adventure, to savour and enjoy.

-End-

ZEUS AND THE ZOMBIES
By Charlotte Langtree

Invisible, he slipped between marble pillars, golden clouds, and sleeping gods.

The sight disgusted him; for centuries he had slaved away, bearing the weight of his position without complaint, while the others had gorged themselves on honeyed treats and rich wine; idled while their names faded into the forgotten, dusty corridors of history.

They would regret that when they heard the news he brought, but it was too late. The damage had been done.

Slight movement caught his eye. One of several hearth fires flared as his sister Hestia added more wood, her red hair blazing as wildly as the flames engulfing her hands. A smile tugged at his lips; she was the only one of them he could forgive. Although she worked ceaselessly, her gentle nature meant the others often ignored her. She would not have been able to persuade them to take action.

He moved on. Hermes, winged sandals and helmet fluttering in the faint breeze, lazily strummed a lyre with his eyes closed. A few feet away, ruddy-faced Hephaestus snored on a cushioned cloud, while his golden-haired wife Aphrodite giggled in the arms of her lover, the war-god Ares.

The cloaked intruder crept on, past the handsome Apollo and his twin sister Artemis, who sharpened her knives with a ferocious concentration. Closer to the throne now, he spotted Athena talking to a tawny owl, and bushy-bearded Poseidon with his silver trident in hand.

He shuddered as he passed dark-haired Demeter, his bitter mother-in-law; if she saw him before he spoke his piece, he'd be lucky to escape with his life.

And there; straight ahead, on a throne of pure gold, idly toying with a sparking bolt of lightning, was his younger brother, Zeus. Sapphire eyes flashed as readily as the lightning in his hand. Zeus' wife Hera reclined on a smaller throne beside him and gazed at her sceptre with a bored expression on her flawless face.

Taking off the helmet shrouding him in invisibility, Hades, god of the underworld, appeared before his brother and bowed his head.

Zeus, white hair surrounding his head like a snowy halo, sighed. "What are you doing here, Hades?"

Behind him, Demeter hissed. Zeus held up his hand

to keep her at bay.

"I have news, brother. Bad news."

Zeus arched his brow.

"While you have all been frolicking your days away on Mount Olympus, the world below has fallen to ruin."

Laughter echoed throughout the marble chamber.

Hades glared at his family. "This is no joke!"

A bolt of lightning crashed into the floor, accompanied by a clap of thunder. "Enough!" Zeus boomed. He turned to Hades. "Why should we be concerned with the world? It has fared well enough without us for centuries."

"That is open to debate, brother. When did you last look down at the world our grandmother created? We are forgotten. Darkness spreads like a plague within the hearts of mortals. I would have noticed sooner, but the business of dying has always kept me busy, until now."

Hera looked up, her eyes sharp. "What do you mean?"

"I mean people are no longer dying when they should, dear sister. Some are, but many are living on in an undead state, their souls trapped by the survival of their bodies. If this goes on much longer, I do not know what the consequences will be."

The other gods rose to their feet.

Zeus' eyes met Hades', and the brothers shared a moment of silent communication.

"Is there a name for this abomination?" Zeus asked.

Hades nodded. "They are called zombies. It is a plague, of sorts, spread through scratches and bites. The humans fall then rise as these mindless creatures, seeking the taste of their fellow men. It is an abomination."

"How could this happen?" Hestia asked, biting her lip.

"It seems humans have become carried away with their own importance," Hades answered. "They interfere with the natural order of things, create dangers in the name of science, and misuse the world they live in. Many things have gone awry in our absence."

Zeus shook his head, his mouth narrowed into a thin line. "Something must be done."

"Perhaps," Athena suggested, "it is time for a new age of heroes."

Hades cleared his throat. "Before we act, you need to see what we are up against. It is like nothing we have seen before."

Grabbing an empty bowl from the floor, Poseidon opened his hand and filled it with clear water. He held it before Zeus and the others. Small ripples moved outward from the centre, and an image slowly appeared.

"Where is that place?" Aphrodite asked.

"Crete."

All twelve gods gasped.

In the water, a young couple cowered behind a closed door. Their tears cut tracks through the grime coating their faces. Loud thuds hammered against the door. Nails scraped against wood. A low rumble, dozens of hungry growls, ebbed and flowed like the squealing grunts of Odysseus' men when Circe turned them all to pigs.

As the wood split, rotting hands forced their way through the cracks, scratching and digging at any piece of flesh they could find. The couple screamed and sobbed. Blood poured from their wounds. The young man, hands trembling, took something from his bag and pointed it at the woman.

Watching in horror, Athena asked, "What's that?"

Hades swallowed. "A gun. A deadly weapon."

A loud bang silenced them.

The woman in the water, eyes glazed in death, slouched forward with a gaping hole in her forehead. Gasping in ragged, wrenching breaths, the man turned the gun on himself and pulled the trigger.

When both lay dead, the horde of zombies pushed their way through the door and feasted on the bodies.

Poseidon threw the bowl of water against a marble pillar.

"We've seen enough," he growled. "We must intervene."

"We can't go down there," Hades said. "We don't know if this virus can infect us; the last thing the world needs is zombie gods."

"Yet we cannot let this continue unchecked."

Athena pinched the bridge of her nose with two fingers. "We are caught between Scylla and Charybdis in this situation. To act may prove unwise; to do nothing may prove disastrous."

A solemn silence filled the heavens.

Ares, black beard prominent on a square jaw, puffed his chest out. "I will inspire new heroes to fight this war."

The others looked at him.

"Which place is most affected?"

"Los Angeles," Hades replied with a shudder. "A lively city where the people worship a breed of imposter gods called *actors*."

"Then I shall call upon one of them to save their people."

With a click of his fingers, the war god disappeared.

"Aphrodite!" Zeus said.

The goddess of love took a mirror from the folds of her gown and held it so they could all see. The glass shimmered before refocusing to show Ares. He materialised in the grounds of a large mansion, deftly avoiding stepping into a swimming pool shaped like a pirate ship. Trimmed hedges had been made to look like anchors, parrots, and human figures with wooden legs and eye patches.

A bronzed man with chiselled muscles looked up from his fruity pink cocktail, eyes wide.

"Who the fuck are you?"

Ares folded his arms across his chest. "I am Ares, god of war. You will fight in my name!"

The drink slipped from the man's fingers.

"You are Brett Withington, are you not?" Ares asked, a little less sure of himself.

"Security!" Brett gulped. "How did you get in here?"

Ares sighed. "There is no time for this foolishness. Your people are dying! Why do you sit here and do nothing to save them?"

"I... I..."

Waving one hand in the air, Ares swapped Brett's revealing swimwear for sturdy leather armour and a sharp sword forged by Hephaestus himself.

Brett's mouth opened and closed as he looked at the sword in his hand.

Ares waved his hand again, and Brett disappeared.

With a satisfied nod, the god of war returned to his family on Mount Olympus and watched through the mirror as Brett reappeared in the midst of several zombies.

"I fail to see why these *actors* are so worshipped," Artemis commented.

Apollo shrugged. "Perhaps they have hidden powers we have not yet seen."

In the glass, Brett held up his sword with shaking hands. A grey-skinned zombie with clumps of golden hair stumbled forward on strange wheeled footwear.

"He's trembling!" Zeus cried. "What manner of god is he?"

A high-pitched shriek cut through the glass mirror. The gods watched, gasped, winced, and finally closed their eyes.

Hera was the first to speak. "I do not think he was a god, nor a hero."

"Whatever he was," Athena murmured, "he's dead now."

Hades shook his head. "His brain was not destroyed; he is not fully dead. Watch!"

"I'd rather not," Hestia said, turning away from the sight of the zombies gorging themselves on fresh flesh.

After a moment, the zombies pulled back. Slowly, as though his body had to remember how to move, Brett rose to his feet, pieces of skin and flesh hanging from his limbs, and the white flash of bone glistening through an open wound in his jaw.

"Sweet Gaia!" Zeus cursed, invoking the name of the earth's mother.

Ares scratched at his beard. "Where are the heroes of this age, then?"

Demeter shrugged. "Perhaps there are none. Perhaps these men would rather steal daughters than save them."

Her deathly glare turned to Hades, who averted his eyes.

Reaching up to stroke the white owl on her shoulder, Athena cleared her throat. "If there are no heroes in this age, then we must call them from another."

"What do you mean?" Hermes asked.

"We will search for history's greatest warriors and bring them here to fight this fight."

"Can we do that?"

Twelve pairs of eyes turned to Zeus.

The king of the gods tugged on his snow-white beard. "It's never been done before, but this is an unprecedented problem."

"If we interfere with time, we risk the wrath of Kronos," Hera said. "And yet, we will need his help."

Zeus growled. "I can deal with my father."

With a flash of lightning, he disappeared.

"Where has he gone?" Aphrodite asked.

Hades closed his eyes. "To Tartarus. Pray that he returns."

***

Zeus descended into the abyss, using bolts of lightning to guide his way.

Tartarus was no place for the weak; even Hades was reluctant to venture into this part of the Underworld. It was a dungeon of sorts: a punishing prison for wicked souls.

It was also the dark place he had banished the Titans to when he defeated them, all those years before. They would not welcome him with open arms. Not even his parents.

"Kronos!" Zeus' voice boomed into the darkness.

The returning silence was deafening.

A rush of wind was the only warning before a wall of fire sprung up before Zeus. A form took shape, moulding itself into the body of a man. With a loud hiss, the flames flickered out and Zeus looked up into the raging eyes of his father; although he was old, there was nothing frail about his bulging muscles and strong shoulders.

"Ah, my life's biggest regret," Kronos rumbled. "To what do I owe this pleasure?"

Zeus dived right in. "There is turmoil above, Father. A plague of undead walks the earth, destroying all that Gaia intended."

Kronos laughed; a deep rumble echoed through the shadows. "Even my powers are not so great as that; I cannot turn back the clock. If I could, I would have eaten you when you were born, as I did your siblings. Curse your mother for hiding you from me."

"I am aware of that." Zeus nodded his acknowledgement. "We do not want to turn back the clock. We have a plan to call upon heroes of the past, and bring them here."

"Why should I help you?"

"It's not for me. If we do nothing, this outbreak will destroy all of nature. Do you wish to watch your mother die?"

Kronos turned to leave, then looked back. "It is that

serious?"

"Yes."

He sighed, the sound eerily like the last breath exhaled from a dying man. With a flick of his wrist, he pulled a brown sack from the air and handed it to his son.

Zeus opened the sack and saw several small stones glowing with tempered fire, the rust and blood and amber swirling behind a shimmer of ancient power. He met his father's eyes.

"Each stone will carry you once," Kronos said. "Use them wisely."

"Thank you, Father."

The old titan bowed his head, suddenly seeming to carry the weight of all time. "Do not come here again."

Zeus blinked, and his father vanished. An unexpected sadness crept into his chest, lingering like the soft touch of his mother's kiss on his brow. He shook it off and began the ascent to Mount Olympus.

***

Aphrodite used the first stone. After searching history books for inspiration, she jumped through time and dragged her unwilling heroine back to twenty-first century Los Angeles.

"Get your hands off me!" the wavy-haired woman snarled, her hands already clutching a shotgun.

"Oh, calm down." Aphrodite clicked her fingers and turned the gun into a single long-stemmed rose.

The woman's mouth fell open. She dropped the rose. "What do you want with me?"

"You are Annie Oakley, are you not? Famous sharp-shooter? Nicknamed 'Little Sure Shot' by the famous Sioux chieftain Sitting Bull?"

Oakley took a step back. "How do you know all that?"

Aphrodite rolled her eyes. "You mortal fools have no clue who we are, do you?"

"Um."

Looking around, Annie saw a long stretch of golden sand and the pretty blue-green of the foaming ocean. Gentle waves lapped at the shore. She turned and looked at an impressive pier stretching out into the water. Several buildings sat atop it, along with a towering wheel that soared into the sky.

"What in tarnation is that monstrosity?" she asked with a gasp.

Aphrodite glanced at it with a bored expression on her flawless face. "I believe it's called a Ferris wheel; people ride in it to look at the views from such heights."

Oakley stared at the wheel, her thoughts churning. A series of grunts and growls drew her attention.

"We're out of time," Aphrodite said.

In the blink of an eye, Oakley found herself transported into one of the wheel's passenger compartments, around forty feet off the ground; more pods rose above and trailed off below. The carriage swung a little with their weight, and her stomach rolled.

She looked over the rail and gulped. "That's a long way down."

Aphrodite clapped her hands; a large pile of bullets appeared next to Oakley's shotgun on the floor of the carriage. "Don't fall."

"I don't understand any of this."

In the middle of waving her hand to leave, Aphrodite sighed. "See them?" She pointed at the zombies, who shuffled closer to the Ferris wheel as they scented Oakley.

Annie nodded.

"Zombies. Bad guys. They'll eat you if they get close enough. Don't let them."

Oakley's eyes widened. "What?"

"Oh, one more thing; aim for the head."

With that, Aphrodite disappeared, leaving Annie Oakley swinging on a Ferris wheel with only her shotgun and a pile of bullets for company.

"Dang it."

The zombies lingered at the bottom of the wheel. A few reached up as if trying to climb. Annie took a deep breath.

It took only a brief moment to load the gun. Steadying her stance, she took aim and blasted off the side of the nearest zombie's head. He reeled back, and was soon caught by his companions, who stopped to feast on his body.

Annie retched. Pushed long wavy hair back from her face. Took aim once more.

Shots echoed across the pier, a cacophony of sharp booms filling the darkening sky like fireworks dancing above the welcoming water.

***

Hephaestus' mind was elsewhere as he forced his

chosen hero through the corridors of time.

Aphrodite had made it clear she preferred Ares over him; his wife was not one to conceal her emotions. What could he do to win her back?

Distracted, he almost didn't spot the heavy gauntlet swinging towards his face. He reached out with one hand and grabbed the armoured fist, stopping it mid-flight. With no effort at all, he lowered the hero's arm.

"Don't do that again," he commanded.

"You will get nothing from me," the tall knight boomed in a deep voice. "I will never betray my king."

"Loyalty." Hephaestus flashed his teeth. "You could teach my wife a thing or two."

"You have my sympathies, sir, but I will not help you."

The ruddy-faced god waved a dismissive hand in the air. "Yes, yes. I know. The legendary William Marshal, greatest knight to have ever existed, would die before betraying his strict code of honour. I don't care about that."

Marshal, encased in armour, narrowed his eyes. "I do not claim to be legendary, sir, but my skill with a sword is unsurpassed. I am the only man to have defeated Richard Lionheart. I tell you this to give you fair warning before I slay thee."

Pursing his lips, Hephaestus studied the knight. "Defeated Lionheart? I thought he was killed with an arrow?"

The Marshal sighed. "Defeated. Not killed. I could not slay my king's son. I knocked him from his horse to teach the young whelp a lesson."

Laughter pounded the air. "Oh, you'll do nicely, my

friend."

There was a sudden jerk, a momentary pause of life; between one blink and the next, they left the corridors of time and appeared outside a circular church beneath a damp grey sky.

"This is Temple Church." Marshal studied the building. "Though not as I know it."

The surrounding area was quiet and empty, but a strange noise emanated from inside the stone building.

"I'd say you shouldn't look inside," Hephaestus said, "but that's why I brought you here."

Marshal placed one hand on the outer wall almost reverently. "I do not understand."

"Zombies seem to have set up a… nest of sorts inside the church," the god explained. "Their queen stays in there, and they bring her people to eat."

"Zombies? People to eat? What devil's work is this?"

Hephaestus shrugged. "I don't know how it happened, but I hear that chopping off their heads works well."

Marshal arched his brow.

One corner of the god's mouth tilted up. He held both arms out, palms up, and a large sword materialised atop them. Solemnly, he handed it to the knight, hilt first.

"What is this?"

"I forged this sword myself," Hephaestus said. "It is unbreakable, and will serve you well in this battle."

Marshal took the sword and tested its weight. "It's light as a feather!"

"And strong enough to topple giants. Good luck."

"You will not join the fight?"

"I'm not risking catching whatever they have; the

world would be in trouble then." Hephaestus shuddered, then patted Marshal's shoulder; the metal armour clanged. "You don't need my help. You are William Marshal; the greatest knight. Let them taste your sword, my friend. Be the hero the world knows you are."

The god tipped his head and vanished.

Marshal swallowed. He checked his armour. Swung the sword to get a feel for it. Pictured his wife's sweet face, and said a heartfelt prayer to God.

"Lord, I am your faithful servant. Do with me as you see fit."

He strode to the arched door and flung it open, pausing to let his eyes adjust to the dim light before striding inside with the confidence of a man who knows God walks beside him.

Inside, dozens of hulking figures writhed and groaned as they gnawed on piles of bones. The metallic tang of blood lingered in the air.

A number of stone effigies lay on the floor, templar knights buried within the church in times gone by. The zombies sat on them, leaving strips of rotting flesh and splattered blood coating the centuries-old stone.

Marshal's stomach turned as he recognised the likeness of his own face on one of the effigies.

"If I am already dead, they cannot kill me." He fortified himself with another prayer and raised his sword.

Several decaying faces turned to watch him, along with the cold eyes of a woman with green skin and blood smeared across her face like war paint. While the others shuffled and slinked, she rose to her feet with the feral grace of a wild animal.

"In the name of God!" Marshal roared.

WORLDS COLLIDE

He threw himself into the melee, swinging his sword with brutal efficiency. Heads and limbs rolled across the sacred space. Teeth and nails fought for purchase on his body, and were thwarted by the strong armour protecting him. Every technique and trick he'd learned in several decades of life came back to help him as he stormed through ranks of ravenous beasts, from the youthful scraps in his lowly beginnings to the chaotic melees of his tournament career and the strategic movements of war in defence of king and country.

Bodies littered the ground, and still they came. The stench of their breath hung like a miasma.

The zombie queen hurtled towards him, sharp claws extended and mouth gaping open to reveal black and bloodied razor teeth. Marshal's muscles reacted before his brain did.

He swung the sword in a tight arc. Bent his knees to strengthen his stance. His aim was true. Sharp iron cut through flesh and bone with a sickening crunch. Her head thudded to the stone floor. Rolled to rest at his booted feet.

The surrounding zombies let out an unearthly wail before rushing towards him, thirsty for revenge.

Once more, Marshal raised his sword.

***

Athena chose wisely.

The woman she'd selected had been difficult to subdue before being brought forward through time, and would no doubt serve her purpose well.

They were in Tokyo, at the Sensoji Temple; a horde

of zombies lingered within its gates. Athena veiled herself and the woman with a cloak of invisibility, temporary but effective, while she instructed the seasoned warrior.

Tomoe Gozen, a figure long debated over whether she was real or merely a literary character, stood beside her. Now, black hair framing her face, and wide-eyed at the five-storied red pagoda across a large courtyard, she seemed younger than her years.

Tomoe said something that Athena couldn't understand. The goddess laid a hand on the young woman's brow and absorbed her language.

"Say it again, please," she repeated in an old form of Japanese.

"Release me from your magic, witch," Tomoe spat.

Athena chuckled. "Hold onto that fire. It will serve you well."

Tomoe pushed her shoulders back. "I am *onna-musha*. Samurai. Whatever you do to me, I will be unmoved."

Athena scrutinised the small woman as she held her still with her powers. Lithe and nimble, she decided. She wasn't strong and muscled like Hercules or other heroes of old. A smile tugged at Athena's lips; she'd had her fill of heroes with large muscles and small brains. Tomoe was perfect.

Aware of time passing, Athena told Tomoe about the zombie outbreak and the intervention of the Olympians. When it became clear that Tomoe could not marry her beliefs with the reality of the situation, the goddess blanketed her in a haze of calm acceptance.

"I'm sorry to do this to you," Athena said, "but we

don't have a lot of time. It will pass, I promise."

"What is it you want me to do?" Tomoe asked.

Athena pointed through the veil to the gathered zombies. "Make sure they stay dead this time."

Lips set in a straight line, Tomoe nodded. She drew two swords from sheaths at her back, and the silver song of steel sliding along leather rang into the darkening night.

"Do not let them touch you," Athena warned. "Or you will become one of them."

Tomoe snorted. "Touch me? They will not even see me."

Tomoe dived through the veil, disappearing into the shadows. The zombies raised their heads and inhaled; they'd caught her scent, but could not see her. She moved too quickly for them to pinpoint where she was.

Swords flashed. Heads fell. Soft feet retreated into darkness.

The zombies roared their frustration into the night.

With a nod, Athena left and returned to Mount Olympus to watch the battle unfold.

***

"It is done," Zeus sighed, scratching his beard. "The pieces are set. Now, we watch."

Several of Aphrodite's mirrors rested on clouds in mid-air, each one showing a hero in the midst of battle. Apollo pumped a large fist into the air as he watched Hercules smash two zombies together on the streets of Athens.

"You can't beat a classic," he said with a wide grin.

Artemis rolled her eyes and turned back to her own mirror. In the glass, Queen Boudicca pierced rotting flesh with her pointed spear, her wild hair flaming behind her.

Whooping and cheering, Ares leaned forward, his body tense, as Attila the Hun drove his horse towards a crowd of the undead. Attila rode with his knees while using his hands to shoot swift arrows into the brains of dozens of zombies before they reached him. In close quarters, he drew his infamous Sword of Mars, and attacked with the ferocity of a snarling wolf.

"Sword of Mars." Ares huffed. "Sword of Ares! He carries my sword, and doesn't even know its true name. Still, he wields it well."

"Attila was not a hero," Hestia pointed out.

Ares shrugged. "He was a killer; nobody specified he had to be a good guy."

Behind them all, Zeus blew air through his teeth.

"What is it, Father?" Athena asked.

"They are strong, but it is not enough. More will need to rise to quell this undead horde."

Athena blinked her owlish eyes. "I might have an idea."

Father and daughter joined hands; Athena bowed her head. Reaching his arm down towards the atmosphere below, Zeus released a slew of lightning bolts that burst the swollen clouds with the suddenness of a thunderclap.

In the viewing glasses, heavy rain fell on the undead and the living, washing away the grime and blood and weight of darkness. Each raindrop was imbued with the soft breath of Athena's call to arms; the goddess of war,

calm and strategic counterpoint to Ares' lust for guts
and gore, inspired the people to rise together to cleanse
their world.

Below, mortals crept out of their hiding places,
weeping joyful tears as they saw others like themselves.
Bands of sisters and brothers joined together; mothers
leapt into battle, inner warriors spitting fire to protect
their children. Young and old, male and female, strong
and meek: all came as one, with guns and blades and
blunt weapons soon put to use.

Some fell, wailing beneath the biting pain of gnawing
teeth.

Others rose, finding their strength and losing themselves in the fight for survival.

On Mount Olympus, arms linked in unison for the
first time in countless years, the gods smiled.

"They will do," Zeus said. "They will do nicely."

***

Months later, on a warm summer day, as the zombie
apocalypse was reduced to small outbreaks swiftly
suppressed, and the world strove to return to a version
of normal, a golden glow painted the sky above the
Parthenon in Athens.

A band of survivors, half wild after months hiding
amidst the ancient marble ruins, looked up in panic
as thirteen rose-hued figures materialised between the
pillars.

They watched as one of the figures, an old man with
bulging muscles, tugged at his snow-white beard and
looked around the crumbling temple.

"We've got our work cut out for us," he said to the others before pointing to a trembling man nearby. "You!"

The man blanched. "Me?"

"Go forth and spread the word, mortal."

He gulped. "What word?"

Zeus flashed his teeth at the same time as he grabbed a bolt of lightning in his bare hand; the snap and crackle resounded through the cavernous temple like the shot of a gun. "That Zeus and the Olympians have returned."

-End-

THE LEGEND OF WYATT APE!
By Teel James Glenn

Prologue: The Lawless Frontier

My name is Lucifer Lawless and I was hung on the horns of a dilemma. On one hand I was cold and tired because of the job I was doing and on the other I was excited because of where I was.

The night was October 26th of 1881 and it was cold and clear in the town of Tombstone, Arizona Territory. Me and my partner were huddled in the deep shadows of an alley beside the Oriental Saloon on Fifth Street waiting for our target to come down the street. We had been hiding there for ten minutes and my partner was already getting bored.

"Why can't we have waited for him inside the nice warm bowling alley," my partner said.

"Because this is where the assassination is gonna happen, you hairy Hadrian, now shut up, just follow the plan and watch."

Tombstone boasted a bowling alley, four churches, an ice-house, a school, two banks, three newspapers, and an ice cream parlor to announce to the world that it was growing in to a world-class town and was 'civilized.' All of this grew up among and on top of a large number of dirty, hardscrabble mines.

The thing that gave lie to the illusion of sophistication were the 110 saloons, 14 gambling halls, and uncountable dance halls and brothels that catered to the wild element who worked those mines.

It was a hard town to police, with the Marshal's office and the town Sheriff doing their best to balance the need for law and order against the frontier freedoms and trail end celebrations that brought in the dollars that kept the town alive.

That night a lone Deputy Marshal was walking down Allen Street, keeping to the center of the street. To his right was the Sampling Room Saloon and Bowling Alley and to his left was the Golden Eagle Brewery Saloon. Both were doing a good weeknight business, raucous but not enough to require '"regulation."

The subject of our watch came along just then, ambling with a long-legged stride, with lambent blue eyes that scanned both sides of the street, missing little. I found I was holding my breath, amazed at the sight of him.

"Just like the series," my partner whispered.
He started to hum a recognizable them tune, even
whispering "brave courageous and bold-' before I had
to smack him on the head to quiet him.

The peace officer, dressed in a long black coat and
broad, black, flat crowned hat was called The Deacon
by many. He was about thirty-six years old, and
weighing in the neighborhood of one hundred and sixty
pounds, all of it muscle. He stood six feet in height, and
a complexion bordering on the blond.

He had a well-groomed handlebar mustachios that
gave a somberness to his handsome features and made
him seem older than his years.

That night he wore two holstered hip guns, both
Colt Single Action Army, 7.5", .45LC. with his long
coat brushed back to give him free and easy access.
Normally he just tucked a single gun in a pocket or
waistband, eschewing the image of a gunfighter.

"I thought he had a twelve inch barrel on one
of his guns," my partner whispered to me with
disappointment in his voice.

"That was the gun that Ned Buntline gave to him," I
said quietly. "There is no evidence that he ever actually
wore it; in fact most anyone who got one of them had
the barrels cut down to a usable length."

"I hate it when the history books get it wrong," he
said.

"That's what we're here for, you jerk," I hissed.
"Now be quiet and watch."

It was still amazing to me that I was watching one of
legends of my youth right in front of me. It made my
skin tingle.

WORLDS COLLIDE

The lawman reached the end of the block and started to turn right onto Fifth Street when the killers came charging out of the Sampling Room with guns blazing.

The Deputy spun with the intent to fire at the two would be assassins but my partner was faster, drawing his twin six-guns and getting off four shots before the lawman could clear leather.

The two failed assassins first had the guns shot from their hands then were spun around by the impact of the bullets in their bodies, to drop and lay still on the dark street.

The Deacon whirled now to face us but I called out. "Easy, Deputy, we're friends." I stepped from the shadows to let him see my hands raised.

"I'm Lucifer Lawless," I said when I stepped closer. "Doc Lawless is the name on my medicine wagon. My partner does a shooting exhibition and I do some magic. We saw those two hooligans stalking you and then come here to lie in wait for you."

The lawman kept his guns trained on me. "You said, 'We're friends,' so let me see who else is in there with you," he said.

"Come out, buddy," I said. "Don't be worried, little guy, the Deputy won't shoot you."

The Deputy gasped when he saw my partner amble out of the shadows; but then, I guess he had not seen a chimpanzee in a black tail coat and flat crowned hat before. At least not one wearing twin six-guns.

"Deputy Earp," I said, "Say hello to the star of the show, Khetar, the world's only six-gun simian!"

TEEL JAMES GLENN

Chapter One: The Six Gun Simian

Let me take a moment to state a few facts. My name is Lucifer Lawless and I hail from Austin, Texas in the year 2011.

I was a Texas Ranger until I had a very strange experience; my doppleganger from another plane of existence tried to kill me! That was when a member of a group that called themselves T.i.m.e. Cops (though the technical name is Corporal Readjustment Alternity Police. That is correct, it spells C.R.A. P. so you can see why they prefer T.i.m.e. Cops) saved my bacon and opened my eyes.

I suddenly was aware that the vastness of the universe was only the beginning. There was a mulitverse out there, planes of parallel existence that all started at once with the 'big bang' and fractured from there.

The passageway between these parallel worlds were big, blue stones we called Philosophers' Stones. There seemed to be at least one on every world that had been discovered so far.

The Terrestrial Inter-Millenium Exchange was put in charge of the stones and of regulating the passage between planes of existence with C.R.A.P. as the active arm.

I became a full-fledged agent and, paired with Khetar Wohl from the world of Chektana, who on Earth we would have called a Chimpanzee.

"We have it on good authority," the Director-general of T.I.M.E.: Kunjar Neh Zorl said to me and Khetar, "that a descendant of William Clanton, who was killed on October 28 1881 has gained access to a portal stone and traveled from their own time to this Universe 6, your Universe Prime, Lawless, and plans to assassinate the lawman who took Clanton's life in order to prevent that death."

"But you can't change your own history," I pointed out.

"We know that, Lawless," he said. "This crosser is from Universe 30. And about two hundred years in the future, which means they have access to transformational technology that will make detecting them very difficult."

"Why should it be easy?" Khetar said. At the meeting the little furball was dressed in a leopard print tank top and baggy pants that looked like he had mugged MC Hammer in the 1980s. "If it was easy you'd just send Lucy here alone."

"Like its going to be easy wandering around the old west with a trial size King Kong in tow?" I said. "I'd keep a lower profile if I brought a florescent singing octopus."

"Agent Skorflum is not available," the chief said. "Agent Whorl will be fine. You can use the traveling show ruse." He pointed a slender six-digited hand at me. "So see you take this seriously, Lawless."

I and my primate partner left the Chief's office with the little hairy reprobate doing his best to keep from giggling.

Even though I knew the stakes were high, I mean, if this yoyo from U30 killed his target he would, effectively wipe me out of existence, but it still could not dampen my delight in getting to go to the old west of my own world!

***

So now we were standing in the streets of Tombstone Arizona with a figure out of my own history and I was trying to act casual about it.

Deputy Marshal Wyatt Earp stood gape-mouthed, and stared at my primate partner who, thankfully did not throw some quip at the frontier lawman, but, instead waddled over to stand beside me with his long, hairy arms folded over his chest like the little wise guy he was.

"He's with me," I said. "And yes, he always dresses like that in our medicine show." I smiled. I pulled out a piece of paper, signed by the town mayor that allowed Khetar and I to wear guns on the streets and showed it to the peace officer.

"I have not heard of your arrival, sir," the lawman said to me, "but I am certainly beholdin' to you." He moved to the two fallen gunmen and checked them over.

"They're both still breathing," he noted.

"I guess they're paid up on their prayer debts," I said glibly. In fact Khetar's superior eyesight and coordination made him a phenomenal shot. We didn't have to worry about using mercy bullets; expcricnce had proven we could not change our own timeline so, as long as I was here, we could never kill anyone that had not died already in my timeline. One of those time paradoxes that had been proven out.

People were pouring out from the two saloons to see

what the source of the noise was.

"You," Earp called to two of the men he recognized in the gathering crowd. "Get the doc over here to clean this up." The lawman then turned to me, "As for you- I want you in my office tomorrow morning. Bring the animal; you'll need a permit." He stood and with a nod headed off down Fifth Street on his rounds as if nothing had happened.

"Nerves of steel," I said with admiration.

"Balls of brass," Khetar said with an annoyed tone. "Bring the animal?"

He showed his tongue and sent a raspberry sound into the darkness after the lawman.

"Knock it off, ya quarter-sized Konga," I said. "We are here to help keep him alive, so we follow him."

"Well, this *animal* could use a drink," Khetar said.

"He's probably heading to the Long Drink to stop in by Doc Holiday's game next," I said. "We can make it ahead of him if we go directly down this street. It is pretty obvious these two goons were just locals with a grudge. Earp's safe as long as there is no audience; this Clanton nut left a note behind saying that Earp had to die publicly."

Khetar did a fair imitation of Gary Cooper as he walked down the street and I could almost hear little spurs jingling. "Try not to be too conspicuous," I cautioned him.

"Well, there is a chance I can smell that transdimentional tech, whatever form this future Clanton takes," Khetar said. "At least as long as the assassin is not down wind of you."

"Keep it up, pal," I snapped. "I'll find me an Apache

who is looking for a scalp and do a wholesale deal for you!"

Chapter Two: High Plains Primate

The legendary Long Drink Saloon was everything I expected and more. There was sawdust on the floor to soak up blood and beer from fights, spittoons set strategically around the room and drunks galore all over the place.

The Tuesday night crowd was a mix of miners, drummers, cowhands, sodbusters and the gamblers who were there to fleece them. The sporting gals who worked the place all looked tired but I detected an excited giggle when my pandimenstional primate partner walked in under the swinging doors. He snorted at me and scampered off toward the bustiest of the bar girls, making mewing noises until she picked him up to snuggle- he had a thing for busty humans- he thought boobs were funny.

I was about to grab him when a bald headed bravo lumbered over toward us with a wooden walking stick in hand.

"What the hell is that?" the bouncer said pointing the stick at Khetar.

"That, sir," I said in my best showman presentation. "Is my partner in the greatest show to ever cross the Mississippi River!" I did a flourish and produced a rose, which I offered him.

He didn't think it was funny, but the watching crowd did. The working girls all snickered. I announced, "I've come to invite you all to see Six-gun Khetar, star of Doc Lawless' Wonder Show, tomorrow near Fly's Boarding House! And for now, a round of drinks on the house."

The only people in the room that did not seem to be affected by the hirsute one's antics and the free beer were a table of card players off to one side. There were five men seated around the circular table. Two women stood by, obviously to attend to the drink needs of the gamblers.

Each seated man had a relaxed attitude in their whole body but their eyes were all but glowing with intensity.

"Another whiskey, John?" one the women asked one of the men. Her smile was a bright spot in the dingy room.

"If you would, dearheart," he said in a soft southern drawl. "I am a bit parched."

Mary Katherine Horony Cummings, who went by the none-to-complimentary moniker of "Big Nose Kate," was not a big woman and not an unattractive one. She had a slight foreign accent (I knew it was from her birth country Hungary) that gave her a slightly exotic appeal. You could see her affection for the seated gambler, but his intense gaze-albeit from beneath half closed eyes so that he appeared sleepy to a casual gaze-were focused on the cards.

"*Doc Holliday and Big Nose Kate,*" I thought. No photo could convey the sheer power of their presence.

Kate looked up at me with a sharp assessment as she walked past me to the bar and her companion threw down one card and drew another to rearrange his hand.

"So, Doctor Lawless," Holliday said to me without taking his eyes off the cards. "Is your anthropoid associate the major attraction of your show or do you have any talent?"

I wanted to answer, "Ask my ex-wife," but restrained myself and said, "I am a premiere prestidigitator and I, of course trained the primordial pippin myself."

The little Chektana native jumped down from the sporting girl and knuckled over to me, looking up with plaintive eyes that were full of 'screw you' attitude.

I held out my arms and he jumped up to whisper, "Trained me?"

"It's a cover, Thing Kong!" I hissed. Then I smiled at Holiday and said in a full voice, "He's a talented little ball of fur."

"And a fast one," Wyatt Earp said as he entered the saloon. He strode across the floor to stand next to me. "I didn't expect to see you two until the morning."

"Just out promoting our show," I said. Khetar held his arms out toward Earp but the lawman ignored him, apparently immune to chimp charms.

Not to be put off, or ignored, Khetar jumped down from my arms and waddled over to stand next to the Marshal, imitating his stance. The gesture brought snickers from any in the saloon who noticed, including Holliday.

"Looks like you have another admirer, Wyatt," the gambler said. His laugh devolved into a hacking cough and Kate rushed back to the table to hand him a whiskey. He threw the drink into his mouth the moment he could and continued as if he had not had the fit. I noticed no one around him remarked at the coughing fit at all. "Seems, the little fellow is angling for a deputy job, Deacon; you think Virgil put him up to it?"

This last remark got a smile out of the grim faced lawman. "I'll have to write mom to see if there are any of my kin I don't know about," he said, "But as to deputies, he seems more in line with Behan's boys."

I watched the lawman and those around him for any sign of any unusual interest in him. Finding an assassin who could resemble anyone seemed an impossible task. Particularly if the object of the assassin had his own set of ready made murderers. We had been given impossible to do before and so far the multiverse was still more or less intact, but as my old dad was fond to say, "Failure is always an option when people are involved!"

Earp stopped at the bar and was given a coffee by the bartender- part of his usual routine- then came over to the gambling table. He said hello to Kate and exchanged pleasantries with Holliday.

My partner had become bored with not being able to speak (have I mentioned he's usually a chatterbox?) so he was knuckling around the room doing his, 'I'm cute' act. I suspected he was trying to sniff out the chemical signature of the transformational device that our assassin might be using.

I took a sniff and almost choked on the thick miasma of smells and smoke. "Good luck scenting out the 'crosser in this," I thought.

Just as the hairy T.I.M.E. agent got to one of the whiskered miners and took a whiff (I did not envy him that moment), one of the not-so-busty saloon gals that he had ignored, pulled a Mac-10 sub machinegun and pointed it at the Deputy!

Chapter Three: Hominid on the Range

I yelled "Duck, Earp!"

Many things happened simultaneously then. The assassin depressed the trigger and began to spray lead, Deputy Earp dropped his coffee and drew his gun, several women screamed, Khetar spun and drew both his .32 caliber sixguns, and I dove into Earp.

My dive took the lawman out of the path of the machine gun and slammed the two of us into the table in front of Doc Holliday. The table tipped over and the two us landed on the gambler's lap.

The bullets licked wood from the heavy table and the assassin screamed in frustration.

I heard Khetar's .32s bark and then the sound of crashing glass amidst the screams and chaos.

I disentangled myself from the two men I'd fallen on as Holliday launched into a debilitating coughing fit.

"Sorry, Deputy," I said. I rose to see that the assassin had thrown a chair through a side window and escaped that way. I saw my primate partner just leaping through the hole.

Khetar yelled, "Follow, Lawless!"

I complied with his shout before Earp could question me, and jumped the jagged glass of the window to follow my simian sidekick. Khetar was in full all-fours chase mode, knuckling down the wooden sidewalk at an amazing speed.

The crosser-Clanton must have been a marathon runner because she was way ahead of Khetar and gaining.

I raised my gun to fire and called, "Alternity Police, freeze!"

The runner did not even break stride and was soon gone around the corner into the darkness. I pulled up short and panted for a moment as I heard a horse take off at a gallop.

In a moment my partner knuckled out of the night and, to my secret delight, he was panting as well.

"She must have cheetah genes spliced in," the chimp said. "I couldn't even get close before she rode off."

We went back to the Long Drink. Once we were inside the chaos that the crosser Clanton had wrought was evident.

The wall of the saloon behind the bar was peppered with bullet holes, the mirrors and bottles shattered.

There were casualties as well, though in her zeal to kill Earp the wounds to the others were minor.

Fortunately no one had noticed that the little furball

had yelled to me in the middle of the attack.

"What the hell kind of gun was that?" Earp asked.

"Some sort of European thing," I offered. Khetar offered a snide snort at my adlib.

"You know, Doctor Lawless," Earp said. "That makes the second time you've save my life tonight. You're getting to be quite a good luck charm."

"Let's hope third time's not the charm," I muttered. My hairy better half elbowed me so I added, aloud, "Glad to be on hand, Deputy, but I'd better be getting this little fella to bed or he'll get cranky. Try to stay safe till I see you tomorrow."

My primate partner ambled at my side and waved to the room before we went to the medicine show wagon.

"You think we can leave Earp alone the rest of the night?" he asked me as he scampered up to a top shelf where he had set up a little nest.

"I think so," I said. I sat down heavily. "This Clanton crosser wants to make a show of Earp's death; apparently her timeline is in the middle of a retro fad that got her obsessed with seeing how things would have worked out if her ancestor had lived."

"Only for this timeline," Khetar pointed out. "It's academic for her, but if the crosser kills him you might cease to exist."

"Thanks for reminding me," I said.

"Thanks to you yelling," he said, "now the crosser knows we are time cops!" He might annoy me like no other partner I'd ever had, but he was a smart simian.

"We didn't do anything any other simian/sapian duo wouldn't," I said. I waited for him to reply but he did something that always annoyed me, he rolled over and abruptly he was already sleeping, snoring like Paul Bunyon rip-sawing Sequoia trees.

Chapter Four: The High Chimperal

Wednesday October twenty six was clear and even colder than the night before.

Ike Clanton had been up all night playing cards and was drunk as a skunk with a full on mad for Doc Holliday, whom he blamed for his bad luck. He was part of a group who called themselves "The Cowboys" and most of the members of the group had reason to dislike the Earps, Virgil, Morgan and Wyatt- who had clashed with them numerous times over various shady dealings on both sides.

I knew that before the day was out there was going to be a violent explosion, a flashpoint of history that might- if we failed- literally erase me from existence. That would suck. Despite that, the fact that I was going to be at that flashpoint- a legendary moment in time- had me almost as excited as scared.

I bought food at a restaurant and brought it outside to feed my fuzzy sidekick. We sat on a tree stump and regarded Fremont Street.

"I think at this point our crosser will wait to do it

near the shoot out; she knows we are after her so my guess is that she has already found a spot to make her move on Earp."

"Well, we know his movements during the day, so I think we should walk over his route, look for likely assassination spots."

"And let's not forget we have a noon show," Khetar pointed out. "Earp will be there and we can shadow him from that point out."

We finished our meal then walked the route we knew that Wyatt Earp would be taking that day, spotting any potential sniper perches or ambush points. Our 'cover' for the trip was the passing out of handbills for our show.

Khetar sniffed at each local, hoping to catch a whiff of our prey. His crime fighting nose came up empty though he made a number of remarks on human hygiene that were unrepeatable.

We stopped by the Marshal's office to get our performance permit and Wyatt Earp accompanied us to see the show.

Earp seemed to particularly enjoy Khetar's display of marksmanship (or was that marksapeship?). The hairball shot a series of clay plates out of the air, a clay pipe from my mouth and did a display of gun twirling using both his hands and his feet.

Khetar's six gun skills and my elementary stage conjuring earned us a healthy applause and I sold eight bottles of Doc Lawless' Cramp Remedy to the rubes. Khetar and I got to keep any profits after corps expenses!

"Nice show," Earp said when we had concluded our last bow. He regarded my furry fellow time cop with a little bit of awe. "How did you ever get that little fella to shoot that well? Even Virgil can't slap leather and hit a target like that."

I made a show being humble about my 'training' ability and stared my partner to silence (I knew he wanted to take full credit but his suddenly speaking might have given Earp a heart attack and done the crosser's job for her).

"Well, see you around, Doc," the lawman said with a tip of his hat. Khetar copied the gesture and Earp laughed. "I gotta bring my brothers to see your show tomorrow. They'll love it!"

"The horses are out of the gate now," I whispered to Khetar. "Better get moving."

"I'll shadow Earp from the rooftops and you head to the corral and try and spot the crosser."

He scampered off to follow the lawman and his appointment with destiny.

***

The actual famous shootout would take place six lots removed from the rear entrance to the O K Corral. It was immediately west of 312 Fremont Street, which contained Fly's 12-room boarding house and a photography studio. The lot was near the West End

Corral on 3rd Street and Fremont, where Ike Clanton and Tom McLaury's wagon and team were stabled.

I surveyed the whole area and decided that two barn buildings across and down the street offered the best sniper's perch if the crosser was going to strike from a distance. I went to the barns to check them out.

Meanwhile, Khetar was following Deputy Earp. The lawman met up with his older brother Virgil at the courthouse where Ike Clanton was being fined for having been caught earlier without turning in his gun in accordance with city law.

Wyatt almost walked into 28 year-old Tom McLaury as the two men stopped short almost nose-to-nose. Tom had only arrived in town the day before.

Earp asked, "Are you heeled or not?"

"No." McLaury lied.

Wyatt saw a revolver in plain sight on the right pocket of the arrogant McLaury's pants. Wyatt drew his revolver and with a lightning swift move buffaloed McLaury with it. He hit him on the head twice with his official revolver. The outlaw went down, bleeding from the temple.

"I don't like being lied to, Tom." Earp said then walked away after taking the downed man's gun.

Khetar, watching from a roof nearby, scampered after the lawman.

I searched the barns then went to the roof of one where I could see the site of the shootout. I settled down to hide from the hider and wait.

WORLDS COLLIDE

I concentrated on trying not to think about the possibility of being 'blinked' out of existence with a new timeline being formed if we failed to save Earp.

I might not just cease to exist, mind you; I might not be directly affected at all, but my world would. It was impossible to know what ripples would come from Earp's death- he had lived a long time, touched the lives of many people from Texas to Alaska and beyond. Hell, he even met Tom Mix in Hollywood!

It would all change if he was not there to interact with them.

Meanwhile Khetar was still shadowing Wyatt who had gone to a gunmaker's shop to talk to some of McLaury's cohorts in an attempt to defuse the situation.

Virgil Earp met up with Doc Holliday and gave a sawed off shotgun to the former dentist, who hid it under his overcoat. He took Holliday's walking stick in return.

Virgil Earp was told that the McLaurys and the Clantons had gathered on Fremont Street and were armed. He decided he had to act. He told his brothers Wyatt and Morgan that things had come to a head and it was time to take the guns away from the Cowboys and, once and for all, prove to the community who was in charge.

A hidden Khetar heard them argue over whether it was the right course of action, with Wyatt arguing for letting it go. Virgil was adamant, however that a showdown had to come.

The Earps carried revolvers in their coat pockets or in their waistbands. Holliday was wearing a pistol in a holster, concealed along with the shotgun. They moved off west, down the south side of Fremont Street.

The Earps were out of visual range of the Cowboys but I could see them up the street. I saw Khetar pop out of a barrel and knuckle along the sidewalk, keeping to the shadows. Even at several blocks distance I could see that the hairy hero was sniffing like mad and scanning the surrounding street for any sign of the assassin.

I was about to give in to the despair of it when I looked across and spotted a gun barrel sliding out from between two boards at the next barn.

The assassin must have been hiding somewhere in the loft of that barn and had sighted in their weapon on the lot where the Cowboys were talking with Sheriff John Behan.

As the Earps approached, Sheriff Behan left the group of toughs though he looked nervously backward several times.

"For God's sake," Behan said with an unsteady voice to the Earps. "Don't go down there or they will murder you!"

The Deacon just bit his lip and stared at the Sheriff with cold eyes. "Let's do this," he said.

The four then moved past the ineffective Behan and marched slowly across the street.

On the roof I tried to move as quietly as possible

and went down the ladder to creep into the next barn, knowing that I would literally be fighting for not only my existence, but that of untold lives to come.

Epilogue: Monkey See, Monkey Shoot

Down in the narrow 18 foot alley I knew the Earps and Doc Holliday were ranged across the open side facing the Cowboys; Tom McLaury, Frank McLaury, Ike Clanton, Billy Clanton and young Billy Claiborne.

I found a ladder in the shooter's barn and moved up it. Once up I could see out the open loft to the alley. The assassin was now lying in the open but I could see the control panel of an electronic camouflage unit.

In the alley I heard Virgil Earp yell, "Hold it, I don't want that!"

Frank McLaury and Billy Clanton drew their guns.

Billy Clanton leveled his pistol at Wyatt, but the lawman didn't aim at him. He knew that Frank McLaury had the reputation of being a good shot and a dangerous man.

Frank McLaury jumped to one side but Wyatt shot him in the stomach. Billy Clanton started shooting.

At that point Khetar popped out from behind a water trough and intervened, shooting Billy Clanton through the right wrist that disarmed him. He always had a hard time 'just watching.'

The crosser screamed at seeing her cross-ancestor hit.

Tom McLaury tried to hide behind his restless horse. He fired over the horse's back then tried to grab his rifle from its scabbard on his horse.

Doc Holliday stepped back for distance and angled around McLaury's horse and shot him with the shotgun in the chest.

I yelled and jumped across the loft at the assassin.

My yell startled the shooter and her rifle fired wild.

Morgan Earp fired at Billy Clanton, hitting him so that he slammed against the wall of the alley with a bullet in his gut.

The crosser screamed again.

I landed on the shooter and tried to grab the rifle from her hands.

"No, Earp has to die!" the crosser screamed. She held onto the rifle with a death grip, clawing and biting at me. I may have outweighed her but her anger (and possibly some chemical help) gave her tremendous strength.

Holliday had tossed the shotgun aside, pulled out his nickel-plated revolver, and continued to fire at the wounded Frank McLaury and Billy Clanton.

Ike Clanton ran forward and grabbed Wyatt, exclaiming "I'm unarmed I don't want a fight."

"Go to fighting or get away!" The Deacon snapped.

Ike ran away unwounded. At the same moment Billy Claiborne also ran from the fight.

Virgil and Wyatt were now firing. Morgan Earp tripped but fired from the ground.

Morgan Earp was shot across the back in a wound that struck both shoulder blades, he went down for a minute before picking himself up.

The crosser heaved me off of her and rolled back to aim the rifle again. I rolled to my feet and made a grab for her but she squeezed the trigger before I could stop her.

Unlike her first shot this one did not go wild but it did not hit her intended target either. My impact on her knocked the sight enough that the bullet thudded home, not into Wyatt Earp but into the body of Billy Clanton, killing him!

Down below Virgil Earp was shot in the calf and cursed. Frank McLaury stumbled to the street and took aim at Wyatt Earp but Khetar fired and the Cowboy went down for good. (Morgan would later take credit for that one).

Suddenly the Gunfight at the O.K. Corral was over. The street was abruptly very quiet.

The crosser was babbling sounds of frustration. She tossed me off her once again and swung the rifle like a club to slam into the side of my head. Abruptly I was counting stars in the Milky Way Galaxy.

I must have been out for a full minute because I was suddenly looking up at Khetar's hairy kisser.

"Up and at it, Lucy," he said. "No amount of beauty sleep is going to help at all."

I sat up too quickly and my head throbbed. "The crosser!" I said.

"Got away on a horse she had out back," he said.

"We better get her," I said shaking off a wave of dizziness. I climbed down the ladder and jumped on Tom McLaury's loose horse. "Hop on!" I yelled to Khetar and we were off to the races.

"Off that way to the right," he said. We were at a full gallop and moving so fast I barely had time to hear the exclamations from the townsfolk as we whizzed past.

It didn't matter now; Earp was alive and there was no point to his murder. The only thing we had to worry about was that the crosser would get the bee in her bonnet to do it all over again in a different timeline, there were at least 45 we knew of.

"Or she could just kill Earp out of spite, you know?" Khetar said.

"You are always so inspirational and uplifting," I said. The horse was moving at a full run now.

"Look," Khetar said, "all you hairless types confuse the heck out of me with your motivations."

"You understand the boobies part of it well enough," I snarked at him. We were approaching the edge of town now and the crosser on horseback was clearly visible.

"Move it, Roy Rogers," Khetar said. "We have to catch her before she kills someone or hits her transit point out of this timeline."

"Shut it, furball or I'll team up with Gabby Hayes!"

We came up on the crosser and I moved alongside. Her features were a twisted mask of hate. When she saw me she hissed like a scalded cat.

She raised a strange weapon but before she could pull the trigger my hairy partner fired, blowing the gun out of her hand.

The crosser was so startled by the shot that she lost control of her horse. She tumbled off her mount and went headlong into the dirt.

I reined myself up and spun, but Khetar was off my back and over at her before I could even come to a full stop.

"Relax, Tex," he smiled up at me, "It's all done now. T'was beauty caught the beast!"

I almost shot him right there, I really did.

***

Tombstone Nugget the next day proclaimed:

The 26th of October, 1881, will always be marked as one of the crimson days in the annals of Tombstone, a day when blood flowed as water, and human life was held as a shuttle cock, a day to be remembered as witnessing the bloodiest and deadliest street fight that has ever occurred in this place, or probably in the Territory.

Not a single mention of a gun toting chimp or a

medicine show magician, which means we did our job. That and the Earps didn't want to admit that a simian six-gun artist had helped them take the Cowboys down.

-End-

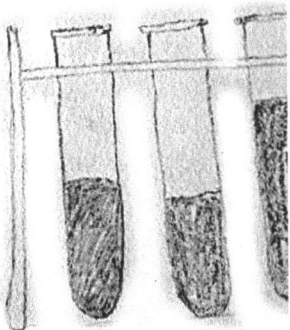

THE STRANGE CASE OF DR BIRCH AND MRS CAMPBELL

By T.J. Berg

"She's peculiar, certainly, dear friend, but if I could just for a moment convince you to step into her workshop, I think you'll find she has exactly what you're seeking." The gentleman, Rialto, his purple velvet jacket tucked tight against the wind with one mechanical hand, held the door with his other. The second gentleman, more sedately dressed in a black waistcoat and yellow shirt, reminded Dr Birch of a nervous bee. She suppressed a laugh, thought how easy it would be with the right potion and a few mechanical modifications, to make him into a bee. Antennae. Stinger. Some fuzz. That probably wasn't what he'd come round for, however.

The bells jingled as the door closed. The mirrors in her work bench showed the bee-man's hesitance. Men were always hesitant around her. Rialto, whose hands she had custom built, visited only to bring her new business. If she came too close, his pointy little beard twitched nervously. She smiled, wiping oil from her fingers onto her smock, then adjusted the cog.

"Dr Birch?" Rialto called. He kept his hands tucked into his pockets, well away from anything in the workshop. He put on a confident smile for the bee man. "Are you in Dr Birch? Belinda?"

Dr Birch twitched, set the screw on her cog. Her set up of audiophones, lenses, and mirrors allowed her to hear and see people enter the workshop. She had to remind herself they couldn't see her. "Bzzz bzzz," she hummed under her breath, giggling. Just one more cog and then she could start setting the Brownian ratchets. And so little time. Always too little time.

"Dr Birch?" Rialto's voice dropped. "Perhaps she's not in."

"Would she leave her door unlocked?" Bee-man followed his question with a panicked shout and leap that brought him crashing into Rialto. A puff of smoke wafted into the air out of the three o'clock cuckoo's beak.

"Oh, drat," Dr Birch mumbled to her butterfly. "I forgot to wind the fireclock. Losing time. Hm. Or is it fast?" She adjusted the last cog and straightened herself, stretching. Her keys, carefully chained round her waist, rattled as she bent and loosened her muscles.

Then she marched down the series of corridors, keying through each locked door, and finally into the workshop where Rialto stood comforting Bee-man. "Bzzz bzz," she hummed happily to herself. Visitors were a pleasure. They stole from her those precious hours before five, but maybe they'd have an interesting puzzle for her.

"Dr Birch," Rialto said. She remembered to look up. Startled, she hopped back. His head had gotten enormous! He tapped his eye. Oh yes! Her teloptics. She rewound them with a soft whir and removed them to a bench top. Better now. Rialto and Bee-man looked normal again.

Except Bee-man's shirt was still smoking. She reached over and patted the burnt sleeve. She risked a momentary glance at his face then hurried back round her counter and busied herself with wiping its surface clean. "And what does the bee want?" she asked, but suspected it was too quiet as neither man answered. She was always speaking much too quietly. She waited a bit longer to see if they would answer, then a little bit longer, just in case they needed time to think.

Rialto made a throat-clearing noise. "What bee, Dr Birch?"

She glanced up to be sure she was aiming her finger in the right direction, then pointed at Bee-man.

Rialto laughed. He had a very nice laugh. "Filbert?" Then, "Oh, oh." More laughter. "Yes, well, Filbert, would you kindly tell Dr Birch of your troubles?"

"Hmm? Yes. It's about my wife."

His wife, it seemed, had been lying in a coma for

nearly a month. "I just want her back. I'm convinced she's alive in there. If only we could find some way to free her mind from its damaged cage . . ." He sighed, was possibly crying. It made Dr Birch feel quite dreadful.

"I'll have to come see her." She was sure once again that they couldn't hear her, as neither responded, so she left them to gather her tool kit.

***

Rialto, great lover of the mechanicals, had one of the newest telautomatic carriages. Dr Birch examined it carefully before allowing herself in. It was going to be a bumpy ride. The suspension was not nearly as well designed as the mechanicals, but it did get them to Saint Ballymore's in a timely manner.

Wireless electricity receivers sparkling atop gothic spires marked Saint Ballymore's as a very well-funded private hospital. Inside, the floors were white marble, streaked through with grey. The wide, pillared entrance hall was lit by glowing wireless gas lamps strung on shining brass chains so that they seemed to sweep like birds through the empty spaces above. A glass dome covered the hall, providing the only natural light, diffuse at such neck cranking distance. The space was walled by a spiralling stair and floor after floor of rooms, walkways protected by polished brass banisters. Up the center of the great room a shaft rose directly to the center of the glass dome, and like spokes on a wheel, glass-covered walkways radiated out to connect it to each floor. Families took the stairs, but nurses and doctors were busy riding the pneumatic plane up and down the central shaft, pushing carts full of clean linens or foul excretions. Dr Birch shuddered slightly at the extent of it all.

"Lina is on floor eight," Bee-man said.

"Who?"

"His wife," Rialto said. "All the coma patients are housed on floors three to nine."

"Yes." She turned away from the view a moment. "What?"

"All the--"

"How so many?"

Rialto took a step closer to her, cheeks turning a charming pink. "Dr Birch, is it possible you haven't heard of the Michaelis-Menten Kineticometer incident?"

Oh yes. "Enzymes are not machines," she muttered. She'd warned them. "No reversing that, of course." She tugged at one of her braids, causing her head to shake. "But the brain lives?"

"Yes, I'm sure of it! It is only the muscles of the somatic nervous system that are affected. All of the autonomic functions are intact."

"Are you a doctor, Mr. Bee?" Dr Birch asked.

"Why yes," he answered, after a quick glance at Rialto. Dr Birch *tsked*.

"Take me to the brain," she said. Then, correcting herself, "The wife."

* * *

The wife was laid out prettily in a bed with bright yellow sheets and a blue checked blanket, hair combed to one side of the pillow. Someone had given her a touch of makeup and a splash of too-sweet perfume. She looked quite alive if one could ignore the unnatural stillness and various feeding tubes. Dr Bee-man buzzed up to her, picked up one of her hands and gave it a kiss. "Lina dear, I brought someone to help you."

Dr Birch sat down and gave the wife a full examination. "Mechanicals hardwired to the autonomic nervous system." She poked and prodded and occasionally removed instruments from her bag. Eyes. Nose. Ears. Heart. What was in the blood? "Hmm. Telaumatics, diffuse broadcast power system dependent. How to restore conscious control through mechanicals? Is it disrupted at the periphery or message center?" She tugged her braids, knocking her head about. "Oh yes, of course, Menten dynamical range modifiers would mean . . ." And she pricked the foot and watched it twitch. "A Michaelis curve linkage restoration should surely . . ." She removed some callipers from her bag, took several measurements, applied an entanglement unit to the wife's head and made some preliminary readings. "Yes yes. I can restore her. Certainly. Yes yes." And she walked out, ready to get back to the lab. There was quite a lot of work to be done. And she was always back in her laboratory by five o'clock.

She was walking beneath the sunny glass dome when Rialto caught up, startling her with a sudden touch on her arm. "Oh!"

"Can you really fix her?"

"What? Oh! Fix. Of course. Give me a few days. Yes, she'll be operational."

***

She only just made it back to her laboratory. She dropped her keys into the harmonic chest and whistled a tune to lock them away. The fireclock, still running fast, had already charred the brass five o'clock cuckoo. It would repair itself by morning, but Dr Birch reset the fireclock before she forgot again. The poor cuckoo. It gargled despondently at her, declaring it was five o'clock. Dr Birch leaned against the workbench, sliding down to the floor. Her legs stuck out and her body fell limp, arms hanging at the side, head lolling down, braids coming to rest against her chest. Ten minutes passed. The workshop ticked and hissed in soft, comforting ways. And when ten minutes expired, Mrs Campbell lifted her head and touched her braids in annoyance.

She stood and stretched, set the fireclock forward several minutes, then removed her key from the throat of the slightly melted cuckoo. The key unlocked the side door to the workshop, which opened into a small, tastefully furnished apartment. Dr Birch had only the vaguest awareness of the apartment, as her memory of Mrs Campbell's actions upon her first awakening were fuzzy. The clothing she'd selected this morning was hanging on the door to her washroom. Her favorite top, shimmery emerald-green silk, the edges embroidered with white violets, a belt of white and silver to cinch it around her waist and flatter her curves without appearing too showy. Her under trousers were a pearlescent white, the front panel, amusingly called the "modesty panel" by fashionistas, was a green to match her top.

But before Mrs Campbell could fully luxuriate in her clothing, she required a good washing. She removed Dr Birch's work clothes, hanging them outside the door to her apartment to air out the noodle and onion smell from that terrible shop Dr Birch frequented for lunch.

Then she gave herself a good hot bath, removing the grease and sweat of the workshop, scrubbed carefully beneath nails, trimming and pruning them, brushed her teeth, washed her hair. She emerged from her wash-room clean and smelling lightly of lavender. Hair dried, coifed, and pinned, she donned her fresh clothing, enjoying the heavenly hints of lemon and rosemary that scented them. Finally, she was ready to go home for the evening.

She picked up her handbag from the vanity, and as always, checked its contents. Keys, wallet, breath mints, lipstick, notebook, pencil, six shooter. The light activated the kittens loaded into the chambers. They hissed, bristling, until they recognized Mrs Campbell, then mewed appeasingly, settling down to purring as she dropped a few feed pellets into the bag. Quite ready, she locked up her little apartment, then slipped the key back into the five o'clock cuckoo before it retreated into its home where it would repair itself, once again locking away the key until five o'clock tomorrow. Then, feeling quite good regarding Dr Birch's activities of the day, she strolled out of the workshop and flagged a carriage to bring her home.

***

Mrs Campbell lived in the city's most fashionable district. The butler opened the door for her, took her parasol, then resumed his position. She checked the kitchen first, to be sure the cook was on schedule and the maids ready to serve dinner, then retired to the sitting room with a book to await her husband.

Miles was everything she'd hoped for in a husband. Handsome, wealthy, well-placed in society, respected, and deeply, hopelessly loving, kind, and naïve. After Dr Birch had given herself the first treatment to make herself more appealing to men, thus creating the future Mrs Campbell, she'd spent several months integrating herself into society and locating just the right husband. Fashion, social graces, flirtation, all those came naturally to her after the injection. What hadn't come naturally was a suitable man to compliment those charms. What Mrs Campbell wanted most was wealth and a position on the stock exchange, but Dr Birch had wanted love, someone to ease her loneliness. Finding someone wealthy and powerful that would fall prey to Mrs Campbell's charms would not have been difficult, but for Mrs Campbell to go on existing, she also had to find someone who would love her, or Dr Birch wouldn't emerge in the morning feeling the sweet contentment of having been loved during her hours away from the lab. It turned out to be much more difficult than she'd anticipated. She'd nearly given up and started to acquiesce to the charms of a rakish young man from a good family. Then Miles became available. He'd not previously been a consideration, already having a wife, but upon her tragic death he suddenly found himself adrift.

When Miles arrived home from work, he found his wife neatly curled on the sofa with a book, looking lovely with her bare feet poking primly from beneath her trousers. She smiled, as usual, the moment she knew he was in the room, and sprung up for hugs and kisses then insisted on making him a drink.

"Wine or a cocktail this evening, darling?" she asked.

"A cocktail, I think," he said, stroking her back firmly and massaging her neck. "An old fashioned?" His voice tipped up in an apologetic query, as if he should feel bad that he enjoyed a strong drink.

"Of course. Anything wrong at work?"

He sat, sighing, on the couch. "I'm so glad Hubert recommended I short sell that Michaelis-Menten Kineticometer stock, " he said. "But it's just been horrible seeing the fallout from that fiasco. So many people in comas who just wanted to improve themselves a little." He took a deep drink. "I know there's no way I could have known that the safety test data had been manipulated, but I still feel guilty for having invested in the first place."

"There's no way anyone could have known, darling." She curled up next to him on the sofa with a glass of wine. "Did you heart that both the scientists involved in falsifying the safety data committed suicide?" Tragic, kitten induced suicides. Her little pets carried many chemicals that could be administered in lethal doses. And how else for a couple of lab rats to send themselves to their guilty end, and absolve Mrs Campbell of any potential links to the MMK corporation? Dr Birch had been very angry about the whole thing. She'd even stopped giving herself her daily injections, but as it turned out, Mrs Campbell emerged each evening at five o'clock anyway--as long as her loving husband awaited her. Dr Birch tried to fight it, but the loneliness won out in the end. However, it meant that Miles must keep on loving her, and never find out about her involvement in the . . . less savory aspects of their wealth. Of course, it wasn't just Miles that benefited from Mrs Campbell's hard work. Dr Birch had proven herself completely unable to profit from her genius. The reality was, if she wanted to keep working, she needed Mrs Campbell. Who else would pay for her wild experiments?

"Suicide is too good for them. I just can't imagine pushing a product to market that you knew could harm people."

"Not everyone has your heart, my love." Mrs Campbell slid a hand tenderly through his hair. He smiled.

"Enough of this. Dinner! Let's speak of cheerier things."

And so, another evening as Mrs Campbell, loving wife. And once her husband dropped off to sleep, content and fulfilled, Mrs Campbell emerged from bed and made her notes. She'd told him in the past that she was not a sound sleeper and frequently woke for walks in the night. That was, of course, the only time she was available to do business. She had investments of her own, under other names, and plenty of cash, but the bulk of her fortune she'd made in her husband's name, as she'd had little money of her own to invest when she'd first entered their marital contract. To secure his fortune, she'd convinced him of the excellent skills of one Mr. Hubert Deluca at the investment firm of Schroder, Mink, and Lorraco. Mr. Deluca, in turn, simply invested as she advised. Having groomed him perfectly for the position after rescuing him from a murder charge--one of which he was wholly guilty--he was happy to do as she wished. Her husband, therefore, was entirely ignorant of her involvement in his financial affairs.

Tonight, she had quite a lot of work to do. Manipulating markets was no simple task. She also had to jump on opportunities when they arose. The MMK scheme had been masterful, profitable for her at every step, from the launch of the company to its acquisition, and its inevitable downfall. She'd expected to leave it there, but now Dr Birch had been called in to possibly rescue the victims of the failed enzomotor platform. Mrs Campbell had to be ready to make her profit. The question was, what would everyone be buying when the victims started waking up? Mrs Campbell had made a killing on life support machinery investments, having known well before the rest of the world the inevitable fate of 75% of MMK receivers. If only she knew exactly what Dr Birch was planning, she could possibly make another big profit.

She would just have to wait until Dr Birch got to work. In the meantime, there was a small oil rich country that was convinced another small oil rich country was planning to invade. They were desirous of some new spy technology, and Dr Birch had invented the perfect thing. They looked just like little desert beetles and reported back only to those they bonded with. Dr Birch, of course, did not approve of her inventions being used in war, but sold was sold, and Dr Birch would only find out after the fact. Mrs Campbell fed her kittens and headed out to do business.

**

Dr Birch woke up in her underwear, head pounding, a gash down her upper arm, and covered in beetles. She really disliked when Mrs Campbell didn't bother to dress her, and even worse, what must Miles think when Mrs Campbell was already gone in the morning? Of course, they'd spent a splendid evening together, listening to the opera after dinner, then discussing the current news. She smiled, then giggled. The beetles tickled. She whistled low and they swarmed down her unhurt arm and formed a ball on the floor, carapaces out. "Good pets," Dr Birch said. Silly Mrs Campbell. She could remember Dr Birch's actions, but not her thoughts. Because the coding process was too technically advanced for Mrs Campbell, she hadn't realized that the beetles had already been coded to herself and couldn't be reprogrammed. At least, not without the coded tune, which Dr Birch was not going to write out. Having taken the precaution of inactivating the tonal centers of the brain during Mrs Campbell's dominance, the only way Mrs Campbell could brake harmonic or melody locks was if Dr Birch wrote out the notes.

Humming merrily, Dr Birch bandaged her arm, dressed, donned a clean smock, and unlocked her keys from the harmonic key chest. Even with the harmonic lock, she always retrieved them early in the morning, to prevent Mrs Campbell getting them. Just as Dr Birch had trouble remembering what Mrs Campbell did in her first few moments of waking, Mrs Campbell had difficulties remembering what Dr Birch did when she awoke. It was a quirk of the treatment that gave Dr Birch her only moments of privacy.

Dr Birch put the uncomfortable actions of Mrs Campbell out of her mind, not wanting to relive the fighting--oh that horrible kitten six shooter! --of the night before. Today was about reconnecting brain to body. The wife! Dr Birch loaded up her pneumatic slug with all the equipment she might need and left directly for the hospital. Its brass plates clanged merrily as it zipped around corners and wove through traffic, its eye stalks bending and weaving to check for the clearest path. Dr Birch sat on his head as she drove, enjoying the warm breeze and the laughing kids waving as she sped by. So much smoother a ride than the more popular telaumatic carriages. She couldn't understand why her slug didn't catch on.

She hopped off at the entrance to the hospital. She squeezed the back of her slug, which popped out a baby slug for hauling her equipment. A porter lurched up with a cart, but she waved him away, too embarrassed to tell him her little slug was much better. She coughed and patted her slug on the head in the correct rhythm for him to compress and park himself. He zipped off and found a shade tree to squeeze himself under.

The porter still hovered, his cart in front of him like an offering. "Mrs Bee-man," Dr Birch informed him as she climbed atop the pile of goods that she had stacked on the baby slug. She waved, smiling, hoping he understood, then whistled a tune. Baby slug kicked into life and hauled her into the hospital and up the stairs.

Dr Birch went to work immediately. The models were all clear in her head. She had to start, however, by neutralizing the pain circuitry. Torture just wouldn't do. Then, careful flaying, mechanizing neuronal telanimators, attachment of replicators and repeaters, and prepping bones for the fitting of mechanicals. Core muscles, limbs, digits, mouth. Mouth mechanicals best braced against teeth, which would require reinforcement to support. Mechanical corset for abdominals and back. And the limbs, most often replaced items but the trouble of re-routing around the defective conscious controls. Can it be done? Can the pathways of the autonomic nervous system be used to drive conscious behavior? This was the hardest part.

A crash behind her. Her fingers fumbled the rivets she held, and they fell, clattering across the floor. She turned. "Dr Bee-man!" She waved. He stood beside his briefcase, open and spilled on the floor. An apple beside his foot. She slid off her stool and swept her stray rivets into her hands.

"What are you doing?" Dr Bee-man said. She could hear his feet shuffle toward her, then stop.

"Picking up rivets," she said. "You startled me."

"To my *wife*."

She found the last rivet and dropped it into her cupped hand. When she stood, Dr Bee-man was standing at his wife's side. He clutched a yellow flat cap in his hands, pressed against his belly.

"No pain," Dr Birch said. "Re-routed pain centers or disconnected them."

"You . . ." His hands convulsed. The hat fell to the floor. He reached out and stroked his wife's arm, now braced with a shining exoskeleton connected to skeletal finger cases. Quite pretty.

"But I can coat it," Dr Birch said. "Any color. Special enamel." She smiled and tapped her teeth.

"She . . . I didn't realize."

"Not attached yet." Dr Birch lifted his wife's other arm. "These are the easy part. The neural diversions . . ." She shook her head. "Several days away. Sorry."

"But I didn't realize she'd be so . . . metal when you were done."

"Like Rialto. I know. Very beautiful." Dr Birch

stroked the wife's arm. She placed her handful of rivets on the armored belly with a rain of clinks. "Strong."

"I . . ." Dr Bee-man dropped his wife's arm and stepped away. "I didn't realize," he said. He was frowning. Frowning?

"Are you unhappy?" Dr Birch asked.

"This will bring her back?" Still frowning.

"Yes."

"I . . . alright." He took a deep breath and held it, then breathed out. "Alright."

Dr Birch went back to work.

It took five days, and Dr Birch knew Mrs Campbell was watching, and that she'd even taken time from her regular business to come and see and feel first-hand what Dr Birch was doing to the wife. Rialto visited once with Dr Bee-man and complimented her on her work, and she blushed and wished Mrs Campbell was there, as she'd have known what to do.

The day Dr Birch put the last replicators and connectors in place, it was nearing five and she knew she must return to the lab. The trial launch would have to wait for the next day.

***

Mrs Campbell woke in a buzz of excitement. She'd been very busy alongside Dr Birch, marshalling supplies and experts. And over the last several days, she'd informed a group of the wealthiest and most powerful investors and politicians that she was to reveal an amazing investment opportunity on very short notice. She'd sent word immediately upon waking that tomorrow morning was the moment of her announcement and sent them the address of the hospital. Then she rushed home with only the most careless of preparation. This was going to make them so much richer. And Dr Birch wouldn't even have anything to feel guilty about! At supper, she told Miles they had an early morning event to attend but would tell him nothing more.

"You'll love this, dear," Mrs Campbell said.

"Not another boring fund raiser?" he asked.

"Most definitely not."

Come morning, Mrs Campbell slipped into her most elegant, high-powered attire. She rarely wore red, but today was a day for red, and a black scarf, and black boots laced in red. Power and passion. She snapped on an elaborate armband, brass, etched, and enamelled in red and black, jointed at the elbow and ending in several spirals along her lower arm. It was a nice piece, and six very sharp throwing stars could be snapped out when needed. A well-dressed woman should always be subtly armed.

***

Mrs Campbell waited in the hospital lobby. Miles kept trying to get hints as to what she was doing, but she shushed him with coy smiles. Once all her guests had arrived, she escorted them up to the hospital room.

"This is an unusual place for a celebration," Miles said, mouth right beside her ear.

She squeezed his arm in encouragement. "This is where many of the MMK victims were taken."

"Then why--" The thin line of concern that had molded his lips since they arrived at the hospital slowly softened. "Has someone found a way to fix them?"

Someone indeed. "Just wait, darling." So many surprises to come, and not just for her guests. Dr Birch had a little surprise coming, too. She'd be helping more than one person today.

***

As 7:30 AM neared, Mrs Campbell shooed away the loitering hospital staff to allow the photographer better access. The last arrivals came just as planned: Dr Birch's dear Rialto--who was so obviously in love with her it was just embarrassing--and Filbert Humphrey Davies, otherwise known as Dr Bee-man. Mrs Campbell, separating herself from the milling crowd, introduced herself to Filbert Davies as Dr Belinda Birch's trusted advisor and apologized for the media leak that led to this all-too-public reanimation of his beloved Lina.

Rialto stood at Filbert Davies' shoulder, eyes narrowed at Mrs Campbell. She beamed and introduced herself and spoke of her dear cousin Belinda and how she'd been quite frightened by the crowd's appearance this morning but had left explicit instructions on how to activate the mechanicals that would reanimate Mr. Davies' wife. At ten minutes to 8:00, Mrs Campbell called the crowd to order, smiled to the camera, and announced that today they would see the successful implementation of the first reanimation of a victim of the MMK disaster, and possibly a little something more.

"It was a simple hope," she concluded. "A hope so many of us have, to improve ourselves in some little way. But MMK sold an empty dream in place of hope. Today, with the help of the elusive Dr Birch, the destruction wrought by MMK ends." She raised a hand to quiet the buzz--excitement, outrage, a few mutterings of "unorthodox" and "miracle-worker."

"If you will allow me a few minutes alone with the

patient," Mrs Campbell said. Then she stepped into the room and locked the door behind her. She removed from her purse the note she'd written earlier for Dr Birch then sat herself in a chair, the note spread in her lap.

***

Of course, Dr Birch didn't need to read the note. She remembered writing it, if not the thoughts going through her head when she did. Horrible woman! She crumpled the note in a fist. She was trapped in this room, everyone outside staring and waiting and Mrs Campbell gone but she was supposed to be her! And herself! Mrs Campbell had left Dr Birch's tool kit just inside the door. Dr Birch scrambled over to it, reached out a hand, then pulled back. Her tools didn't have the same comfort they normally carried. Mrs Campbell had touched them. Dr Birch carefully tapped the handle. It felt quite like it usually did.

Dr Birch opened the tool kit and gazed inside. All was as usual. She picked up the telekineoautomator and tuned it by ear, then strode over to the wife/brain. *Just turn her on, open the door, walk to your Dr Bee-man (his name is Filbert Humphrey Davies by the way), ignore everyone else, then lean in and whisper to him, "She's waiting for you. Go in and say hello." After that, you can leave if you want. Just vanish.* Mrs Campbell's note made it sound so simple, and here she was, trapped. If she didn't play the part--and what *was* she wearing? --Dr Bee-man would be sad, Rialto would be ashamed of her, everyone would ask her questions. What if they discovered Mrs Campbell? She couldn't just leave. She was trapped.

Dr Birch activated her telekineoautomator. It vibrated in her hand, warming her palm. When the frequency was correct, she applied it to the temples of the wife. It took only a few moments for the replicators to activate, the broadcasters to initiate, and remote and direct connections to the mechanicals to develop circuitry rerouting protocols. Then the wife's eyes fluttered open. She raised a hand, eyes fixed on Dr Birch. Dr Birch slipped the telekineoautomator into her belt and turned to the door.

When she threw it open, everyone was staring. Sweat salted her upper lip. Her hair, normally so neatly tucked away in braids, felt like an elaborate bird's nest on her head. What if it had a bird in it? She touched her waist, where her keys should be, but there was nothing but a large belt and her telekineoautomator. She spotted Dr Bee-man and rushed through the crowd. She grabbed his shoulders and pulled him close to her, trying not to meet anyone's eyes, especially Rialto's.

"She's waiting for you," she whispered. Then, panicking, worried that he didn't hear, she raised her voice and repeated the words. He flinched away. "Go in and say hello," she said, lowering her voice again. Then she let go of his shoulders. He met her eyes.

"Really?" he said. She nodded.

He rushed past her, and she hurried toward the stairs. The crowd all seemed to follow Bee-man. Someone caught her by the arm, and she spun around. Rialto. The metal of his hand was cool against her bare skin. He didn't say anything. His pointy beard twitched. She dropped her eyes to the floor. He tapped the armband Mrs Campbell had put on curiously, then tilted up her chin to study her face.

"What's going on?" Miles stepped up beside them.

"Who are you?" Rialto asked.

"Miles Campbell," Miles said. "Her husband."

Rialto didn't look away from Dr Birch. "No, you," he said. "Who are you?"

Then, screaming. Dr Birch ducked out of Rialto's reach. Several people were running out of the door to Mrs Bee-man's room, many splattered in red. Dr Birch cut her way through the crowd, found herself at the door to the room.

Mrs Bee-man was crouched on the bed, holding an arm, and tearing flesh from the bone, gnawing and gulping down huge bites. Her re-enforced teeth clinked against bone. Her face was covered in blood and gore.

Dr Bee-man was on the floor against the wall and a nurse was injecting him with something while another applied a fibroblast bandage. Dr Birch ran to his side. His eyes were glazed.

"She's just hungry," he said.

"You told me she was conscious inside!" Dr Birch slapped him, then fell back, shocked by the feel of his flesh against her hands.

"My love my love, how could she have been gone?" His head rocked back and forth.

"HUNGRY!" Mrs Bee-man roared.

"You said you were sure," Dr Birch said. "What measurements did you make? How did you know?"

"I had faith. How could I not believe? How could I not hope?"

"HUNGRY!" Something clattered to the ground. Dr Birch turned to see Mrs Bee-man crawling off the bed.

The arm bones, scraped clean, gouged by her teeth, lay on the ground.

Dr Birch scrambled, grabbing up her tool kit and Mrs Campbell's purse. "What's happening?" Miles stepped into the door, paled at the sight of Mrs Bee-man.

"Re-routing around inadequate cerebral cortex functions. Cerebellum initiating control."

Rialto stepped up behind Miles. He gasped. "What?"

"Run!" Dr Birch turned around and shouted it again, this time at the nurses. "Run run run!" Mrs Bee-man pounced on her weeping husband and bit into his face. "Oh no oh no oh no."

Screaming from the hallways, everywhere, all over the building. The nurses helping Dr Bee-man tried to pull Mrs Bee-man from him, but she flung them aside with ease, her mechanicals too strong for them. One of the nurses hit the bed, stumbled. The other hit the wall and fell unconscious to the floor. Dr Bee-man, drugged, struggled only weakly.

Dr Birch dropped her tool kit and charged up her telekineoautomator. She ran to Mrs Bee-man and tried to fit it round her temples from behind. A quick swat from her mechanoamplified arm sent the telekineoautomator flying. It crashed against the wall and Mrs Bee-man resumed the devouring of her husband. Dr Birch scrambled back and tipped open her tool kit, searching frantically, thinking thinking. Something. Something to deactivate. Then, a scream and a crash and Rialto was swearing and pushing Miles into the room. Behind them. In the hallway, people screaming and running and several of the previously comatose patients, clumsy and poorly structured, stumbling by.

"Oh no, Mrs Campbell, what have you done?" Dr Birch moaned. She dove back into her tool kit. Over the past few days, Dr Birch had installed seeding elements into all the comatose patients, to make them ready for activation once proper mechanicals could be engineered and fitted. Mrs Campbell must have employed someone to fit them with prototype mechanicals instead of waiting for Dr Birch's custom work. Not nearly as nice, but sufficient to start them walking once the seeding elements were activated. More slowly, of course. But they did. Secondary waves from the telekineoautomator. Oh no oh no. "Oh no."

"Belinda, what's happening?" Miles asked, coming up behind her.

"Belinda?" Rialto echoed. A piercing scream from the hallway, and a bellow of "HUNGRY!" A naked gentleman stumbled through the door and threw down a leg with only a few remaining shreds of meat. He reached a mechanically re-enforced arm toward Rialto, who threw his own--far superior--arm up to block the thrust.

"You have to get out!" he shouted, throwing the man back with the full force of his mechanicals.

"No no no. How to interfere?" How to re-route circuitries, remote neuronal interference patterns? But they're strong and protected. How to reach so many. Hundreds. Heads would have to be detached.

"HUNGRY!" It wasn't a word so much as some primal network activated howl of basic animal desire. Mrs Bee-man shoved her mostly eaten husband aside and narrowed her eyes at Dr Birch. "HUNGRY!"

Miles stepped forward to block Mrs Bee-man just as

she pounced. He threw up his arm to block her, but he had none of the strength of Rialto's mechanicals, and she sunk her reinforced teeth into his flesh and gripped his arm in her mechanical hands.

"Hey bitch," Dr Birch snarled. She found herself on her feet, dizzy, confused, angry, hands pulling throwing stars from her arm band and whipping them into the air faster than she might have imagined possible. "Get off my husband." Mrs Bee-man howled. She shoved Miles to the ground. No pain from the injuries, but she knew she was being attacked.

"Belinda, watch out!" Rialto called, just as Miles, too, called her name. She ducked as Mrs Bee-man pounced. She rolled under the attack and opened her purse, pulled out the kitten six shooter. Steady on her knees, she levelled the gun. The kittens mewled. She hummed a tune, setting their programming. Then she shot.

A kitten launched from the barrel, yowling in a horrifying scream of kitty ferocity. It landed on Mrs Beeman's face with all four paws out, claws sinking in, injecting the cocktail programmed by the hummed tune. Belinda ducked sideways as Rialto threw one of the patients from himself. She shot again. Another kitten hissed through the air. It landed on the patient's arm but quickly scampered to his throat, biting and clawing and injecting.

"I'm going to need more kittens," Belinda said. Then, "Oh yes, I see." They would return to her. All she needed was to keep feeding them. She pulled out the make-up bag and found the baggies of kitten feed stashed inside. Miles pulled himself up using the bed.

"What are they?" he said. Mrs Bee-man collapsed, still. The kitten crawled up Belinda's boot, hitched onto her skirt, then scampered up to her arm. Belinda reloaded it and gave it a bit of feed from the bag.

"My kittens," she said. "Dear."

The second kitten scampered across the floor, mewling. She bent and reloaded it. It purred as she fed it. Rialto, in the doorway, said, "There's hundreds out there."

Belinda looked between her husband and Rialto. "We'd best start disabling them, then. Think you two can do kitten feeding and retrieval duty?" She strode out of the room and into the chaos.

The hallways were filled with screaming people, stamping feet. A nurse rammed a dirty laundry cart into a patient and sent it hurdling over a railing then snatched a little girl from the arms of a man with his head caved in and started running for the stairs. Six patients had cornered a visiting family in a doorway. It would be easier to go for the kill if she let the patients start feeding. The woman shoved a teenage boy behind her and took her husband's hand as the patients closed. Belinda ran in shooting. Rialto flipped open his arm to expose a cutting edge and lopped off the head of one patient. The kittens went to work on the others. Miles lagged behind, stunned.

"Honey, the kittens please," Belinda said. He hung back, panting shallowly. Belinda tried to think. What could she say to get him to help? She ran back, took him by the shoulders. "Darling, I love you, and I need your help." She wrapped his fingers around a bag of kitten food, gave him a quick kiss, then a shove. He stumbled toward a dead patient and scooped up a kitten, feeding it before tossing it to Belinda. It landed claws out, clinging to her dress, and held on. A spray of hot blood hit her from behind and drenched the floor around her. She ducked, spun. Rialto swiped another head off of an attacking patient but four more were coming up behind him. She felt kittens hitting her dress, tossed to her by Miles. She reloaded.

***

Four hours later, Miles stepped up beside her, a kitten cradled in his cupped palms. He stroked it and it purred. Belinda plucked it up by the scruff of its neck and dropped it into the chamber. Two of its companions had been torn apart in the fighting, and one had lost its back left leg. This one bent its head around to its wounded neighbor and mewed, licking its nose. Belinda tore off a scrap of her skirt--largely shredded during the fighting-- and wiped the blood from Miles' face.

Rialto, finished with his sweep of the four upper floors, joined them. Everyone had been evacuated while the three fought the risen coma patients. The immediate threat gone, Belinda was not sure what to do. Not sure what to think of what had happened, what she had done.

Rialto sat on the stone edging around the gurgling water wall, now pink with blood. Belinda sat beside him, then Miles beside her. She placed her six shooter in her lap and fed the kittens the last bits from her bag. She'd have to go out soon and let the police know it was safe to enter. And explain? But how to explain? Belinda wanted nothing more than to sit quietly. She'd done this, all of this. All these people were dead, would never come back, unfixable.

"Who are you?" Rialto asked.

"You know," she said. Miles said, "She's my wife," nearly at the same time.

"Who are you?" Rialto asked again.

A murderer. An inventor. An opportunist. A wife. How to make them understand? She wanted to cry. She wanted to take it all back. As much as she didn't want to be both, she was, and she couldn't take it back. "I'm Dr Birch," she began. "And Mrs Campbell."

-End-

ABOUT THE AUTHORS

DEREK POWER is the author of the Filthy Henry series. Hailing from Dublin, Ireland, most of his stories tend to involve Celtic myths and legends to some degree. He has also featured a couple of anthologies and spends most of his working day dreaming about Hollywood knocking down the door for the movie rights. This story was based off an entirely throw away joke he said one day.

T. J. BERG is a molecular and cellular biologist working and writing in Sweden. She is a graduate of the Odyssey Writing Workshop. Her short fiction has appeared in in many places, including *Talebones* (for which it received an honorable mention in *The Year's Best Fantasy and Horror*), *Daily Science Fiction, Caledonia Dreamin', Sensorama, Thirty Years of Rain, Tales to Terrify*, and *Diabolical Plots*. When not writing or doing science, she can be found travailing the world, cooking, or hiking. To find more fiction or odd musings, check out www.infinity-press.com and, very occasionally Twitter @TJBergWrites.

RACHAEL BOUCKER doesn't know how she got on this planet, but she sure as celibate, shelved Seans doesn't know how to get off it.

She's settled in the Forest of Dean, a hub for peculiar beings, with her human Richard (enslaved in a long term relationship) and three hybrid semi-sentient miniatures (the oldest of which has turned grunting into a new language).

With a tentative connection to the hive mind, Rachael listens in on strange stories spanning multiple dimensions, and passes these eavesdroppings off as fiction, mostly horror and fantasy. Sci-fi can be triggering, dredging up memories of the spacebound life she left behind, but she does occasionally indulge in this genre. Look out for her upcoming Night Order dark fantasy series, being published by Eerie River Publishing.

www.rachaelboucker.com

https://m.facebook.com/RachaelBouckerAuthorArtist/

JOSEPH DOWLING has pursued many interests and diverse career paths, always knowing he would write seriously one day. In 2020, now owner of a small but previously thriving chain of retro arcade bars temporarily shuttered due to Covid-19, he fell into an obsession. Since finding the passion, Joseph can't imagine life without the stories constantly rattling around his head. Eager to make up for lost time, he's in the habit of writing every day, becoming a keen student of the craft. The 'Worlds Collide' anthology was his first acceptance, and his rejections seem to be getting nicer by the week.

ELLA ANN enjoys reading and writing in a wide array of genres. Born and raised on the West Coast of the United States, she currently resides in Southern California. While attending graduate school, she found her passion in creative writing. She types most of her stories late at night, with a snoozing pup near her feet.

L. T. EMERY is a British author, with a love for Horror, Sci-fi and Fantasy genres.
He is the proud father of one and husband to the love of his life. Outside of family life, he is an avid reader of novels, genre magazines, comics, manga and just about anything else he can get his hands on. With a particular love of long-form fiction, he is currently working on a fantasy novel which he hopes to publish in the future. He can be found online at https://ltemery.wixsite.com/home and twitter.com/ltemeryuk

TEEL JAMES GLENN, winner of the 2021 Best Novel from Pulp Factory Awards, 2012 Pulp Ark 'Best Author of the Year.' Epic ebook award finalist. P&E winner 'Best Thriller Novel',"Best Steampunk Short", Multiple finalist "Best Fantasy short stories," Collection" Member HWA, MWA, HNS, ITWA visit him at Theurbanswashbuckler.com

DEBORAH DUBAS GROOM is a Westcoast writer and artist. She has been published in 20+ anthologies and other print in Australia, the U.K., the U.S., and Canada. She's a member of the Langley Writers Guild, former medical social worker and vintage sci fi geek. She is the mother of Josh and grateful daughter of Stan and Helen. This story was written with my sister Heidi in mind.

CHARLOTTE LANGTREE is a poet, aspiring novelist, and writer of short fiction. Raised in West Yorkshire, she has a deep love of hills, berry-picking, and her unique accent. The themes of her writing encompass life's all-consuming emotions: joy, fear, love, and loss. She has been published in several magazines and anthologies, as well as online. In September 2021, she was voted the winner of the Great Clarendon House Writing Challenge. Dragon Soul Press selected her story 'The Shadow Queen' as an Editor's Pick of 2021. You can find her online by following the links below:

Website: www.charlottelangtree.wordpress.com
Facebook: www.facebook.com/CharlotteLangtreeAu-

thor
Twitter: www.twitter.com/CharlotteLangt5

TIM MENDEES is a horror writer from Macclesfield in the North-West of England that specialises in cosmic horror and weird fiction. A lifelong fan of classic weird tales, Tim set out to bring the pulp horror of yesteryear into the 21st Century and give it a distinctly British flavour. His work has been described as the lovechild of H.P. Lovecraft and P.G. Wodehouse and is often peppered with a wry sense of humour that acts as a counterpoint to the unnerving, and often disturbing, narratives.

Tim has had over eighty published short stories and novelettes along with five stand-alone novellas and a short story collection.

When he is not arguing with the spellchecker, Tim is a goth DJ, crustacean and cephalopod enthusiast, and the presenter of a popular web series of live video readings of his material and interviews with fellow authors. Tim is also a co-host of the Innsmouth Book Club podcast. He currently lives in Brighton & Hove with his pet crab, Gerald, and an army of stuffed octopods.

https://timmendeeswriter.wordpress.com/
https://tinyurl.com/timmendeesyoutube

Born in the usual way, author, **MICHAEL D. NADEAU** found fantasy at the age of 8 with Dungeons & Dragons. He loved being different people as well as casting magic and in time he discovered his love for reading. He has read hundreds of fantasy books, living in each of their worlds, and after a while, he created his own. He is the author of the Lythinall series: The Darkness Returns book 1, The Darkness Within book 2 & Tales From Lythinall. He also has several stories in Gestalt media anthologies, Fractured Mirror publishing, and Eerie River Publishing. He is rep'd by Skullgate Media.

PATRICK WINTERS is a graduate of Illinois College in Jacksonville, IL, where he earned a degree in English Literature and Creative Writing. His work has been featured throughout several magazines and anthologies. A full list of his previous publications may be found at his author's site: http://wintersauthor.azurewebsites.net/Publications/List

The anti-villain character known as **JASIAH WITKOFSKY** is an independent author of dark speculative fiction and harrowing tales of swashbuckling adventure derived from myth, legend, and history...although he attempts other non-fiction literary projects when time allows. He also forays into editing, pragmatic philosophy, gardening, dabbling in the arts, rock n roll, and rabblerousing amidst the majestic Sierra Nevadas of Northern California. To date, his works can be found on both hemispheres, three continents, and several companies including Summer Storm Press, Black Ink Fiction, Crow's Foot Journal, Iron Faerie Publications, Black Hare Press, Breaking Rules, and Raven & Drake

Publishings. Find Josiah on Facebook at Jasiah Witkofsky Author Page.

Lightning Source UK Ltd.
Milton Keynes UK
UKHW040946310522
403752UK00001B/329